SIEGE

Also by K.F. Breene

DARKNESS SERIES
Into the Darkness, Novella 1 – FREE
Braving the Elements, Novella 2
On a Razor's Edge, Novella 3
Demons, Novella 4
The Council, Novella 5
Shadow Watcher, Novella 6
Jonas, Novella 7
Charles, Novella 8
Darkness Series Boxed Set, Books 1-4

WARRIOR CHRONICLES
Chosen, Book 1
Hunted, Book 2
Shadow Lands, Book 3
Invasion, Book 4
Siege, Book 5

SIEGE

By K.F. Breene

Copyright © 2016 by K.F. Breene

All rights reserved. The people, places and situations contained in this ebook are figments of the author's imagination and in no way reflect real or true events.

Contact info:
www.kfbreene.com
Facebook: www.facebook.com/authorKF
Twitter: @KFBreene

CHAPTER 1

SHANTI SQUARED OFF against Kallon, the two most promising fighters the Shumas had. One had already been declared leader by the death of her father. It was universally thought that the other should step into the leadership role, traditions notwithstanding. Times were changing. Their people were under threat. As a people, they must look to who would lead them to victory and fulfill the duty of the Chosen.

But he hadn't been chosen.

Shanti's fist tightened on her practice sword as her grandfather looked on, his face stern but expression devoid of his desired outcome of this fight.

Kallon stood patiently with a passive face. Clearly, he wanted her to make the first move.

Shanti took a hesitant step to the right, wondering if she should circle him and feint a few times to try to draw him out, or just rush him. She'd failed at both often enough that her body was decorated in bruises.

It wasn't fair. Kallon was a couple years older. That was the only reason he was stronger, faster, and more *agile. He'd already grown into his body, and he'd been doing this longer. His perfect technique and quick learning enhanced his natural ability, like anyone's would. Like hers would, eventually. For now she was nothing but a lanky eleven-year-old, gangly and jerky, but by the time she hit her mid-teens, people would say the stars were* her *limit, as well.*

She feinted forward, ready for him to block her pretend thrust so she could stab him in the side. Her sword hit its zenith and slowed as her eyebrows rose, needing him to commit.

Just be fooled, blast it, Kallon! *she thought in desperation.*

He didn't so much as twitch. He watched her with those cool gray eyes.

She pivoted and put more force behind her sword, bluntly thrusting it the rest of the way. With a flash of movement, Kallon swung his wooden blade in an arc, knocking away her sword as he stepped to the side. He resumed his patient pose instead of going for a kill strike.

He wasn't the fool, she was. He was making that perfectly clear.

Shanti jogged backward before noticing her grandfather's expression darkening.

Oh yeah, she wasn't supposed to retreat.

She jerked to a stop and placed a hesitant foot to the left. Time to circle. She needed to think this through.

Truth be told, she hated this slow approach. How would this help them? The enemy, when they came, wouldn't just stand around and wait for her to come up with a perfect sword thrust. They'd charge her, and then feel the wrath of her Gift.

This was a no-Gift fight, though. They'd gang up on her if she used it...

"Blast it." *She sent a hard thrust with her mind, ramming his shield with her might. He staggered backward.*

Her grin was short-lived.

A moment later, her brain was scored with hot needles. Fire blistered her eyes and knives racked her body. Blood oozed down her skin like acid, burning away everywhere it touched. Her scream sent birds to flight. She hit the ground in a ball before a shock wave of her Gift speared the others, lashing out at the minds attacking her. The pain diminished enough for her to uncurl and stare at her limbs.

No blood.

Another wave of attack punched her, but she was ready. She grappled with the power before stabbing out, hard bursts of power beating away her attackers.

She snatched her sword off the ground, and with a wild cry, barreled into Kallon with everything she had. She hacked at him before her body crashed into his. She ignored the pain that set her scalp on fire and sent two hard punches into his sides. Their bodies hit the ground. He rolled her under him and brought his fist away to deliver a blow.

Her power blasted *him, making him hesitate. She head-butted him. The cartilage in his nose cracked. The mental assault lessened slightly.*

Shanti heaved with all her strength, knocking him to the side. She squirmed and twisted, using all the muscle in her smaller body to turn him the rest of the way. Blood gushed down his face as she straddled him in a haze of violence. Her hands worked quickly, peppering him with blows as the mental assault from everyone else in the clearing tore at her thoughts.

Pain blossomed in her side. Kallon's fist struck a second time, smacking against her ribs.

"Just let me beat you!" she yelled.

She pumped more power into her mental attack as something niggled at her awareness. A presence of some sort. It wasn't the pain and power she'd known all her life from the people in this clearing; it was the distant aura of something foreign.

She froze. A fist knocked her backward, tumbling her off Kallon. The mental assault from the others died away as hers did. Kallon scrambled to his feet, ready to claim his victory.

She stopped paying attention to the fight and focused in on that mind. It was analytical and precise, male, and searching. A mind was like that when it was hunting.

"What is it?" *Kallon asked, crouching down beside her.*

"Someone…" *Shanti closed her eyes and followed her training. She spread her* Gift *farther, covering their lands in a circle. Behind them, in the villages, lay the mental hum of those she recognized, going about their day. She felt no unusual fear or anxiety. She peeled her* Gift *away and directed it toward the mind that was slowly working closer. He was en route to the most northern village. Her village.*

"There's someone coming…" *She was on her feet in an instant. She wiped her arm across her face, smearing blood across her cheek.*

"Is he Gifted?" *Her grandfather motioned for the others to file in.*

"No." *Shanti jogged to her sword. After strapping it on, she glanced around at the others. Her grandfather stared at her expectantly.*

She needed to take charge. It was her birthright.

She still didn't really know how.

Her grandfather had told her that it would come naturally, like it had with him. Like it had with her father. He'd tried to guide her, with little success.

She glanced at Kallon. A silent plea for help.

"Should we move closer and observe, or should we surround and capture?" *Kallon asked with battle-ready eyes.*

A few people shifted. They knew he was guiding her. They would question whether he was helping...or trying to take over.

She couldn't think about that now.

Her chin rose and she met her grandfather's expectant stare before letting her gaze travel over the others who had gathered, all older. Kallon might've been the best, but she was the youngest to ever reach the top tier of fighters. That had to be good for something.

"We'll surround him silently," she said. "I will then step out. I want to see his reaction and feel his purpose, if I can. Is he Xandre's eyes, or is he merely curious? Hopefully this will give us some insight."

She barely noticed her grandfather's curt nod.

Without delay, she started jogging through the trees, feeling the others jostle in behind her, a little too close for comfort. "Fan out," Shanti said in a low voice. "Stay silent."

"We need to join our mental Gifts, Chosen," Kallon said. "We can't feel things the way you can. Our range isn't as great."

Shanti mentally kicked herself. That should've been the first thing she'd done.

She felt the battering of Gifts hitting against her. Some came in with a weird heat, stuffing into her head like a hot poker into the fire. Some slid right in, cool and certain.

"Stay calm," her grandfather instructed, his breath coming in fast pants. He was getting too old for their fast pace. "Keep your Gift *contained. Retain your focus. You must attack your adversary with a level head."*

She would attack her adversary with a sword and a snarl, actually, but she didn't say anything. They were getting close now.

"Can you feel him through me?" she asked Kallon beside her.

"Yes we can. Just like in practice. We're close enough for most of us to be able to feel him ourselves, now." Kallon glanced behind him before motioning for the others to spread out. She gritted her teeth and held a hand up to slow everyone down, regaining control. She slid behind a tree trunk and stopped. The stranger moved toward them, no more than fifty steps away. She mouthed, "Wait."

Kallon's expression transformed into one of frustrated confusion. He shook his head.

"We wait," she whispered.

His face cleared. Many of the others nodded and fanned out a little further.

Shanti closed her eyes, analyzing. The stranger seemed intelligent and cunning, processing the area around him quickly and efficiently. Though he moved swiftly, she didn't hear him. There were no snapped twigs or swishing foliage. He knew how to move through wilderness without being seen or heard.

Shanti moved slowly, putting herself in line with his forward movement. Confusion and frustration colored the fighters around her. She waved her hand, trying to get them to keep their positions. Mela wrinkled her brow and shook her head. Dannon glowered.

They had no idea what she was trying to do. There had to be a better way to communicate silently...

A soft footfall reverberated in Shanti's ears. The slide of a hand on bark.

She took a deep breath before slowly easing her sword out of its sheath. She glanced at Kallon, raising her eyebrows with the slightest of nods. Ready?

His brow furrowed and he shook his head. Duh...

Unable to speak for fear of being heard, she hoped her people would understand as she stepped out from behind the tree. The stranger straightened up in surprise, his eyes going wide and his hand reaching to the knife on his belt. The black of his uniform with its three red stripes burnt into her brain. A surge of rage made her tighten her hand on her sword.

"Why are you here?" she asked, willing for the level head her grandfather spoke of.

His eyes darted around, no doubt looking for other Shumas. They came back to rest on hers. "Looking for you, of course. My master, the Being Supreme, would love to speak with you."

A feeling of violence whispered into the mental thread. Shanti ignored it, wondering why they weren't fanning out around him. Why they were sitting where they were, watching. "He has asked before. We told him no."

"Actually, you killed the messenger."

"Same thing. Why did you really come?"

A sickly grin coated his face. "Your people were a mystery. Now they are a riddle. Soon they will all be in the Being Supreme's possession, as they should be. But you...he has great plans for you. You should be honored."

Shanti sneered. "A man who kills innocence should be killed. Surround him!"

In a rush of movement, he tossed the knife up and deftly grabbed the blade. A shock of fear had Shanti diving to the side as the knife sailed past her, just missing her shoulder. She hit the ground, yelling, "Don't kill him. Capture him!"

The man was running as Kallon leapt out, his sword in hand. He bent to Shanti, checking to see if she was okay.

"Get him!" she shouted, scrambling to her feet. She latched on to the intruder's mind as he fled, ready to deliver a soft blow to halt his progress.

Sayas tripped over Tulous, as both tried to slip between the same trees in pursuit. Mela had taken position in a small, open space, sighting an arrow.

"Don't shoot!" Shanti yelled.

Too late. Mela let go of the bowstring. An arrow zipped out as three people stabbed, or struck, adding to Shanti's punch. As the intruder's body stumbled, already dying from the mental assault, the arrow hit him in the center of his back.

He hadn't had a chance.

Neither had Shanti.

It was her first real attempt at leading, and she had failed. Miserably.

"Flak," she said as she slumped.

"They are coming more often now," Kallon said with his hands on his hips. "That must mean the battle is getting closer."

"They could've been coming all the time." Mela lowered her bow, her eyes still on the downed body. "Shanti—I mean Chosen—is better with her Gift. She has felt the last three spies."

"Xandre is gathering information." Shanti's grandfather stopped beside her, his disapproval plain on his face. He'd expected more from her. "When he has all he needs, he will attack. If that is soon, then we won't be ready."

Shanti watched him walk away with a stiff back. His message was plain: if she didn't form a cohesive fighting team from her people, and then again when they joined the Shadow, she would fail as the prophesied. She would kill them all.

CHAPTER 2

SANDERS WALKED OUT of the gate with a surly expression and a can-do attitude. What the hell women were doing wearing britches and toting bows he had no idea, but lately it had become part of his life whether he liked it or not. His apparent ease in accepting Shanti had made him perfect for the role of overseeing the new female recruits...or so the Captain said.

Plain foolishness, that's what that was. He hated the post. A bunch of know-it-alls, the lot of them. And why point out that he stank every time? It wasn't like he could take a bath in between training sessions.

He had a wife. He didn't need any more women to argue with him.

They did not respond well when he explained that.

Grinding his teeth, he glanced up at the sentry. A cold-eyed Shuma stared back down at him.

Tingles worked through Sanders' body. His fists tightened in response. "You should be scanning your surroundings, not watching me pass by your tree," he barked.

The Shuma—Kallon—tapped his temple. "I am watching without my eyes."

"Anyone ever tell you staring was rude?"

"Yes."

Sanders grunted and continued by, feeling the sentry's gaze pound into his back. It was impossible to tell if Kallon was joking or being dead serious, but neither would change the constant, assessing stare that seemed to follow everyone and everything around. Annoying, that.

"Quit standing around, lollygagging!" Sanders yelled as he got within earshot of a bunch of chattering women standing in a line. A couple jumped, their hands flying to their chests. A few flinched and their arrows went off course. Three released their arrows, completely cool, as if unaware of him. The points of all struck the target. One was a bull's-eye.

Those three were great finds. It almost made dealing with these training sessions worth it.

"Is it really necessary to yell like that?" Fabienne scolded.

Sanders gritted his teeth, refusing to answer the older woman at the end of the row. "Maggie, excellent shot. Alena and Ruisa, also great job. The rest of you, you need to work on blocking everything that's going on around you when you're focusing on the shot."

Sanders felt a presence off to his right. He turned, belatedly spotting one of the female Shumas—Mela, he thought—crouching amongst the foliage. The woman was as quiet and still as the grave, watching him with luminous, sorrowful eyes. Turbulent eyes, desecrated by war. It was enough to make a man want to hug her. Almost.

"What are you staring at?" He let his hand rest on his sword.

"Not block out…take in." Mela drifted closer with the graceful slide of a skilled swordswoman. "Try to ignore and all you do is hear. Accept your surroundings, and become one with it."

Sanders clasped his hands behind his back and squeezed his eyes shut for one moment. Pulling patience out of his ass and hoping it would stick around, he forced a smile. "Thank you for your insight, but in our army, we have a chain of command. They answer to me, and you answer to Shanti. I'll do my job; she'll tell you what yours is. How does that sound?"

Mela's eyes started to twinkle. "*Chulan* told me to help them. She is above you in this chain, yes?"

Ire started to rise, heating Sanders' face. He leaned forward just a little, trying to keep from seeing how far he could throw her. "She is outside of my chain of command, actually."

"Then we are partners."

Sanders tilted his head and showed his teeth. Mela smiled at him. She clearly knew that he was rapidly losing his temper. "And have you made any progress?" he asked.

Her smile dwindled and she looked down the line. "Half of them are wasting time here. They are too old."

"I beg your pardon?" Fabienne put her fists on her hips in indignation.

Mela gave her a flat look and glanced down the row. "A seasoned fighter can be retired to a mostly stationary position when hurt or old. When his body fails, he must move less. By then, aim and focus is second nature. These old women have not learned, they cannot move, and have trouble standing for long periods of time. It is a good hobby, but otherwise, they are wasting their time, and yours."

"Maybe we *could* learn if you would *show* us!" someone shouted.

And here came the arguments.

Sanders willed calm, ready to try and lead these women in a few exercises, when Mela said, "Maybe. I do not know you. First, I watch. I learn how you move. Then I try to fix, teach, or tell you to go home, depending on what you need. It is *Chulan's* way, and very effective."

"Well…" Fabienne shifted, looking at the other women. "I would be content to just watch. But I want to make sure these women get their instruction. They are part of the army, too. Shanti said it was to be so, and the Captain agreed. It's bad enough they are pushed out here in the trees like some kind of secret—I want to make sure they aren't forgotten about entirely!"

"Fine. Would anyone else be more content to watch?" Sanders rocked back on his heels, then stepped to the side as a quarter of the line shuffled out of the way. Ten women stood their ground.

"Yes, that is better." Mela stepped away and crouched again. "Those who need to learn should learn." She braced her forearms on her knees. "Everyone who is not good should not distract the fighters. They should find something useful to do."

Sanders couldn't help a grin. "Okay. Looks like you got this. This is one of two groups. I'll assume you'll watch both." He nodded at the ladies still on the line. "If you have a problem, take it up with the Shoo-lan. Looks like the Captain is letting her run this donkey show."

"Now hold on just a minute," Fabienne said, but Sanders didn't wait around. He'd just been given a free pass and he intended to take it. He'd go back to where men did as he said, and if they didn't, he was allowed to punch them in the ear.

He passed by the stables and pretended not to flinch when one of the male beasts growled at his presence. Apart from harm coming to Junice, Sanders wasn't afraid of much. Those beasts were at the top of a very short list.

"Everyone good here, Rufus?" Sanders asked Cayan's assistant.

The smaller man looked up from his clipboard. "Yes, sir. Our food stores are handling the additional animals just fine."

"And the extra Shadow that keep arriving to join us?"

Rufus licked the tip of his finger and peeled a sheet of paper up from his clipboard. "I believe another group of ten just arrived this morning," he said after surveying the contents for a moment. "They've been stationed with the others. We have space for a couple dozen more, but then we'll need to make some decisions."

Sanders tightened his lips before nodding and walking on. That made four dozen Shadow that had arrived since Sonson's party three weeks before, with more coming every couple days. At any time, Shanti would win the battle with the Captain and give the signal to be on their way. Word was constantly coming in from Burson about the movements and whereabouts of Xandre. Other messages came in about movements of what could only be Shanti's people, stuck behind layers of well-trained Graygual. Still more news came in about each new barrier delaying the Shadow from reaching the main land. So far the Shadow had fought their way through, but that wouldn't continue for much longer if Xandre was any kind of strategist, and if the battle in the Shadow Lands taught him anything, it was that Xandre could form a plan or two.

Sanders hated to admit it, but Shanti was right. Xandre was tightening things up and locking in the Westwood Lands. Soon they'd all be trapped by a sea of the enemy, cut off from help.

He blew out a breath.

But to leave would be to leave their family and friends vulnerable. It would not be an easy decision to make.

The early afternoon was fresh and vibrant as Sanders made his way through the city. Efforts were still being made to clean up after the battle, but the city people were working diligently, combining their efforts. A soft breeze blew against his face, bringing the vital smell of trees. He'd gone through a lot of shit in his day, but to protect his home, he'd go through ten times more to protect his home.

He turned a corner that led toward the eastern side of the city. The Shumas had been placed close to the eastern gate so they could escape out into the trees as often as they wished. He clasped his hands behind his back and gripped them tight, willing the patience he knew he was going to need.

It only took one second in their midst to prove

those efforts futile.

"What in the holy hell is going on here?" Sanders marched into a front yard where the oldest of the Shumas was standing, looking at a blooming pink flower. A corset wrapped around his middle. His manhood dangled between his legs.

The man—Tulous, if Sanders wasn't mistaken—glanced up with a surprised expression.

"You're naked, man!" Sanders barked. "And wearing women's undergarments. Care to explain?"

"What is problem?" Sayas, the most lighthearted of the Shumas, walked up with a brisk pace. He wore a creased blue army uniform.

Sanders stared for a full beat, waiting for Sayas to figure it out for himself. When the other man gave him a quizzical expression, Sanders pointed at Tulous' exposed bells and whistle. "We don't have outside bathhouses in this neck of the land. We wear *clothes* when we're outside. This has been explained to you people."

"Ah yes." Sayas nodded in understanding. "You tepid."

"Tepid? You've gotten some words mixed up there, man." Sanders glanced around, noticing two women standing opposite the lane, gawking. "Well? Move along," he yelled. "This isn't something for you to see."

"They are curious," Tulous said.

"Want inspect." Sayas grinned and slapped Tulous on the back.

"They're married with children—they know how one of those works, and now they're probably horrified and headed straight to the Women's Circle." Sanders pinched the bridge of his nose. "*Why* is he wearing women's undergarments? How could this *possibly* be normal where you come from?"

"What's going on?" Shanti jogged up before taking one look at Tulous and cracking a giant smile. She rattled off something in her own language.

"And he's got it on backwards," Sanders growled. Two giant, empty cups stuck out from the man's muscular back and the lacing wound down his stomach, a little off center. The device was obviously meant for a larger woman—how else would it fit Tulous? Somewhere around this city, someone was waltzing around with two huge breasts swinging free.

That would probably be the next fad.

"My life was so quiet…" Sanders mused as Tulous spoke to Shanti in their language. Two Shadow ducked out from between houses, looking around in confusion. Another ran into the street three houses down, appearing as if from nowhere. "What the hell are they up to?"

Shanti laughed. "We are training. I'm trying to teach the Shadow the way we communicate through our *Gifts.*" She gestured at Tulous. "His back is strained. He was looking for a brace and found this. He was given permission to borrow it."

"Granted the right—" Sanders cut off and started walking away, shaking his head. His patience was all used up. Soon he'd just start stabbing people, and that sort of behavior was frowned upon when there was no enemy present. He bet Tulous hadn't been given permission either—he probably wandered into someone's backyard, naked for all the city to see, and demanded the garment from a shocked and embarrassed housewife. Of course she was going to say yes. She was probably terrified for her life, scared that the riffraff would do something violent if she refused.

"Take care of it," he demanded of Shanti over his shoulder. "We don't need a bunch of dicks wagging around this city."

"You already have a bunch of dicks wagging around the city," Shanti yelled back. "They're the ones barking orders."

Sanders clenched his fists as the peal of laughter followed him up the street. He stared down a Shadow with a shock of blond hair, daring the other man to challenge him in some way. All these cultures being confined within the same walls was jarring, at best. If someone wasn't wandering around naked, he was bathing in a pond, or roasting a pig in his front yard. Two Shumas were caught having sex in the trees in the large park, and Shadow loitered in all the parts of the city, quiet and deadly. Sanders was open-minded, sure, but this was just ridiculous. Lord only knew how they'd get along when they left to find Xandre. That would be an all-out clusterfuck, if he was any judge.

Halfway to the practice yard, he found two of the Honor Guard skulking toward the trees.

"What are you doing?" Sanders shouted.

Xavier jumped and swung around with wide eyes. He moved a garden spade and hoe behind his back. Gracas stepped out from behind Xavier holding another couple of gardening items, both with purple handles.

"Nothing, sir," Xavier said, standing straight and tall.

"What've you got there?" Sanders gestured to the items in Gracas' hands.

"Just some, uh, gardening equipment, sir," Xavier said.

"I was thinking about planting something, sir," Gracas said with a straight face.

Sanders stared at Xavier for a beat, then Gracas. They stared back, not blinking.

"The women are dressing as men, the men are wearing women's underwear, and the young men are taking up gardening instead of chasing women or punching stuff. I do not understand my life anymore." Sanders took a deep breath. "I assume this is free time?"

"S'am's orders, sir," Xavier said with a snap to his words.

Of course it was that woman.

Muttering to himself, he continued on. He didn't have it in him to care about gardening equipment or what those two might be up to. It was easier that way.

A few minutes later he walked onto the practice yard and saw the Captain and Lucius standing at the edge, watching the proceedings. Sanders headed straight for them. He could feel the stress and confusion break away, uncoiling. *This* made sense. This place. Training, swords, physical exertion—everyone knew where they stood in the pecking order, and if they didn't, there was a clear way to settle the matter.

"Captain." Sanders sighed gratefully as he came to stand right next to the solidest man this land had to offer.

The Captain glanced at him before looking back out at the surging, moving mass of bodies. "How are the female archers faring?"

"Mela, one of Shanti's countrymen, has taken over at Shanti's behest. I would've chased her away, but she was as blunt and pushy as Shanti. She cut away the fat in three seconds and she hadn't even started to work with them."

"Good. You weren't making any headway."

Lucius chuckled. "Does that surprise you? Everyone

knows Junice runs the house."

"That shouldn't have anything to do with the army," Sanders growled. "This whole city is in chaos."

"Roles have been called into question. People are figuring out what they're good at and changing their destinies. When everything settles, it'll make us stronger. We need that if another section of the army plans to leave in the coming months." The Captain's focus shifted for a moment as Shanti and a team of Shumas and Shadow entered the practice yard on the opposite side. She glanced at Cayan, nodded in *hello,* and turned toward the Pit.

Without a word, or even a glance in their direction, her people fanned out into the practice area. Only Rohnan went with her. The rest took up stations evenly along the outside, their focus on the army, their orchestration perfect and silent. In opposition, the Shadow looked confused, jerking to a stop in some cases, and then altering their final destination. But no one opened their mouths to ask for directions.

Sanders had to admit, it was a damned effective way to communicate. He half wished he could use it with his own men.

Sanders noticed the stormy-eyed Kallon, one of those slinking off to the side. He rested his forearms on his knees, his gaze rooted to the Captain.

"How you have not answered that challenge yet is

beyond me," Sanders said, crossing his arms and hoping that Shumas would direct his fire-sparked stare in Sanders' direction. "That warrior is sizing you up."

The Captain didn't even shift. "He's still deferring to me."

"It doesn't look like it," Lucius said in a low tone, watching one of the female Shadow lunge forward in the sword practicing area. Her wooden point struck her training partner in the side. He bent and held up a hand, yielding.

"They are always connected to Shanti, as am I." The Captain didn't sound pleased by that. "The Shadow are starting to merge in as well. They are trying to learn Shanti's elaborate system for silent communication. Within that merge, Kallon is deferring too. Until he doesn't, I can't challenge. I would be seen as insecure."

"You have more patience than me, sir." Sanders dropped his hands, ready to yell at a cadet who was wandering too close to the archers. Before he could open his mouth, the boy staggered and grabbed his head. He looked around in fear and confusion, connecting eyes with one of the Shumas. She shook her head no before pointing at the line of archers. The boy, his eyes rounded, jogged away in the other direction.

"Effective," Sanders said. "And she didn't even have to get up."

"We've gotten word." The Captain's stare was still

rooted to Kallon's. Sanders could almost see the electricity and violence crackle between them. "Xandre has moved a large faction of his well-trained men. They are still to the southeast, but are slowly headed in this direction. Burson's messages are coming daily, and each one is more disconcerting than the last. He says our window of opportunity is closing."

Sanders stayed silent, as did Lucius. There was no point in beating a dead horse.

"Daniels is working on the map. He spoke with Rohnan about their prophecies." The Captain's jaw clenched. He looked away from Kallon. "I want more information before I leave the city again. I need to know that they can protect themselves in our wake."

"Are there any more strong Shadow on their way?" Lucius asked. "If so, we could leave most of those currently in the city behind to lock it down and meet up with the others."

"Sonson knows of a few more groups on their way." The Captain looked out at Shanti. "They are coming from a different direction than the remainder of Shanti's people."

"Then we take those here as the others arrive." Sanders' gaze skittered across a pair of light blue eyes. He did a double take, seeing that woman Mela staring at him. "They have some serious social issues."

"Shanti thinks that her people will find her if we

cause a noteworthy event." The Captain shifted. "That is in line with what Daniels is thinking. They have very similar thoughts about what comes next."

Lucius said, "Causing an event?" as Sanders asked, "What kind of event?"

"We would need to take a Graygual stronghold. Or maybe another Inkna stronghold. That would send a message about our ability to the land. Shanti's people would know where to find us; Xandre will react, and hopefully reveal his location. Those hoping to join our cause would see that we are a strong adversary. Burson is adamant that we will bring others to our cause—they are just waiting for the sign. Taking a Graygual or Inkna city would be that sign."

"So, let me get this straight, sir." Sanders frowned at Mela before directing his focus elsewhere. He didn't have that mental mumbo-jumbo. If she kept staring, Sanders would take that as a challenge and rock her world. The practice yard was used on *his* terms. "You want to take some of these warriors and go pick a fight?"

"Basically, yes. Hopefully it'll force Xandre to show his hand. Or at least his general location. After that we disappear for a while, and get in position."

Sanders shrugged, his gaze returning to those light blue eyes. "Sounds like a treat, sir. Now excuse me—I have to go kick a woman in the teeth."

CHAPTER 3

MARC ROSE SLOWLY, peering over the hedge. Ten feet in front of him, sitting next to an open window, sat a freshly baked, golden-crusted, beautiful pie. Steam wafted invitingly, daring him to come closer and have a taste.

He licked his lips.

A head popped up over the fence on the other side of the yard. Leilius scanned the empty space in front of him before dropping back down.

Marc rolled his eyes. They were supposed to be working together to steal this pie. Without speaking, they had to sneak into the yard, steal the pie out from under the fiercest, most observant cook in the whole city, and bring it back without getting caught. Somehow, being good at this was supposed to make it easier to read the Shumas, who rarely spoke in battle.

Eloise seeing them, and accosting them later, would count as getting caught. She couldn't run with her bad knee and excess weight, but she didn't have to. One word to Marc's or Leilius' parents, or even to one of the other women, and they'd be as good as dead. Or worse. Shitting liquid for a month was not on his wish list.

Marc shivered as he glanced at the open window in time to see Eloise's large bust. His legs went limp, dropping him down to the dirt. She had been bending to put another pie in the window. If he had been in sight, she would've noticed him. The woman was too observant by half.

How the hell were they going to do this?

Marc rose up again, finding Leilius across the yard looking in his direction.

He lifted his eyebrows and widened his eyes. *Well? What should we do now?*

Leilius lifted his eyebrows, brought an open hand up, and shook everything.

That wasn't even sign language. It was gobbledygook. Couldn't Marc have been paired with Xavier or someone who always took charge? It would've made things so much easier.

Marc shook his head and mouthed, "What?"

Leilius stared at him. He scrunched his brow and put a hand to his ear.

"I can't yell it, you freaking idiot," Marc muttered. He glanced at the window. Empty apart from the two pies. They needed to hurry. Eloise only let her baked goods rest for a short time before she took them away in anticipation of serving them to the ladies' luncheon.

Marc waved Leilius toward the open window before he dropped back down and started creeping closer. He'd follow the hedge until it met the wall, then he'd climb over, out of sight, and continue close to the ground until he was under the window. After that, it was lift, snatch, and run. Easy.

A queasy feeling swirled Marc's stomach. He hoped timing was going to be on his side.

At the wall he peered over the hedge again. Seeing the way was clear, he scrambled over as quickly and quietly as possible. The branches bent and cracked. What was once a trimmed rectangle turned into a haphazard spray of green, the ends at all different angles.

Now he *really* couldn't get caught.

A large thump came from the other side of the yard. Leilius scrambled toward the wall before bending down to check his leg. He must've caught it on the wooden fence.

He was their best spy?

Staying low, Marc half crawled before hunching under the window. Leilius met him there a moment later before nodding in acknowledgement and sliding down to his butt. Leilius put his palms toward the air and shrugged in a *now what?* type of way.

Marc pointed at him then pointed upward. *You go.*

Leilius waved his hands in front of him while vehemently shaking his head. He pointed to his eyes, and then ran his finger through the air, indicating he'd be lookout.

Of course he would, the coward.

Knowing they didn't have time to debate it, and also that Leilius was as stubborn as a mule, Marc took a deep breath and turned so he was facing the house. Slowly, a fraction at a time, he rose. His legs started to burn almost immediately. Sweat dribbled down his forehead. He neared the ledge and paused, his knees shaking. Now or never.

As his eyes cleared the ledge, he saw a round face in the window staring at him.

"What are you doing, Marc?" Eloise asked in a deceptively calm voice. It was the voice someone who had a blade to his throat might use.

"Oh shit!"

Without thinking, only knowing he needed to complete the mission, he snatched the pie off the ledge and spun around. His legs pumped of their own volition, his feet slapping the ground in a harmony with Leilius' panicked, harried breathing.

He reached the hedge and dove over, clearing it with room to spare. He landed on his side. The pie bounced out of his hands and tumbled onto the ground.

Leilius jumped over the hedge after him as Marc scrambled up and scraped the pie contents back into the ceramic dish.

"It's ruined!" Leilius accused.

"No one said it had to be edible. We just had to get it."

"We weren't supposed to get caught. She said your name!"

"I panicked. What was I supposed to do?" Clumps of dirt and apples piled high in his wake, Marc took off at a jog. Looking back, he saw the blank face of someone that would soon make his life a living hell. "I should've left it there. S'am's punishment only hurts for a few hours. Lord only knows what Eloise will do to us."

"THOSE BOYS!"

Shanti stifled her smile, feeling Marc and Leilius scamper away from the house in terror as Eloise bustled into the living room with one pie and a surly expression. The older woman, the loudest voice in the Women's Circle, looked around the room with thunder in her eyes. Her gaze settled on Shanti. She pursed her lips, obviously suspecting Shanti of putting the boys up to their mischief.

Rohnan leaned away from Shanti with a grim expression.

"Hmm." Slowing down, her expression turning contemplative, Eloise put the pie on the small table between the couches amid the half-dozen gathered women and Rohnan. She straightened back up, eyeing the small plates and utensils placed strategically on the surface for the sake of appearances. "Molly, we need the tea."

"Yes, of course." Molly bustled into the kitchen.

"Which boys?" Valencia, the women who was equally skilled at killing pigs and Graygual, glowered. "Because yesterday my gardening equipment went missing and I had to pull weeds with my bare hands. If I find out who was messing with my things…"

"But yesterday was your gardening day," Tabby said with a furrowed brow. "I can't imagine someone could've grabbed them out from under your nose. Maybe they're just under the leaf pile. You know you tend to let your mind drift and—"

"I checked under the leaf pile!" Valencia glowered at the room in general. "I remember distinctly." She ticked off a finger. "I cleared away the petunias." Another finger. "I planted that pretty, leafy plant—I can't remember the name, but you remember, the one that blooms that pretty pink flower in the spring?" The ladies nodded and murmured. "I went to get the watering can, and when I came back, they were gone. Vanished. Someone must've taken them!"

Shanti's lips tweaked upward and her eyes sparkled. That would've been Xavier and Gracas. Impressive.

They were really coming along.

"I think you should check the leaf pile again." Tabby got up to help Molly set the tray of tea items on the table amid the baked goods.

"What went missing, Eloise?" Valencia asked, ignoring Tabby.

"Nothing." Eloise lowered down into her chair. Her fingers tapped on the arm for a moment, making a steady rhythm. "Nothing. I'll take care of it." Her gaze skewered Shanti. "On to important matters. Our enlisted women have grown more than twice since the battle. I've given orders for them to be supplied with bows, as you've suggested, but now what?"

"I have someone helping them with training," Shanti said, kicking away her bulbous skirt from around her legs.

She'd been invited to attend this meeting under the condition that she wore a dress, as befitted Cayan's wife. Since she was not Cayan's wife, and didn't want to go, she'd refused.

The invitation had been amended. As the woman giving commands alongside Cayan, she was required to go, for the good of the city. But she would still need to wear the dress.

She'd then amended her refusal: wearing a dress would prevent her from reacting quickly if anything should go wrong during the hourlong meeting.

If it hadn't been for Molly shadowing her for two days, explaining the importance of meeting with the Women's Circle and how her refusal would look on Cayan, Shanti would've ignored Eloise's assurances that in no way would the dress interfere with anything that could possibly happen.

The woman was as tenacious as mold on old cheese.

"Yes. I heard about Mela's instruction." Eloise pursed her lips again. "Even so, she is a great resource."

"It got me out of messing around with bows and arrows." Fabienne looked down at her splayed hands. "I have blisters."

"That's because you don't do anything," Valencia said with a sniff.

"Is that right?" Fabienne leaned to the side enough to put a fist to her hip. "You don't think I work my tail off to—"

"Ladies, enough!" Eloise took a cup of tea from Molly. She looked at Shanti. "We all want to make sure the women who want to be trained will be."

"I cannot make that guarantee," Shanti said matter-of-factly.

The room fell silent. Rohnan shifted uncomfortably.

"Please explain," Eloise said in a level voice.

A shiver raced up Shanti's spine. She now realized why Sanders gave these women a wide berth. An enemy running at her with a knife was much more appealing than this near-silent threat.

Shanti matched Eloise's tone. "We will only train those with potential. Just like with the men in the army, those who don't have sufficient ability to learn will be given a different task."

"But your Honor Guard, as you call them, were nearly sent to the mines." Eloise sipped her tea calmly. "If it hadn't been for you, we would never have seen their skill. Yet you are not training the women. What if they are passed over because a blind man judged their worth? Or worse, a man who only saw a woman…"

"Sanders doesn't just see women." Shanti sipped her tea. Then grimaced. It was awful stuff. "But since he is too easily pushed around by your city's women, I've put my people on it. They are great judges of talent."

"Why are you training them out in the middle of nowhere?" Valencia asked.

"We need to pick those who have potential, train them to a reasonable level, then move them over to the larger army. I didn't want grown women learning beside boys. That would reflect poorly on the women."

"Most of the army is okay with women learning to fight," Rohnan said in his musical voice. It had the pleasing benefit of defusing the growing tension. "They understand that they need as much help as possible to protect the city. Those that object are doing so loudly, however. It's best to bring the women into the fold only when they can make the loudest statement."

"What about when you leave?" Tabby asked from the back of the room. "What happens to us?"

Shanti kicked at her dress again. "We're not sure who's going yet, but a few commanders as well as some of the Shadow will be left behind. As Rohnan said, everyone understands how valuable capable fighters are when it comes to defending the city. Women as well as men. When needed, the women will be used. I guarantee it."

"Fine, fine." Eloise stretched out her leg with a pained expression. She settled back and took a sip of her tea. "Let's move on to other matters. We've had some problems with nudity in the city." Eloise looked at Shanti over the rim of her cup.

"I apologize." Shanti shook her head at Molly's proffered piece of pie. "They know the rules, but occasionally they forget."

"Now, I don't mind an attractive, nude male body—let's get that right," Fabienne said. "The issue is, we have to maintain some sort of decorum or else everyone will think nudity is the way to go. And we have more unattractive bodies in this city than attractive ones…"

"I think you're focusing on the wrong part of this problem," Eloise said.

"The problem is, the men are going to be standing around, gawking, and grabbing themselves," Molly offered. "You know, if it's a woman who's naked."

"No—Well, partially, yes, but that still isn't exactly…" Eloise scratched her head.

"Young girls don't need to see saggy balls." Fabienne nodded at Shanti. "It could traumatize them."

"That's not—" Eloise stared at Fabienne.

"It's just not our custom, is that what you're trying to say, Eloise?" Tabby asked.

"Having women in the army isn't our custom, but we're pushing for that," someone in the rear of the living room said. "I say let the attractive young men be naked. Old farts like my mister wouldn't wander around with his tackle out. I don't think we need to worry about that."

"It isn't just the men who go around with their bits uncovered, though." Valencia turned on the couch to look back at the speaker.

"I don't mind getting a little air under my dress," someone else said quietly. "I'd try going nude. It would be liberating."

"You'd sag to the floor!"

"So?"

"Think of the children!" someone else shouted.

"Ladies, ladies!" Eloise rolled her eyes. "You are completely missing the point."

"Until you resolve this, I'll have a word with them," Shanti said, trying to hide her smile. She would laugh in

Sanders' face if these women decided nudity should be more freely expressed.

"Fine—"

"Put this on the table for discussion, though," someone cut off Eloise.

"You are too old for running around without a top."

"Ladies!" Eloise scoffed. "Of all the things to get worked up about." She took a deep breath as the room filled with the sound of shifting fabric and heavy breathing. "Now," Eloise said when things had settled. "The next order of business is the Captain's proposal. Where do you stand on that?"

"So romantic," someone sighed.

"It's not romantic to bring it up at a Circle meeting," Valencia said with raised eyebrows.

"Did she refuse him?" someone asked from the back.

Shanti shifted, feeling something niggle at her awareness. Suddenly a blast of warning ripped through her mind. One of the Shadow sentries was sounding the alarm.

"I have to go!" Shanti jumped up and immediately stepped on the hem of her dress. She staggered, clutching Rohnan, who was there in a moment. "Get me out of this thing."

Heart racing, fear tingling her fingers from memories of the past, she made herself stand still while

Rohnan peeled her out of the expensive dress. Underneath she had a tight top and leggings, garments that would allow her to fight without being overly restrained under the dress.

"What's happening?" Eloise asked as she heaved her body upward.

"Someone is in our lands." Shanti kicked off the slippers and raced toward her sack at the door before ripping out her boots. "I should be halfway out there by now, not trying to get dressed."

"Point made," Eloise said somberly.

Rohnan, who had also been required to dress up, stripped off the silk top and pushed down his trousers.

"Now this I don't mind," one of the women said.

"Let's go!" Shanti said through gritted teeth as another pop of warning blared through her mind. "There's more than one."

"I feel it." Rohnan snatched up his sword and strapped it on as Shanti opened the door.

They raced out as Shanti pinpointed where everyone was. Her people were running toward whichever one of the city gates they were nearest to. Shadow did likewise, feeling the urgency and taking up their posts. She could feel Cayan's anxiety, aware of what was happening but having to rely on speech to get his men in position.

Another warning blasted. *"Flak!"* Shanti said, veer-ing right.

"Where are you going?" Rohnan kept pace.

"Horses…" Her breath came out in fast puffs. "They can…run faster…than we can."

The first foreign mind solidified in Shanti's consciousness as the cobblestone of the street ended and became torn-up dirt. The smell of horses assaulted her nose. She ripped open the stall to the Bloody Bastard as Sonson ran in behind her.

"Should we turn loose the beasts?" he asked, running toward his horse.

"Will they run rampant around the city?" Shanti launched a foot over her horse's back and scrambled on. There was no time to saddle up.

"Tunston has been working diligently to train them where to exit the city. He's confident." Another gate squealed as Sonson went after his horse. "Those cats, though…"

Shanti locked on to the strange mind in her range, waited for more, and was immediately rewarded with another two. "The cats will wait for Cayan and I, I have no doubt."

She was lying. She had a lot of doubt.

"Leave the beasts for now. There are only three. We aim to capture, not kill."

More Shadow, and now the army started to file in. Shanti felt others running outside of the city, getting into position to surround the intruders.

"This is not an attack," Rohnan said for Sonson's benefit as he climbed on his horse. "This is Xandre's way of collecting information. He has no problem sending men in, even though, toward the end, he rarely received any back."

"He's talking about before the battle that ended our way of life," Shanti said, clutching her horse's mane. He pranced impatiently. "We waited for them to come with force. We cannot make that mistake again. We need to leave before it's too late. Hopefully these men can give us information about Xandre's plans."

"They never have before," Rohnan said quietly.

"Yaw!" Shanti dug her heels into the horse's flank. The animal lurched into motion, his power and speed jolting Shanti backward.

"Bloody...hell." She gripped with her knees and adjusted her balance, feeling the horse's speed pick up to almost alarming levels. "No, no!" She clutched the coarse hair in her fists as she tried to steer around a corner. The horse's hooves clattered and skidded, the animal stumbling before it righted again. "Too fast for—Look out!"

A woman screeched as she hustled out of the way. Others in the busy street ran to the sides, shock or disgruntlement on their faces. The Women's Circle would no doubt put this on their agenda.

The open gate loomed in sight. Men stood around the chain, ready to close the doors and secure it if they received the command. "*Now* run, you bloody horse!" Shanti dug her heels into its flanks and leaned forward.

With a burst of speed, the horse rushed through the gates, stretching its legs and putting distance between it and those behind her. She held on for dear life, her jaw clenched tight, fighting for control.

Another mind came within her range. Like a vivid dream, Shanti clearly remembered the type of mind she felt. Cunning and analytical, he was a quick thinker but slow mover, plotting his way forward with careful steps. It was Xandre's ideal type for recovering information—he was making plans. They were a lot closer to battle than she'd realized.

A wash of fear had her leaning to the right, directing the horse as much as it would let her. Trees streamed by. Sentries looked down at her, she felt many within her *Gift*, waiting for the emotional cues they knew would come. They'd had so little time, but they'd made great progress so far.

Yet another mind came into her map. The same type of man—she could feel his watchfulness as he neared one of the first sentries. A blast of fear colored his mind. He'd recognized the sentry as a Shadow, she had no doubt. He'd know the Shadow could feel him with the *Gift*.

For a moment everything seemed to freeze. A decision was left in the balance. And then the man was in action. He moved away quickly in the direction he'd come.

"No! We have to get him!" Shanti urged her horse faster, before her heart jumped into her throat. Warning sirens pinged through her consciousness like pops in a fire. All round the city, one after the other, the sentries scrambled out of their trees and ran, aiming back for the gates.

In another few moments, she knew why.

A wall of enemy, surrounding the city, was advancing. This was the first wave of attack, and there had been no warning.

CHAPTER 4

SHANTI YANKED ON the Bloody Bastard's mane as hard as she could, preparing to jump off if the accursed animal didn't slow. Thankfully, the horse complied, almost throwing her as it jolted and bounced to a stop. She schooled her emotions to send a message to her people, making them run back toward the city.

The thunder of hooves behind her started to slow. "What is it?" Sonson's eyes went wide and the color drained from Rohnan's face. They could feel what she did.

"This isn't like him," Rohnan protested, turning his horse.

"Which is exactly why he's doing it. He is way ahead of me." Shanti ripped the mane around and dug in her heels. "Hurry!"

A black shape flashed by, followed by two more. The cats had found her and anticipated their direction. Good. They could be of use in the city. If anyone got over the walls, hopefully these animals could help take them down.

Shanti monitored the sentries. The Shadow and Shumas had been warned ahead of time. They'd collected their horses and would make it back without any problem. But they hadn't stopped to inform Cayan's people, who were relying solely on their eyes. The *Gifted* weren't making themselves clear to those without it.

"Shortsighted," she muttered in agony, slowing for the second time. She'd just discovered a gaping hole in her training.

Before she could turn the Bastard, a large black stallion barreled out of the city gate. Behind him came sleek and shining horses ridden by some of Cayan's elite. She felt fighters with single-minded focus exiting through the other gates.

"He means to get the sentries," she heard Rohnan say behind her. Cayan had figured out what she had, and reacted ten times faster.

That was why he was the Captain.

"C'mon!" She urged her horse on, riding to meet up with the others. When she was close, the Bastard fell in line naturally, easily keeping pace with Cayan's stallion.

Spreading her mind along the line of enemy horses, thundering down on the sentries, some of which were only now climbing down from their trees, she *wrenched*.

Equine screams rode the breeze. She *stabbed*, feeling the turmoil in the riders as their mounts bucked and kicked, dizzy with fear.

"Save your strength," Rohnan shouted behind her.

He apparently thought she was a novice.

Behind the line of panicking horses rode another line, and then a horde of men on foot.

How had this many men moved so close without the Westwood Lands being warned? It didn't seem possible.

A man in blue emerged through the trees, frantic, riding for all he was worth. A hundred yards behind him, between Cayan's team and the Graygual, limped another. Determination radiated from him even though his situation had looked hopeless.

"Lucius!" Cayan called over his shoulder. The wind whipped his words away as the thundering of hooves drowned them out. But Cayan had his own way of communicating, built from years of working with his men.

He veered to the side, sending a feeling of *distance* to Shanti, having her veer the other way, opening up a hole to run around the struggling man so Lucius could make the grab.

And then they were on them.

Graygual looked up the instant before a thunder of power rocked the line of enemy. Men screamed, clutching at their chests. Shanti hit them a moment later, *slashing* through their brains and driving men to their knees.

Sunlight glinted off a sword as Cayan slashed downward. The Bloody Bastard hit the line a moment later, screaming wildly before rearing, lashing out with his front hooves. Red splashed as a head caved in. Shanti slashed a neck, dropping the man before readying another blast of power.

"We're here long enough to get everyone secure," Cayan shouted, piercing a man's face with his blade before hacking down at someone else. His strokes were vicious and powerful.

Shanti monitored those around the city, identifying who was still outside the gates. On the far side, where the second largest cluster of Graygual approached, someone was in agony.

"We'd never make it in time," Cayan yelled, feeling her discovery.

Shanti sent a request for aid to her people, hoping they remembered the difference between *her* needing help and someone else. She sliced down at an arm even as she tried to focus with all her person on the downed man.

A spark of understanding came from Kallon before she felt his action. Mela and Sayas were the next to give that spark of understanding. She didn't know if they'd read her right, though. The system, despite their years of practice, was still imperfect.

"Shanti!" Lucius' voice cut through her mental focus. She registered her surroundings a moment before she saw a black uniform with five stripes bear down. The flash of a sword announced a strike aimed right for her.

Reacting, she *struck,* piercing his brain before her arm could even lift to block. The sword kept coming; the Graygual officer had trained against excruciating mental pain and was not deterred. Suddenly she was weightless. Her body flew through the air, ass over end, as a horse scream cut through the clang of metal and shouts of men. Her body hit the ground in a painful thud as the scream sounded again.

Hooves swung up to the sky before crashing back down. The Bloody Bastard reared again, kicking out with his front legs. Blood dripped onto the ground below him. The sword must've sliced into his breast. Another scream and he turned, before bucking out with his powerful hind legs. The kick landed, punching a huge gash in the other horse to match the rips and scrapes from his previous attempts. The enemy animal reared, screaming his pain.

"Mesasha!" A large hand reached into Shanti's line of sight as the Graygual toppled from his horse, a knife sticking out of his ear. She grabbed the hand and allowed Cayan to hoist her up as she *slashed* with her mind, cutting into man and animal alike, taking down anything near her horse. He might be an asshole, but he

was *her* asshole.

"Are you hurt?" Cayan asked as he threw her over his saddle and turned his horse toward the city.

She realized, belatedly, that another round of fighting had kicked off near the downed man on the other side of the city. Kallon had understood. He was fighting off the enemy to get to the fallen sentry.

"No. I don't know. How's my horse?"

"Hurt. He's following us. Do you feel any pain?"

Shanti bounced and jostled, lying awkwardly across Cayan's lap with the pommel digging painfully into her side. Her breath came hard, and her right thigh pounded.

"I'm okay. Probably." She bent to try and look behind them. It was a futile effort. "How hurt?"

Cayan's irritation was overridden by his anxiety. She felt his large hand on the center of her back before the horse picked up speed. Her body bounded on his lap, sending waves of pain through her middle.

"We have to go faster!" Lucius yelled from beside them.

"I can't go any faster with her like this," Cayan said. "And I can't stop to right her. We'll make it."

"That grab was poor planning." Shanti's words came out as little more than a collection of grunts.

Shanti felt the enemy, chasing them back toward the city. Only a few were mounted, and she *seared* the minds of horses and riders at the same time. Screaming sounded behind them.

"Save your strength!" Rohnan yelled.

"For when? After they've caught us?" Another collection of grunts.

"We'll make it," Cayan said again. More hooves passed within Shanti's sight before Cayan's horse slowed. Shouts and voices grew louder as Cayan's horse went through the partially opened gates.

Once inside, he stopped his horse and helped someone take her down off the saddle. She looked up and felt a rush of relief as the limping and bleeding Bloody Bastard trotted forward, his head hanging and his sides heaving.

"See to my horse!" she cried.

Someone ran forward, only to flinch back as the Bastard tried to take a bite out of the man's shoulder.

"Damn you, you stupid animal." Shanti felt like slapping him, but under the circumstances, that might be a little abrasive. Instead, she put a hand on his neck firmly, hoping he knew that she *would* slap him if she needed to. "Let someone help you."

"That animal doesn't understand you, you know." Sanders marched up with a hard expression. "Gates are all closed. Archers are positioned on the walls. Everyone made it back in."

Cayan gave Shanti a long look, no doubt trying to

ascertain if her stance meant she was in pain. It did.

"I'm fine," she said as someone hesitantly stepped closer to the Bastard. She paused long enough to make sure the horse would allow treatment, before she moved away with Cayan. "That came out of nowhere. How was that possible?"

"I don't know," Cayan said, rage lining his voice. "We've heard nothing about their approach."

"The Graygual with the knife in his ear had five stripes." Shanti checked her weapons, making sure she had everything. "I didn't expect Xandre to engage so soon."

"I saw two others with three stripes," Sanders said, surveying their surroundings as they walked.

Up the street people bustled, rushing for the hold that would hide them away from attack. It wasn't impregnable, and not everyone took refuge there, but if a small number of the enemy made it over the walls, most of the city people would be safe.

"They didn't have any larger units able to break into the city," Cayan said as they rounded a corner and headed to the practice yard where the majority of the army was getting prepared. "I was in front of the largest horde of Graygual, and I didn't even see a battering ram."

Like ghosts drifting out of the mist, Shumas jogged in from the sides, falling in behind Shanti, awaiting direction. The three large cats moved among them, sleek and deadly. Shanti noticed Sonson up ahead, his flare of red hair catching the sun as he waited with his men and women at the edge of the practice yard. Among them were the three beasts on chain leashes—as if that would help if those animals went berserk.

To Shanti, Cayan asked, "Did you sense any Inkna?"

"None. The upper-tiered officers would usually be protected. Not this time."

Cayan shook his head, marching onto the packed dirt of the practice yard. "This doesn't make sense."

"What are your orders, sir?" Sanders asked, standing in front of the army.

"Reinforce the gates. They don't have enough to surround the city with any density. Our archers can easily take down anyone that nears the wall. Get women up there, too. The time for hiding them is over. Make sure we have men and horses on the ground in case they produce a battering ram we haven't seen. Take down anyone that comes within range."

To Shanti he said, "Station the Shumas and Shadow around the wall with the archers. I want immediate communication if anything comes up."

"With the amount of power we have in the city, we can kill or cripple them with a single surge," Shanti said, motioning Sonson over. "We don't have to get our hands dirty."

"That'll severely weaken us. I don't know how he moved this many people without word reaching us. I wouldn't have thought it possible. We have no idea how many more are out there, and I don't want to leave us defenseless against a mental attack."

CHAPTER 5

Cayan stood at the top of the wall, looking out at the lands beyond. He couldn't see the enemy waiting out there patiently, but he could feel them. They remained out of sight, sticking to the trees and foliage. Their minds were watchful but at rest, not preparing for an attack or expecting one from the city.

What were they doing here if not waging war?

"Captain, we're set." Commander Sterling came to a stop beside him, forcing one of the dozen female archers along the wall to make room. "Commander Sanders has the ground forces ready, as well. Shanti is monitoring the mental workers. Maggie, the woman with the exploding devices, has teams set. We're ready for the next move."

Cayan clenched his jaw and shifted his weight. He didn't like making strategies when the enemy's intentions weren't clear. It left too much up to guesswork.

He looked along the wall, eyeing those waiting. Eyes hard and bodies squared, his people were primed and ready. Not one harbored a spark of fear, not even the women or younger men. All were determined and ready to defend what was theirs. His people would not let someone invade again. They were warriors.

A swaying branch caught his eye. Nothing but the wind.

"We wait. They want us to come to them; I can feel it."

"They are trying to draw us out?" Sterling braced his hand on the hilt of his sword. "Or maybe they're trying to keep us put? Cut off our supplies?"

"With so few?" Cayan shook his head. "Doubtful. They have orders. I just can't fathom what they are." He turned toward the stairs leading down. "We wait. Let's see if they make a move."

"Yes, sir."

Cayan nodded to ready the men and women as he made his way through the city. Commander Daniels was in Cayan's larger office, bent over the maps of the land. Various points had been dotted in blues and grays, denoting known Graygual and Inkna forces. Other colors represented their various allies, minuscule in comparison.

"What do you think, Commander?" Cayan asked as he felt those with mental power moving around the city, shifting position. Shanti was using the opportunity to train them in mental communication. It was genius, though sometimes extremely hard to grasp, even with their *Joining*.

Daniels' bloodshot eyes glanced up before he tapped the neighboring land. "I bet the Graygual have been collecting in the Mugdock city. They could trickle in there slowly until they had a large enough host, then they moved this way. That would seem the most reasonable explanation."

It made sense. Since the Mugdock attacked all those months ago, they'd been unnaturally quiet. Cayan's traders had remained unmolested; they'd had no more threats, and reported no real sightings. "You think the Graygual wiped them out after the Inkna made use of them?"

Daniels straightened up, wincing as he rolled his shoulders and massaged his neck. "There is no way to tell, but it seems likely. We've been so preoccupied with the larger issues, we haven't checked in with our turbulent neighbors. Who's to say what has been going on?"

"That could be why the Hunter was left unchecked. Xandre had his eye on the situation from close enough to get his prize if it was going to be easy pickings. I never thought he would be the kind of Commander to allow important pieces to slip through the cracks." Frustration welled up in Shanti suddenly, turning into violent energy. She was getting restless. She hated waiting for an enemy to come to her. Cayan knew how she felt, but he also hated chasing an enemy that might be laying a trap.

His hands thudded against the desk as he leaned over the map. "He couldn't have assembled a large force in the Mugdock lands. Not with the host he had in the Shadow Lands. There hadn't been enough time to move that many people."

"That many *valuable* people," Daniels said. "Kallon gave me the impression that he encountered a great many men who were little better than militia. They were starved out of their lands and given very little choice but to join the Graygual army. The Shadow Lands had good warriors and enlightened tacticians. That doesn't mean the men waiting at our walls are of the same caliber."

"But why are they waiting?" Cayan pushed off the wood and crossed to the window. The street beyond was empty, nothing but sunshine gracing the cobblestone. "Anything new from Burson?"

"Just the latest urgent plea to get moving."

"Have any other reports come in?"

"The land is strangely quiet."

Cayan turned around to find Daniels was looking at him with an unreadable expression. His shoulders were tight, and not just from the fatigue of constant planning. Something was worrying him.

Cayan thought about the port city of Clintos after they'd returned from the Shadow Lands. The people there kept to themselves. Only low murmurs and the clink of eating utensils graced the inn's common area, where dice games and the raucous laughter of the drunk would usually vibrate through the space. The town had been plagued by the Graygual, and yet they were lying low. Sonson had said they were waiting for the Wanderer.

Was everyone?

The situation crystallized in Cayan's head. Everything from the solemn looks of strangers to the glimmer of hope in the downtrodden. From the desperate acts of the Hunter when he was trapped to the hesitation of the army at their doorstep. Everyone, including the enemy, was waiting for someone to push back.

They were waiting for Shanti.

She was the ultimate wild card, entirely unpredictable. Things she found so logical were chaos to most, including her own people, and yet her plans always seemed to work. Even nearly succumbing to death in the burnt lands worked to her advantage—she had found him, and grown stronger.

She was the key, and he was holding her back. He was trying to tame the wildness in her instead of embracing it. He needed to set her free, hold on, and take what came. It was the only way.

Cayan moved toward the door. "Put the plans in action. We're leaving." He paused with his hand on the cold metal of the handle. "And Daniels…"

The graying man looked up.

"We'll head to the Mugdock lands first. We need to clean out that infestation and then plant some eyes there in case they come back."

TWO INCREDIBLY SHORT days later, armed men waited at the gates of the city at dawn, ready to ride out and cut down the enemy. Preparing had been a hectic affair, all while the enemy was growing in size outside the walls. They hadn't attacked, though. A few had ventured closer each day, and each had been brought down by a well-aimed arrow.

"I had no idea you were this ready," Shanti said from beside Cayan. "This horse is too tame, though. It does run, right?"

Cayan glanced at her warhorse, one of the best they had. It waited under her patiently, as it was supposed to do. Her own wild horse would have to stay behind. The gash in its chest wasn't life-threatening, but would severely hinder taking a rider. "Ideally, I would've loved to stay within the city and somehow also beat Xandre, but that wasn't logical. We've been preparing for this day since we took our city back."

Cayan glanced behind him and saw Sanders walk up the line of horses. His Commander paused at the mare bearing Alena. He said a couple words Cayan couldn't hear, nodded, and continued. "I worry about taking such inexperienced people."

Shanti followed his gaze before checking her weapons. "Ruisa was more inexperienced. It'll be fine."

Ruisa hadn't been his choice, either. It had been Burson's.

"We're ready, sir." Sanders threw a leg over his horse's saddle.

Cayan braced. There were so many ways this could go wrong.

He looked at the men and women lining the walls. The Shadow he was leaving behind stood firm and ready, their power unyielding and their viciousness unmatched. They'd protect this land as their own—hearing Sonson speaking with them had confirmed that. Their home would be protected.

Cayan had to make a move. There was no other way.

"Let's hope there's no one waiting just outside our mental range." Cayan looked up at Commander Sterling, who was watching for Cayan's signal. Cayan nodded.

"Open the gates!" Sterling put his hand in the air for the archers.

"He's testing you," Shanti said for what seemed like the millionth time in the last two days. "He's waiting to see how long it'll take you to engage."

"Xandre couldn't possibly be willing to sacrifice this many men." Cayan tightened his grip on the reins.

"We only saw one higher-ranked officer. Just one. I bet these men aren't his best stock." Shanti stared down at her horse again. "I never thought I'd be sorry that I had complete control of a horse. It's boring."

"The things you bitch about," Sanders growled.

A wave of expectation assaulted Cayan as they waited. Horses started to fidget. The grind of the gate echoed off the buildings behind them.

"No movement," Sterling said from the wall.

The enemy minds that were awake remained idle. They obviously couldn't see the gates opening, and without mental ability, they couldn't feel Cayan's people gearing up.

"Strike fast, kill quickly." Shanti took her sword from its sheath. "If there *is* someone waiting beyond our range, we don't want to be half-dead with fatigue when we face them."

A flare of *ready* came from the south gate, followed quickly with the west.

"Why is Sayas' team taking so long?" Shanti turned as if she could see across the city.

The last flare filled Cayan's awareness. "Move out!" He urged his horse forward, walking until he was out of the gate, and then started to trot.

Shanti fell behind immediately.

"Kick its sides!" Sanders shouted.

"I did!"

"S'am, you're doing it wrong!" Gracas said.

Bursts of what Cayan could only describe as realization rose up from the enemy, followed by confusion, rage, thrill, and action. This was not a synchronized army, but they knew battle was coming. Right now.

"Charge!" Cayan shouted, sword in hand.

Shanti was beside him a moment later, and the others fanned out behind. Trees whipped by as the enemy scrambled, probably only starting to realize what was happening when it was too late. The thunder of hooves soon competed with shouts and yells as they penetrated the beginning of the enemy lines.

An arrow zipped by from behind before striking a black uniform mid-chest. Another caught an enemy in the arm. Up ahead the Graygual camp was a frenzy of activity, men stuffing their arms into protective tunics as they rushed for their horses, while others ran forward with bows in hand.

"Cut 'em down!" Cayan burst into the center of their camp with his sword already in motion. He sliced through a black uniform as his *Gift* rolled before him, not strong enough to kill, but enough to immobilize. Men screamed. More power struck to the sound of louder screams, making men sink to the ground.

"Take them out," Shanti yelled as she jumped from her horse. She descended on a cowering group who held their heads in agony. Rohnan dropped down beside her, his staff twirling in his hands.

Cayan directed his horse through the tents, catching a man with two stripes as he ran. Two more sprinted away, one with his shirt only half on. They were not preparing to fight—they were running for their lives. These must've been the militia Kallon was talking about.

A figure jumped out from behind a tent with an arrow swinging upward. Cayan kicked his horse, making it lurch forward, trampling the man. He took his own bow and nocked an arrow before turning in his saddle, away from the running men. He loosed toward someone with three stripes running at one of the Shadow's backs.

His horse neighed as Cayan tugged the reins to the right, running out of the cluster of tents, aiming for another group. He released an arrow, catching a man running at him on a finely bred horse. To his right, a man fell from his saddle, an arrow in the side of his neck. Alena emerged from the trees, quickly nocking another arrow.

Great shot.

Spirals of fear announced the presence of enemy from the side, hidden in the trees. Flushing them out was quick and easy, but as Cayan stared down the length of his arrow at the two dirty and terrified men, he couldn't relax his fingers for the kill shot. He couldn't cut down two men who might not have had any other option but to join the Graygual army. They probably didn't even know why they were fighting, or who. They were just trying to survive. Like Shanti was.

"Damn it!" Cayan dropped the bow before yanking on the reins. That decision might very well be the death of him in the end, but he wouldn't sacrifice his humanity. If he did that, he would lose no matter the outcome of the war.

His bow sang at the sight of the next multi-striped Graygual. Then the next. They came at him with three or four stripes, straight-faced and hollowed-eyed. A sword-wielding blond warrior exploded from the trees to his right, aiming for two Graygual on foot. They faced him with fierce expressions before the Shadow hacked down at them, catching one before his upswing caught the other.

Behind him ran a riderless wild horse. It whinnied before it ran on, the white bandage around its chest peeling away in places. Shanti's horse had gotten free somehow, and followed everyone out of the city. The thing was crazy, but it had possibly saved her life in their charge. Cayan would give it a lot of allowance for that.

A black-clad man ran from the trees, bow at the ready. Without warning, a streak of black lunged, white teeth flashing before they clamped down on the man's jugular. Another of the great cats gave its feline roar, joining in the kill.

Panting, with sweat glistening from their brows and blood dripping from their swords, Cayan's army slowed, looking for more.

The enemy were either running in terror all around the city, or dying. Few were left after such a short time. The enemy had been largely unprepared. Shanti was right—they were here to test Cayan's resolve. One or two officers were likely to have escaped to make a report of their findings, while the lower-tiered men would die. The question was, where were those officers headed?

He hoped it was to the Mugdock lands. If so, he'd see them soon.

CHAPTER 6

"Woman, you are not holding that right."

Alena jumped as Kallon drifted out of the trees like a phantom. The Shumas came out of nowhere. All of them were so quiet, even when traveling through dry leaves. She knew they'd blend into the bright green of spring as easily as the dull gray of winter, even those with bright blond hair. It was crazy.

She was a little envious, if she was being honest.

"This is how I was taught." Alena frowned at the bow, as if that would reveal the answer to the problem. She glanced at the sky, annoyed that the sun was sinking and taking the last of the day's light. They'd traveled all day, nearing the horrible Mugdock lands. They'd reach the border sometime tomorrow, and a battle might come soon after.

Butterflies took over her stomach as the striking blond man came to stand right in front of her. His hair fell around his face in a wave, accenting strong cheekbones in a chiseled face. He was incredibly handsome, not just striking. If it hadn't been for his stormy eyes, so haunted and riddled with pain, he'd probably have set her panties on fire. As it was, his dangerous edge had her body tingling in a way that wasn't entirely pleasant.

Mostly.

"I j-just…" She jerked her bow up and scowled down at it, trying to rid herself of the stammer. "I thought I was doing it right."

His intent gaze surveyed her for a moment before his hand drifted out from his side to the bow. Electricity crackled as his warm hand graced hers. She flinched and dropped the bow. Her arrow tumbled to the dirt.

"You are jumpy." He bent to the bow and arrow, picking them up with graceful movements. He held them out. "Take them. I'll show you."

"Yup. Oh-kay." Face on fire, she took the bow and held it as she was taught, only shaking a little more. The man was rattling her. He was just so *intense*.

He stepped to the side and waited. She fitted the arrow and pulled back, sighting. As she had been taught since childhood, she let her mind go blank. Her breathing came even and slow. She zeroed in on the red splotch in the middle of the target, ignoring all else. Trying to block out the wind ruffling her hair and the heat of the man standing a little too close.

She let go at the same time as blinking. That meant she'd also jerked just a tiny bit. "Dang it!"

The arrow was at the edge of the target, just as she'd

suspected. "I'm better in the middle of battle. Or action. Just standing here…I think I'm too caught in my head."

Tingles worked down her back again as the man surveyed her. "You are trying too hard. You are not giving in to it. Are you a virgin?"

"*What?*" she sputtered.

"In sex, there is a point where you can give in totally. Have you been to that point?"

"That's… This…" She moved a step away and circled the air with her pointer finger. "That's none of your business."

His eyes sparkled but the sentiment didn't reach his lips. He barely nodded. "Let's see."

"No!" Alena flinched away. "I barely know you!"

This time the corners of his lips pulled, hinting at a smile. "Let's see you hold the bow again."

"Oh." She tossed her head, which would've looked a lot better if her hair had been tied in a bun and therefore unable to flick behind her shoulder. "Okay, then."

She raised the bow a second time and quickly reached back for an arrow, but stopped when she felt strong fingers wrap around her wrist. "Wait," he said.

He moved her arm back in front of her. "Speed is good, but technique is better. Do not move faster than your experience level. It will cripple you in the end."

"You speak our language well," she blurted.

"Yes. Now, try again."

Biting her lip, she reached back slowly, feeling his direction as she did so. The change was minute, barely more than a flare of her elbow, but it felt so much smoother. Like a greased machine instead of a rusty one. "Weird."

"Try again."

She reached back, feeling his hand directing her. "It feels smoother when I do it your way, but at the same time, it feels like I am reaching wider somehow. Like it'll take longer. It's not the shortest distance between my bow and the quiver."

"You are not using your muscle groups properly. You are thinking too much. Learn to listen to your body. *Feel.* Try again."

Alena didn't just try again—with his instruction and patience, she must've reached back ten more times, before being instructed to keep trying. "I think I have it," she finally said.

"Yes. Your form is perfect. But to remain perfect, you need to teach your body. You are still thinking. When you stop thinking, you will have it. Let's see you shoot."

Alena's sigh was a little too loud. Her arm was growing tired from all the reaching.

She sighted, and then let her mind go blank. Her breath evened out, and then came quickly again when deft fingers danced across her shoulders.

"You are too tight through here." He tapped her shoulder muscles.

She tried to relax, but he was standing really close. He didn't have the same respect for personal space as her people did. And also, he smelled really good. Like wild forest and springtime.

"Okay." Alena dropped her bow and stepped away. "Can you just…wait over there?"

"If you would prefer." He took two smooth steps away.

This time, with relaxed shoulders, she focused on her breath. She blocked out the breeze and tried to settle into the shot.

The hand on her shoulder made her jump. She hadn't even heard him walk closer!

"You are blocking your surroundings. That is dangerous in battle." Kallon stepped in front of her again, his eyes sweeping her face. "Mela noted that your people are trained incorrectly in that regard. It can be mastered, doing as you do, but it is so much harder, and shortsighted. Your Captain does not use this approach. Your commanders don't. Yet everyone still tries to train with it. It seems those with natural ability find the best way, while those without stand in line to get killed."

Alena frowned. That was a harsh thing to say. Surely there was some stock in their training if they could produce the army they had.

"Try again." He stepped around her, his body nearly touching hers as he stood to the side.

She pulled back the string, sighted, and paused while he adjusted her elbow. His hands applied pressure to the side of her hips, turning her a fraction.

"Mela approved of my posture." Not to mention that when she'd adjusted her body, it had been in a more formal way.

"Mela wasn't noticing what I am noticing. You are beautiful. I want to drink in the sight of you. Vulnerable and fierce at the same time. *Chulan* was like that, once. We all were. I barely remember."

"That's… This is…" Alena felt like she was trying to swallow a boiled egg. "You aren't helping."

"I am distracted." Kallon touched her elbow again. His fingers grazed her hips. "Look at the target."

The red splotch swam into view, but her shoulders would not relax. Her breath came unevenly. This was not helping.

"Release."

A blast of awareness tore through her a moment before she did as instructed. In that brief time, she saw the red; she felt her body; she noticed the strength of the wind and the sweet smell of his breath. Most importantly, in that brief moment, her body went fluid and reacted to the task at hand. She didn't think, she just did.

The fletching quivered in the middle of the target.

"Oh wow." Kallon forgotten, Alena dropped the bow in surprise. "I was not ready to release when you said release, and then I just did, and…wow."

"You think too hard. Do not block out your surroundings; become one with them. Accept them into you. If a man is sounding his death scream at your side, hear it. Let his suffering wash over you, and then leave. React through it, not around it. You can save the nightmares for after."

"That's…helpful…" Or horrifying, she wasn't sure which.

"You are a natural." He moved in front of her again. His eyes delved into hers, making her feel uncomfortable. "Before you release, think of me. Maybe that will help."

"I don't…" She nearly pushed him away. This was becoming a little overbearing. "I don't know about that. But thanks for your help."

She was walking before she even knew where she was going. Before she was out of earshot, she heard Mela's voice. "You came on a little strong. These people are not so bold."

Mela had been in the area and Alena hadn't even noticed. They could all have been there for all she knew. With Kallon in her personal space, and touching her—he was really distracting. The whole people were really distracting, including S'am. She gave a *look* when she was in fighting mode and everything Alena was thinking dried up right before a warning in her body urged her to run.

Alena had a long way to go before she was as battle hardened as the Shumas. In a way, she hoped she never made it there. She hoped this would all end peacefully somehow.

Her scoff was lost to the approaching darkness. *Fat chance.*

SHANTI SAT HIGH in a tree away from the camp, reveling in the silence of nature, interrupted only by Gracas and Leilius creeping closer. She picked at a leaf, and then tore it apart before letting the wind blow it from her hands.

They'd reach the Mugdock lands soon, engaging in just one stage of the overall plan. They would be asserting themselves as Chosen at last.

She tore another leaf apart.

All the things that could go wrong filtered through her head, one by one. They were a small host, and even combined with the Shadow, and reunited with more of her people, they wouldn't have enough. There was no way they'd ever be able to enter into a straight fight with Xandre and win.

So the question was, how could they even up the disastrous odds and stay ahead of an incredibly strategic mind, to complete her life's duty?

It didn't seem possible.

But then, it never had. Somehow, she'd made it to Cayan, and together, they'd made it farther than she could ever have expected. Ever hoped.

Taking a deep breath, she allowed a tiny kernel of hope to work into her middle. Her duty still seemed impossible, but…

She let the wind take the fragments of leaf as the two boys drifted within view, quiet as field mice. They stopped a moment. Leilius examined a tuft of grass where she had trodden earlier, then looked around the area, unaware of where to go from there. She hadn't tried to hide her tracks, but she hadn't advertised her position, either. She hadn't wanted to be disturbed by busybodies like Sanders, who had already wandered by an hour ago. He pretended to hate the very thought of her, but then worried when she went missing. He was a severely emotionally repressed individual.

Leilius shrugged. "I think she was here, but then her tracks just vanish."

"Do you think maybe she made it this far and an animal killed her?" Gracas said with wide eyes.

"There'd be blood, you moron." Leilius peered through the bushes in front of him.

"Oh yeah."

"She has to have gone *somewhere*." Leilius sounded completely put out.

"What's the point of finding her, anyway? This isn't a training exercise. She'll probably kick us in the head if we disturb her. Remember that time we caught her peeing in the Shadow Lands?"

"She didn't care that we found her that time. She cared that you pointed at her and stared."

"*Well?* How was I supposed to know women squat to pee?"

"You sound like you're twelve. They don't have dicks. What did you think they did? Dribble down their legs?"

"She still had her pants on, you idiot." Gracas punched Leilius. "How the hell was she not peeing all over her clothes?"

"They learn how to do it out of necessity. And they're smarter than you. It's a wonder you don't pee all over your pants even with a dick!"

They were yelling, and if they had been in enemy land, they'd be dead. It was funny, though. And a great distraction. Instead of letting them move on, as they were about to do, she used a soft, raspy voice and said, "Oooooh!"

Gracas jumped so high he was airborne. Leilius dove into the bushes.

Both boys froze for a moment. Not even their eyes moved.

A second later Gracas charged into the bushes directly under Shanti's location. He stomped the ground like a madman, tearing at foliage and roots and weeds, looking behind and under everything he saw. He never thought to look up.

Leilius, on the other hand, did. His gaze went skyward, looking through the leafy trees. He wasn't looking high enough, though. She could never jump down on them from her height, so he didn't think of anything above the lower branches as a threat. He'd forgotten about the use of bows. She'd have to rectify that.

Sweaty, with leaves and branches sticking out of his shirt and the waistband of his trousers, Gracas marched back toward Leilius. Hands on hips, chest heaving, he said, "What the fuck, right? I mean…" He looked around as if his horse had gone missing. "You heard that, right?"

"I'm in a bush, aren't I?"

"She would've pounced on us by now. Shit." Gracas' eyes widened. "What if it's one of those cats? Or one of the beasts?" He froze, his body rigid, staring out to his left, listening. One quiet beat, two…

He jumped at some phantom sound, and then surged right, without any destination in mind. He just sprinted away from whatever imaginary thing he thought he had heard.

Leilius poked his head through the top of the bush like a mole, first looking where Gracas went, then turning just his head, swiveling on his neck, looking back in terror in the direction Gracas had been looking when he startled. He was frozen for a second, listening.

A rodent scurried away into the undergrowth.

"Shit!" Leilius started thrashing, trying to escape the bush, squealing like he was being eaten alive.

Finally escaping, he ran after Gracas, wild and panicked. Shanti just barely heard, "I think I pissed myself…"

Shanti almost fell out of the tree, she laughed so hard. After climbing down, Rohnan drifted out of the brush, having been completely missed by the boys. A moment later, the dying sun caught a flare of bright orange hair as Sonson strode into their vicinity. "Found you."

"By cheating," she said, heading back to camp. "Why is everyone looking, that's the question."

"Dinner is being set out. The Captain insists that the women get their plates first. I'm hungry. Chop, chop."

"Mela loves how the women are favored in this land," Rohnan said softly.

"Whatever keeps them from bitching." Sonson flashed Shanti a grin.

Shanti rubbed her eyes as she entered the camp.

Steam rose from pots set over the fires as stew bubbled. A dozen or so Westwood women awkwardly held spoons as men scooped up their dinner and slopped it onto their bowl. Other men waited for their turn to crowd in and get some grub.

Shanti met Mela at the end of the line. "Where are the other Shadow and Shumas women?"

Mela pointed off to the right. Another campfire was surrounded by women who were happily talking and eating. "*The Westwood women made a fuss that the men wanted them to go first. If it hadn't been for that handsome Captain, the Shadow and Shumas men would've agreed with the Westwood women,*" she answered in the Shumas language before laughing. "*Such foolery. I'm hungry. If these men want me to eat first, I will gladly oblige.*"

"*The women don't want to be treated any differently,*" Shanti said, noticing Maggie's surly, defiant expression. "*They want to be equal.*"

"*They fight the same.*" Mela shrugged. "*That makes them equal. What does eating have to do with it?*"

"*Their culture is changing. It is a slow process. Instead of being grumpy, however, the women need to realize that at least they weren't asked to cook. It is a step forward.*"

"*It would probably taste better if they had,*" Rohnan mumbled, eyeing the lumpy brown stew.

"The food is not good?" Mela bent to the side to see the man scooping out the stew. *"The food in the city was great."*

"That was made by cooks. This is made by men who have lost their taste buds." Rohnan looked away, unimpressed.

"Then maybe I'll have to cook. Or Sayas." Mela scratched her jaw, contemplative. She loved her food.

Ruisa slowed in passing, holding a dirty bowl from a finished dinner. She nodded at an uncomfortable Alena, hesitantly holding out her bowl at the front of the line. Ruisa shook her head. To Shanti she said, "This chivalry wears off quickly. I tried to tell them all to take these niceties while they can get them, because as soon as these men think of us as warriors, and not woman warriors, they become men again. The spitting and the farting is annoying. I'm going to enjoy this social etiquette stuff while it lasts."

"Why did you get to eat?" Marc asked as he wandered closer, shooting a scowl at Ruisa. "You're not new."

Ruisa gave Mela and Shanti a suffering look. "See? I'm one of the boys. They pretend I don't have a vagina." Marc made a face and stepped away. Ruisa gave a sly grin. "And the younger men really hate the word."

She started walking again, throwing a verbal *vagina* at Marc as she passed. He flinched and then scowled harder, staring after her.

"*Strange,*" Mela said, glancing at the two younger people.

"*Yes. It's best not to question.*" Shanti grinned.

"*Didn't need to be said.*"

Shanti grabbed two bowls and went to find Cayan. The flap of the tent sprinkled dirt on her as she moved it aside. Cayan, Daniels, and Lucius stood inside, squinting down at a map.

"Dinner." Shanti set the bowl on the very edge of the makeshift table, careful not to disturb any of the maps. She would've put it on the ground if she wasn't worried about one of the cats—which were lying, curled up, in the corner—getting it.

All three men straightened up and looked at her as if she'd appeared out of thin air. Lucius stretched, not as worried about being as proper in Cayan's presence. Daniels rolled his neck, keeping his signs of fatigue to a minimum. He clearly pretended that Cayan couldn't sense his tiredness and desire to be done with the day.

"Are we set for tomorrow?" Shanti asked, sinking to the ground in the corner, cross-legged. Her cat looked in her direction. "Don't get any ideas, you." She pointed at it before hunching her food away a little.

"Please excuse me, sir." Daniels nodded at Shanti as he ducked out through the flap of the tent.

Cayan glanced back down at the map. "It's a two-day trek. We'll stick to a relatively unused travel-way. The land is easy to traverse. It mostly skirts along the base of a mountain. I doubt we'll see anyone tomorrow. That is, if the Mugdock have been taken over, as I fear."

"You fear? I thought you didn't get along with the Mugdock?" That was a nice way of putting it. The two peoples had been at war for generations. Shanti speared a soft potato.

"No one deserves to be taken over." Cayan took up his bowl and handed it to Lucius.

"No, go ahead." Lucius waved the stew away. "I'll get mine shortly. I'm sure they'll save some for me."

"I wouldn't count on it," Shanti warned. "The younger men can eat more than is natural."

"More than Sanders?" Lucius grinned and made for the flap. "I can't believe it."

Shanti noticed his grin and the elation pouring off him as he left. He wasn't like most of the others, somber and slightly anxious. He was almost joyous at the prospect of action.

She shook her head and speared a soggy carrot. "He's happy you brought him. He can do more than fret in a prison cell, is that right?"

"Yes. I should've left him behind to help run things. A lot falls on Commander Sterling, but…" Cayan lowered to the ground next to Shanti, for once adopting her way. Usually he'd insist on bringing over a chair and getting her out of the dirt.

"You want a childhood friend around, or is it you couldn't deny him coming?" Shanti nudged Cayan with her shoulder. "Getting soft, Captain."

Cayan nudged her back. "Both, I think. I thought he'd died at one point. That…hit me. I didn't make the decision with logic, as I should've."

"We're human. Sometimes we need to feel our way instead of think it."

"I've come to that conclusion." Cayan gave her a sideways glance before digging his fork into a piece of meat. "What do you think we'll find in the Mugdock lands?"

Shanti's hunger evaporated. She pushed the contents of her bowl around. "You were there when we took down the Inkna-occupied city. You saw it firsthand."

Cayan's eyes went distant. A spark of rage flared inside him. He bent to his bowl and lifted a piece of carrot slowly to his mouth.

"We should have less trouble than with that city," Shanti said quietly, forcing herself to eat. "From what I've heard, the Mugdock don't have much of worth. The Inkna or Graygual will only be there as a gathering point closer to the Westwood Lands. I doubt Xandre has filled it with competent fighters. Not yet, anyway. As you said, he couldn't have moved so many across the land that fast. Not without us hearing about it."

Cayan didn't speak for a moment. He finished the rest of his meal in silence, and then just sat for a moment, waiting for Shanti. When she'd finished, he rose and helped her up before opening the flap for her to pass through.

"Your women are unhappy you let them eat first," Shanti said, forcing a lightness to her voice she didn't feel.

"They aren't used to army life, and the cooks never make enough the first couple nights. I didn't want them to be pushed to the back and then go hungry. Plus…I want them to fight for their pecking order. I don't want it given to them."

"But aren't you giving it to them now by making them go first?"

"I'm making them angry. The anger will overcome any hesitation to assert themselves. Hopefully. Do you want to sleep among your people, or inside my tent?"

Shanti slowed as her cat glided ahead of her. Two army men backed out of the way, and then swiftly changed direction. Cayan's people were still leery about the animals.

Cayan's expression was unreadable, and strangely, so were his emotions. She couldn't decipher what his intentions were. "Why, don't you want me with you?" she asked.

She could barely make out the ghost of his dimples in the flickering firelight. "I will stay with you. I wondered if you wanted us to be among your people?"

"Oh." His forearm was smooth as she let her fingers drift down and into his hand. She wrapped her fingers between his. "Your tent. I was never one of the pack in that regard. It has always made me stand out."

"And Rohnan?"

"He'll probably stay with one of the women. Which one, I have no idea. He always has more than a few options."

Cayan's deep chuckle drifted into the night. "Then let's retire. I have some things I want to do with you."

As always, her worry about what lay ahead shed from her like a coat in summer. Cayan's gentle tug into their secluded quarters turned into a loving embrace and a deep kiss. His hands roamed her body before shedding her clothes, coating her skin in a soft touch. She slipped into their furs and accepted him between her legs, sighing when his body entered hers. It was hard to imagine she could ever cross the line into being the monster Xandre could create with Cayan to keep her grounded.

Hard, but not impossible.

Her climax stole her breath, but the horrors Xandre was capable of were not erased from her mind. The worst might yet be to come.

CHAPTER 7

Sanders held up his hand to stop the train of horses behind him. He braced in his saddle as Shanti jumped off her horse—that bastard animal who wouldn't let her ride any other stallion, regardless of the fact that he was still injured. She paused beside him and placed a hand on his foot.

Her gaze scanned down the line. "There are bodies within our mental range," she said in a low voice. "I think they are Graygual. I can't be certain from just their minds, but there is a familiarity that I wouldn't have with the Mugdock. It is likely this place has been conquered, as Cayan thought."

"Okay." That was why they were here.

"I realize your people don't like the Mugdock, but they are not complete strangers. There is no telling what we will find in that city. If the Graygual are of a lesser caliber…it might not be something your army will want to witness. Knowing the victims, no matter how disliked, will hit harder."

Sanders blew out a breath and leaned back. "What

are you thinking?"

She glanced back at Cayan, and then at Rohnan. "We'll take a team closer to feel what we can. If possible, we'll go so far as it takes to be able to see. It depends on whether there are Inkna. We'll take the hardest fighters in first, and see what we're up against."

"And you're asking me which are the least sentimental?" Sanders turned in his saddle. The more experienced men would have no problems. His gaze skittered across a few of the women, and kept going. Except for one.

He did a double take on Maggie. She sat straight and tall in her saddle, her eyes hard, her mouth set. In one hand she held an explosive, not armed. She was fast and deft at mixing the chemicals now, with perfect timing in her throw. More than that, she was open to the ways of the army, to the Shadow, and somehow fit with Shanti's people. She was a career man, dick or not.

He nodded to himself before scanning the boys and picking out another handful of people. "Horses?"

"No. We go on foot." Shanti tapped his toe. "My damn horse might follow anyway, though. I can't get rid of the bastard." She turned back to the Captain.

Sanders jumped down from his saddle and rounded up those he'd chosen. If it proved to be too many, he knew who he'd leave behind, in order. As he motioned Maggie down, Alena said, "What about me?"

Sanders didn't bother looking at her. "No. Thank me later."

"But—"

Sanders caught her gaze as his temper rose.

"Don't push it when he looks at you like that," Marc mumbled, turning his gaze to the horn of his saddle. "Trust me."

Alena's mouth had already snapped shut, though. Unlike the boys, she wasn't an idiot.

"Let's go." Sanders led the dozen to a gathering in front of the horses at the head of the line. Half the Shadow, all the Shumas, and the higher officers waited on Sanders to stop within their fold.

The Captain said, "We are going in waves. Shanti, myself, and her kin will go in the first wave. Sonson, organize your team to follow." Sonson reached back to tie his hair in a bun at the top of his head. The Captain's piercing blue eyes hit Sanders. "You will come with Shanti and I, and Lucius will lead our army. You've been within the Shumas before."

Sanders grunted. It was disconcerting when a group of people expected you to know what they were doing without actually telling you. It involved so much more work than just talking.

He got all the shitty jobs.

"We are just gathering knowledge," the Captain said to those gathered. "We will not be engaging, if at all possible. I want to know what we're up against."

No one moved. This team was experienced, and lethal.

A chill arrested Sanders. The army had become something else with the addition of Shadows and Shumas. He wasn't sure what to expect.

"Let's go." The Captain turned and started off at a fast walk, Shanti at his side.

Sanders stepped forward before the Shumas swarmed around him. No one took out their swords. Instead, they armed themselves with knives in silence. They were ready for the stealth kill.

Another chill raced up his spine. Shit had just got real.

Without a word, the pace slowed. The Shumas fanned out to the sides, Kallon giving him a tiny nudge as Sayas plucked at his sleeve from the other side. Apparently they wanted him to follow Sayas.

"Just say it," Sanders whispered.

"You read language when words steal us." Sayas flashed him a grin. "Hope you learn speed, yes?"

"Never mind. Don't say it. You're out of your league." Sanders followed the thinner man to a covering of trees. Once there, they advanced slowly. Sanders marveled at the soft steps and careful feet of the Shumas. With exceptional balance, they let a foot hang in the air before deciding where to put it, avoiding anything that could rustle or crackle. Often, with the foot off the ground, they would also contort their bodies, avoiding dried leaves or low-hanging branches.

"You're putting me to shame," Sanders mumbled. The sound deadened on his lips.

After about a hundred yards, they stopped and crouched. Sanders, not able to feel anything, crawled forward on his hands and knees, and then dropped to his stomach.

A couple of hundred yards in front of him, cleared of trees, squatted the dingy wall of the Mugdock city. Great holes marred it in places, crumbling the stone into rubble. One side of the gate was ripped from its hinges and lay to the side, a bent and damaged mess. A black-clad man stood at the mouth, leaning against the wall.

Thick fingers drummed Sanders' shoulder. He looked back.

Sayas used those fingers to point to the right.

Sanders followed the vague point and saw another pointed finger.

Words. Words were so much simpler.

Sanders crawled backward until he could stand, and then went in the direction of the waggling digits. He found the Captain.

Sanders dropped to one knee as the Captain started speaking in a low tone. "I'd say a battering ram took down that gate. The wall wasn't made of strong stuff—it might've fallen with the forced entry. The Mugdock never worried that we'd come for them—unless they'd stolen something of ours. They've never needed a heavy defense."

"They attacked us, though." Sanders shook his head. "The Inkna initiated the attack, using the Mugdock. Why would the Mugdock agree to work with a people that forced their way in?"

"I suspect they didn't at first," Shanti said, still facing the city. "The Inkna probably offered material rewards. Then when the Mugdock didn't fulfill their obligation, the Inkna would've had no use for them apart from their city. If the people aren't needed for harvesting goods, then they are disposed of."

The Captain's knuckles turned white on his sword hilt. "Their mental power would've pushed them away from the walls, leaving the Graygual free to force their way in."

Shanti pushed forward onto her knees. "I can identify one higher officer. I know their type. There might be a few sex slaves, but…" She lowered her head in concentration. A small movement had her turning toward them. "I think they might be prostitutes. They are there for some purpose, not out of fear. I would guess a working woman."

"Know something of them, do you?" Sanders

growled.

"Yes," she said.

Sanders knew a shocked moment before he let it go. That was the Captain's problem.

"How many Inkna?" Sanders asked.

"A handful, only one with higher power," the Captain answered, moving away from the crest of the hill before standing. Sanders did likewise. "We can take them down easily."

Shanti's people flocked in from the sides. "A host of Graygual, kept in line by a few officers. It is like the Hunter's camp, only with much less skill."

"Are you sure about that?" the Captain asked.

"Mostly," Shanti answered.

"Oh, well, that's reassuring." Sanders spat to the side.

"Let's talk with Daniels." The Captain pushed through everyone, headed back to the line of horses. "I only want to bring as many forces as we need."

"All due respect, sir," Sanders said as he kept to the Captain's side. "We may not need all our number to take out the enemy, but we do need to learn to work together. We have some greenies with us—we have three different peoples, plus one or two of the Duke's men thrown in for kicks. We need some none-too-threatening practice before the time comes when we *will* need our whole force, and then some."

The Captain paused. A low equine moan made his head snap up. A warning flashed through his blue eyes, shutting Shanti's animal up. "You have a point," the Captain said, fingering his chin. "A very good point. I'll speak with Daniels. Let's aim for tomorrow at dawn."

"No. We should go tonight. At dusk." Kallon shot a sharp look at the Captain. His tone brooked no argument. "Don't let inexperienced fighters stew all night over what is to come. Let them go while their adrenaline is at its peak. There will be less dying."

"That counts as a challenge in this land, Kallon," Shanti said in a singsong voice. "Now you've stepped in it."

The Captain's jaw clenched and his eyes flashed for the second time. His arms came away from his sides a little, lending just a little more size to an already large, muscular man. Sanders would not like to be in Kallon's shoes. Not for all the peace and quiet in the world.

"We'll deal with this another time, you and I," the Captain said in an even tone. The hair prickled on Sanders' arms. Shanti's lips spread into a smile.

The Captain stalked away but Shanti lingered behind. Her smile grew brighter. "Here's what went wrong." She ticked off a finger. "You're assuming he doesn't know how to lead and you do." She ticked off another finger. "You are forgetting the days before I developed our communication technique and the chaos during even small battles." Sayas started laughing as she ticked off a third finger. "You challenged a man like that." She patted him on the shoulder. "And won't admit that I still don't want to fuck you."

The rest of the Shumas bent over in laughter as Kallon's expression flashed confusion. "I thought *fuck* meant something gone wrong… It means sex?"

They all laughed harder.

Sanders shook his head and moved away to his horse. "I miss the quiet life where everyone had some kernel of sanity." He poked the air with his index finger, picking out people. "Scout out the location, get sentries organized, and see if you can find the places to hunker down."

"Yes, sir!" they shouted in unison.

"And remember that we're in enemy territory. Keep your voices down."

"Yes, sir." Still too loud.

Sanders stalked after the Captain. Battle was on the horizon. Sanders wanted to know exactly what he was going to be up against.

CHAPTER 8

MARC PATTED DOWN his sleeping fur, trying to make it so nothing could crawl in when he wasn't around. He glanced up at the sky, mapping out the stars to make sure he knew which direction he faced. It would look bad if he wandered around the camp in utter confusion—he was part of the *experienced* group now. He'd been through a few battles, and he knew what to expect. He was supposed to look out for the first-timers.

Or so Sanders had said. Marc was under no misconceptions that he could help.

His foot cracked a twig as he made his way to the main eating area. He flinched and then paused, staring at the huge pools of inky black ahead of him, hoping no one popped out with a sword and a manic smile. The sentries had mental ability, but you just never knew. Someone could get through. Weirder things had happened.

The broken twig crackled as he shifted his weight to look behind, and he flinched again. Shanti would punch him in the head if she heard him. He was supposed to be better at this.

Seeing no movement, he continued ahead through the brittle grass. Shapes to his right caught his eye, a small group of people sitting in a cluster. He glanced up at the moonless sky, and then tweaked his direction. More shapes moved away left. A horse huffed. Continuing on, he ducked into the trees and immediately put out his hand to feel his way. Visibility was so poor that he had no idea how other people got around. Some passed him at a normal walk, wandering by like it was broad daylight.

He felt something soft and warm slide across his leg. He jumped and stepped away. His foot caught the edge of a stone and rolled, sending his body pitching to the side. Arms out wide, he windmilled and then staggered, grunting as his chest met someone else's.

That someone was a woman. With round, full breasts.

A fist caught him just below the ribs, offsetting the tingling in his body.

"Sorry!" he wheezed, clutching his side and staggering away.

"What is your problem?" Ruisa hissed.

"I can't very well *see*, can I?" He looked around his feet. "Those big cats are around, aren't they?"

"The Captain and S'am are in the officers' area talking over tomorrow."

Marc stared at her face, waiting for more. He didn't get any. "So?"

"So the cats usually stick around the Captain and S'am, which are right over there." Her shadowed hand went out to the right.

"Ah." He straightened out his uniform. "They make me nervous. They're like ghosts."

"Me too." She turned and started away. He followed, hoping it was in the direction of food.

The murmur of voices rose up from those sitting in clusters. The wild grass thinned out, making it easier to step through without being able to see. He threaded his way around a group and then turned sideways to avoid the thinner frame of what was probably a Shadow or Shumas.

Finally they reached a large circle of people sitting in the darkness. Judging by the lack of a line or any larger men, this wasn't where he thought he'd been heading.

"I thought you were going to get food?" Marc glanced up at the sky and then looked out to the right. Why he bothered was anyone's guess. He couldn't tell what was out there any more than he could tell what was in the other direction.

"The Captain had the women's rations separated, and apparently lumped the Honor Guard in. We brought it here." Ruisa sighed and dropped to the ground. "I'd thought we'd get the preferential treatment a little longer."

"You don't deserve it." That sounded like Rachie's voice. The speaker shifted on the other side of the large circle.

Marc shuffled in next to Ruisa, hoping the hulking frame that looked like Xavier didn't have his fingers resting on the ground. If Marc accidentally sat on them, he'd surely get a punch. Coming from Xavier, that wouldn't feel great. His ribs still hurt.

"Do you need to be right on top of me?" Xavier huffed before backing out of the circle a little, making more room for Marc.

"Here." Ruisa crawled forward to the center of the circle, and then came back with dried meat, bread, and cheese. "This is what we've got."

Marc would have eaten a raw fish he was so hungry. He tore a chunk out of the lump of bread.

"I overheard Sanders talking," Ruisa said, crossing her legs and leaning her forearms on her knees. "He said their defenses seem minimal and there aren't that many on the inside. That they probably sent everyone to attack our city."

"They didn't attack—they just kind of…camped out." That sounded like Gracas.

"Whatever. You know what I mean." Ruisa huffed.

"Sanders didn't think the Graygual thought they'd be attacked. The ones here, I mean. I don't know what was going on with the ones in our lands."

"That guy Kallon." That feminine rasp sounded like Maggie. "He said it would be better to go quickly so we didn't have all night to stew in fear. That it would be bad for the inexperienced to wait."

A great many shadows around the large circle shifted. Feet scraped against the ground and heads ducked. Maggie had hit on the worry that a great many were clearly feeling.

"You didn't have the Captain when you were trapped in the city," Xavier said in a firm voice, "so you wouldn't know that he is an excellent leader. Even S'am is impressed with him, and she's rarely impressed with anyone. She led Kallon, and she lets the Captain lead her into battle. So that should tell you where Kallon ranks in all of this."

"The Captain is going to *squash* him when they fight." Gracas shifted, but for a different reason than the women.

Marc rolled his eyes and ripped off another mouthful of meat.

"But…what he said made sense," Alena said in a slightly shaking voice.

"Nah." Xavier waved the thought away, ramming Marc with his big shoulder. The guy didn't know how much room he took up. "They need time to plan. Once they have that, they tell all the officers, and then *they* tell us. So each group is banded together with directions. We'll get some sleep, refresh, and then we'll be ready for tomorrow."

"I don't know how much I'll sleep," one of the women said.

"Even so, you'll be with experienced warriors," Ruisa said. "I was scared at first, but Xavier is right about the Captain. And Shanti is always monitoring everyone—us especially. Between the two of them, it works out."

Xavier shifted again, jarring Marc's elbow. Scowling, he scooted back as Xavier said, "Every time I get anxious about what's to come, I think of what the Captain says sometimes: Overcoming fear is the best way to gain confidence. Skirting fear is the fastest way to a hollow bravado. And he's right."

Someone blew out their breath. Stillness settled, slow and heavy, expectation so thick it was palpable. Marc finished off his dinner, savored to the last and not quite enough. "I remember my first battle," Xavier said, bracing his forearms on his knees. "It wasn't even much of a battle. Not the part I had. It was when the Mugdock attacked and S'am told us to guard our family and friends. I was terrified."

"I'm always terrified," Marc admitted. There was no

sense in denying it—everyone knew that fact.

"But S'am saw us through," Xavier continued. "The Captain led the defense, his commanders did their job, and we picked up the slack. We all worked together, and everything worked out. Put your faith and your life in their hands, do what they tell you, and they'll bring us out."

"S'am will pull a win out of her ass, don't you worry," Rachie said. "She's gone through some serious shit, and made it out. The woman is a miracle worker."

"We'll watch your back," Gracas said, all bravado.

"They'll watch ours, actually," Xavier said. "They're the archers. They have a longer reach."

"But...you know..."

Movement around their circle interrupted Gracas' struggle for the right words. Shapes darted, graceful and silent, skirting by their number. A long shape in a hand announced the brandishing of steel.

"What's happening?" Xavier said, standing.

One of the shapes slowed in its jog. A woman—possibly Mela—said, "All of you get into the trees. Stick together. Our perimeter has been breached."

"How many?" Leilius asked, but Mela was already moving away.

Marc felt a jolt of adrenaline. Before he even made the decision, he had a knife in his hand and was clutching Ruisa's shoulder. She shrugged him off before

Xavier's hand covered Marc's shoulder and started pushing.

"With me, everyone," Xavier said.

The circle collapsed toward Xavier like paper crumpling.

"What do we do?" Gracas asked Xavier when they slithered around two tree trunks and stopped in the undergrowth.

"Get the more experienced people on the outside of this group," Xavier said in a hush. "We have no idea how many there are. The mental people can feel the intruders, but that doesn't mean they can get to all of them in time. Especially if they are fighting with Inkna."

Marc shoved someone out of the way and stepped forward, his grip too tight on his knife. Trying not to fall into shallow breathing that would make him eventually black out, he focused on the sounds surrounding them, currently drowned out with talking.

"There can't be that many," Gracas said. "Or they would be louder, right? This can't be an attack."

"It can if they are like the Hunter's men," a woman said. "Those guys didn't say much. They just killed."

"In the middle of the night?" Rachie said in disbelief.

"Maybe we should shut up so they don't realize we're here." Marc's words scratched against his too-tight throat. A bead of sweat ran down his temple.

The chatter died away, leaving the utter silence of a nearly black night. Marc widened his eyes, trying to take in more light to see through the black. It was a fruitless effort. The press of silence suffocated him and made it hard to breathe. His hand shook a little; he was more afraid of the unknown than of a shape running at him.

A shout sounded to the distant right, followed by an agonized scream.

Marc flinched and pressed into those around him. The group moved and shifted as the scream rattled off into silence. Into death.

Silence drifted back in like a fog. Ragged breathing sounded behind him. Someone was about to hyperventilate in panic.

Marc slowly worked backward, careful not to make any sound. He picked up his feet slowly, letting them hover in the air before gingerly setting them down. His heart hammered against his ribs and a pulsing rush blared in his ears.

Someone moved out of the way, but didn't ask him what he was doing. He felt another body shift before he was standing next to a woman with a heaving chest. Her hands held a shaking bow in front of her, terror clearly drowning out her thought. She was very dangerous at that moment.

Marc let the calm of his profession settle over him. She needed help, and it was his job to give it.

"Hey," he whispered. "I'm going to put my hand on your arm. Are you ready?"

He wouldn't have been able to see her nod even if she gave it. The outline of her head was lost to the darkness of the trunk behind her.

"I'm reaching over," Marc said, his words almost coming out like a melodic hum. He'd learned that from Rohnan. "I will touch you now."

Her flinch almost made him jerk away, violent as it was. She clutched her bow harder into her chest, crushing his hand.

"We have you surrounded," Marc said in that same melodic voice. "The Shadow and Shumas are out there, tracking these people down. And if all else fails, those cats are out there, hunting. You are safe with us. Just stick with us, and you'll be fine."

He desperately wanted to believe the words he was saying.

The ragged breathing slowed a fraction. Her arms relaxed just a little.

"Now, I want you to drop that bow—just for now." He winced as the wood and her skin pinched him. Dropping the bow didn't seem to be an option. "Okay, hang on to the bow. No problem. Just don't try to shoot it. You might hit one of our people."

Her body shook. Probably a nod, because he didn't hear any sounds of crying.

"You're going to be fine. We'll take care of you."

She shook again. Definitely a nod. Her breathing had slowed even more, now not nearly as ragged. Hopefully, she was calming down enough to at least be able to think straight.

"I'm going to go back to the front and kill anyone that comes, okay?"

He wanted to believe that, too.

Another shake.

"So just hang tight." He took his hand back as another shout trumpeted in the night. A bright glow lit up a halo of orange to the right, drawing Marc's eyes like a moth. Shadows danced and swayed, distorted at their distance. Yells and the ringing of metal made everyone draw in closer.

"We need to move away from that," Xavier said, looking in the opposite direction of the fire. "We'll be silhouetted against that flame."

"But if we're near the flame, we can see a little," Maggie said, nocking an arrow.

"Not if they come from the other direction," Alena said in a shaky voice. "Xavier is right. We should—"

"Women, Xavier is in command. This is not a debate. Shut up and do as he says." Ruisa moved toward Xavier. That instruction worked because it came from a woman, Marc had no doubt.

Silence rained down. Followed by a strange awareness that niggled at Marc's senses.

Xavier moved ahead, having everyone follow like a line of ducklings. Except for Marc. Something wasn't right.

Pressure pushed on his chest. His heart started to hammer.

Something definitely wasn't right.

The sound of metal clashing echoed through the trees before a man cried out.

"Why don't they just use their mental power?" one of the women asked.

"I don't know," someone answered.

Marc felt a hand on his back. "Go."

"Shhhh!" Marc stuck out his elbow, pushing the woman away so he could turn. His eyes trained on a spot of black amid a sea of darkness. Something waited out there, in the night. Something dangerous. He would bet his life on it.

Marc closed his eyes, cutting off the desire to see. He let his other senses fill in the gaps, doing exactly as S'am taught him.

Almost immediately he felt that pulse of danger he attributed to S'am.

A warning surge of electricity worked down his spine. She wouldn't be using this as a training exercise. Not right before a battle.

The cats, maybe?

Marc spread his arms, trying to make himself bigger. Just in case.

Footsteps approached him from the front of the line.

"What's—"

Marc punched Xavier in the side, eyes still closed. Xavier grunted, but said nothing. He knew to trust Marc's violence—it always preceded danger.

Marc took a deep breath, trying to slow his wildly beating heart.

A rustle sounded in front of them, blaring through the dark. Xavier's feet scraped the dirt, pivoting. He must've heard.

Marc took another deep breath. Xavier's footsteps moved away. More soles scratched the ground, others turning toward the danger. Xavier was getting everyone in position.

A soft crunch of a boot shocked through Marc's senses.

It wasn't the cats.

Oh shit.

"Graygual," Marc mumbled, trying to deaden the sound as much as possible.

"What?" Rachie asked, almost a yell in the silence.

"Should we run?" Marc whispered, his whole body shaking. Anything that could be that quiet through pitch black in the middle of battle had to be excellently trained. They didn't stand a chance.

"We wouldn't all make it," Xavier whispered back. He must've come to the same conclusion.

Marc didn't have the heart to say it.

Sweat dripped down his neck. Another soft crunch, half as close as a moment ago. He or she was still moving in their direction.

Marc swallowed a lump of acid. He really hoped he was wrong and it was S'am. He really, really hoped.

"Run, Marc!" Words like an explosion pierced the night. S'am. She was not in front of them. And her voice was laced with panic.

"Go!" Xavier screamed, shoving Marc with rough hands. "Go!"

Something parted the air close to Marc's head. A *thud* hit a tree behind him.

A throwing knife. *Shit!*

Marc turned and pushed the girl behind him. "Get out of here. Hurry! All of you!"

Soft footfalls pattered against the ground. Fabric swished, barely heard. It was coming right for them.

Adrenaline ignited in Marc's body. He took out another knife, gripping one in each hand. Not thinking logically, knees bent, he stepped forward to intercept whatever it was that was coming right at them. Xavier was right there with him. The other Honor Guard filed in, their steps blaring in contrast to the stranger in the night.

"Get out of—"

A flare of light cut Xavier off. Bright orange sparked at eye height.

A man dressed all in black with a strip of fabric over half his face was moving toward them at a half-jog, sword held out, moving as lightly as a dancer.

"Oh no—it's one of them?" Leilius whimpered.

The flare left Maggie's bow and zipped through the night, the tip of the arrow on fire.

With movements precise and perfect, the man flicked his sword, knocking the arrow out of the way.

Marc's mouth dropped open.

"I have no *Gift*." S'am's voice was calm yet elevated as she sprinted toward them.

Another flare lit up the area, but this time, Maggie aimed at his feet. Fire licked the grass before spreading out like a hungry thing.

The man danced to the side, his focus on S'am rushing toward him. "Get out of here, boys!" she yelled, slowing as she got within sword-striking range.

Marc had never seen her slow when taking on an enemy.

"What is he?" Marc asked with a quivering voice.

"Death," Leilius said in a breathy rasp.

The man's eyes crinkled in the flickering light. Words came out, musical but unintelligible. He spoke to S'am in a friendly tone.

She lunged, her strike precise and elegant. He blocked with an effortless flick of steel. S'am didn't immediately counterattack, or notice that the Honor Guard hadn't departed. She stared at the man in front of her as smoke curled around her feet.

She stepped to the left, starting to circle. He stepped diagonally, cutting her off. He brought one hand up and waggled it slowly. His words made no sense.

S'am attacked, her style changed to deliver fast, brutal strikes. Her sword glimmered in the firelight, smashing down, getting blocked, and coming in again at a different angle. Fast and hard, her body worked in perfect symmetry. But for every strike, he had a counter-strike. He wasn't blocking anymore; he was meeting her attack with one of his own.

His body, moving in a circular style Marc hadn't seen before, dodged. He feinted, then struck. His sword clattered against hers.

Her attack came immediately, her steps beautiful yet deadly. He matched each movement, then counterattacked, his sword narrowly missing her. She lunged, her point snagging his shirt but missing flesh.

They were two masters in the fight of their lives.

"Shoot him!" Xavier yelled at Maggie. "Help her!"

"They're moving too fast. I might hit her!"

A sleek black shape skirted the fire, followed by a

feline cry that could only be described as frustrated. S'am and the man stepped through and jumped over the growing flames, swords still moving in that incredible dance.

"Should we charge?" Marc heard himself ask. He licked numb lips. Quivers from his body made his teeth chatter.

"You'll distract her," Gracas said in a level voice. "We can't let anything distract her."

Another black cat joined the first, staying away from the flame. Eyes fixed on the man S'am was fighting.

Feet thumped through the night. Large swinging shoulders and a powerful stride announced the Captain, followed by the lithe movements of Rohnan.

"Over here, sir!" Xavier shouted.

The man danced away from S'am, uttered a few garbled words, and then sprinted into the darkness. The cats launched after him, but before they could reach him, a scream rent the night, followed by a fierce feline snarl. The third cat had been waiting to ambush him as he ran.

Shapes ran forward around Marc, shaking him out of his disbelieving stupor. Women were stamping at the ground, trying to put out the flame.

"Help them," Xavier said, following suit.

Moving like a man made of sticks, Marc lurched

forward, stomping through, thinking about that fight. It didn't take long for someone else to voice his fears.

"That guy was just as good as S'am," Gracas said, his customary excitement at all things to do with fighting missing.

"He was one of those guys that guard the Being Supreme," Leilius said in barely more than a whisper, standing with a rigid body and wide eyes.

"How do you know?" Marc asked as his body succumbed to shaking.

"I remember seeing guys just like him. From the Shadow Lands when I went into the Trespasser Village. It might not have been the Being Supreme, but S'am thought it probably was."

"They're the best." Xavier stomped at the ground more heavily. "And he was here."

"Are you guys okay?" S'am jogged back into the area with Rohnan on her heels. One of the cats kept pace at her side. Wetness glistened around its mouth and down its throat.

"Did you get him?" Xavier asked, panting.

"The cats did." S'am glanced down at the dying flame. Her gaze then scanned the line. "Everyone accounted for?"

Xavier and Maggie both checked faces as Marc watched S'am. While her body moved just as fluidly as normal, there was a tightness in her shoulders, which always meant concern. Then there was Rohnan, who wore his worries on his face for the world to see.

"What is it?" Marc asked, though he didn't really want to know. He'd rather curl up under his bed covers and pretend danger didn't exist.

"They have someone with the same *Gift* as Burson." S'am put her hands to her hips and glanced down at her feet. "Just one, I suspect, and his or her range doesn't seem as large. But they have someone. There is no telling how close they've come or how much information they've gained. They could've been checking out Cayan's city while we were there, for all I know."

"But they followed us?" Leilius asked in a tight voice. "They are here, which means they didn't leave anyone behind."

"Seems like it." S'am dropped her hands and looked behind her. "We're sending someone back with a message, anyway. Where the *Gift* is blind, the eyes can still see. The Shadow are familiar with going without their *Gift*. They won't even balk at the new situation."

"So we're still going along as planned?" Maggie asked.

S'am looked at her for a long moment. "Yes, but with more caution. If anything, Xandre has shown his hand. We have a better idea what we're up against."

"But the number of people you felt in the city yesterday might not be accurate," Xavier said.

"That is why we have to be cautious." S'am glanced behind her again as the Captain stalked into view. His gaze swept those gathered before looking off to the east. S'am turned back. "Get some rest. We'll have a plan bright and early."

"But what if there are any more?" Alena asked.

"The beasts are free," the Captain said, taking a few steps away. "What we can't feel with the *Gift* we can hear, and what we can't hear, the animals will find. We'll sleep close together, as planned, and we'll be fine."

It was too dark again to see if the tightness in S'am's shoulders had relaxed, but judging by the way Rohnan hovered around her, it hadn't. They weren't as confident as the Captain sounded. Tomorrow might not go as planned.

CHAPTER 9

SHANTI SAT ASTRIDE her horse, waiting for the final pieces to fall in place before Cayan gave the signal for all of them to move out.

"Think we'll run into those warriors from last night?" Sonson asked in a low tone, picking his nail with his knife.

"No," Shanti said softly as a soft breeze blew from the west and a pale sun was heaving itself up over the horizon. "They had not meant to be seen last night. Cayan's man spotted him. Shadow and Shumas did not."

"So you think the enemy can only sense those with *Therma*?" Sonson glanced back as Sanders barked orders at the women. Many would be sectioned off as archers with Lucius, Maggie was being promoted, and a couple would join the Honor Guard. "Was Burson like that?"

Shanti shrugged with a shaking head. She didn't know.

"These Graygual seem prepared to let their own get

stomped on." Sonson put away his knife. He adjusted the sword on his hip. "I wouldn't be surprised if the guy last night, whoever he was, lets us kill them all and then follows us out."

"I wouldn't, either." Shanti's stomach flipped over. "If that's the case, and we don't find him, Xandre will know everything we do. It will take away our largest advantage."

Cayan stalked into their midst with Lucius and Daniels. He stopped next to her and placed a hand on her knee. "Stay safe, *mesasha*."

She met his gorgeous blue eyes. "You too. Don't do anything stupid."

He winked before his eyes hardened again and he turned toward his horse. Shanti patted the Bloody Bastard before stepping into the stirrup and throwing her leg over. As expected, before she could even get her foot in the other stirrup, he was prancing and moving, ready to get running.

"You shouldn't be riding him yet," Rohnan warned, climbing onto his much calmer mount.

"Remember what happened yesterday? Now we have two damaged horses."

Rohnan hefted his staff. "A few bite marks won't prevent that horse from carrying you, but your horse's gash might slow him down."

"Even slow, he'll still be faster than the other horses."

"Not mine."

Shanti rolled her eyes.

At Cayan's nod and his hacked-up sense of *go* through the overall mental link, Shanti leaned forward slightly. The Bastard pranced sideways. "Don't make me look a fool in front of everyone, or I will never ride you again." She softly touched her heels to his sides.

He lurched forward and started at a fast trot. The Shadow kicked their horses into motion directly after, following her out before the army would file in. The Shumas, who were best at mental communication with Shanti, would take up the rear until they could spread out more.

She directed her horse to the track that led down to the city, and noticed the wild growth on each side. If there were regular wagons coming through here bringing large amounts of supplies, wheels would've cut lanes and stripped away some of the vegetation. She hoped the absence made them correct in their earlier assessment of how many people were in that city.

She pulled the reins to slow her horse as she reached the crest of the hill. The Shadow tightened up their formation, allowing the army to do the same. Slower than she would've liked, she rode over the hill and quickly swept the area with her gaze.

The man at the open gate lounged, just like before.

Minds in the city seemed dull, probably going about monotonous tasks. The few women were idle, spread out and in a state of boredom.

The city would not have heard the few cries of pain in the night, and neither would they have been warned. Last night's small but expertly trained force had a different agenda to the people in this city. Not only that, but they were instructed to keep to themselves and let this contingent of Graygual die and rot on their own.

If that didn't sound like Xandre, nothing did.

Shanti picked up the pace. Cayan's power boiled through the merge with high intensity, ready to be unleashed. Her people's power, tranquil, simmered just below, keeping adrenaline low until the battle began. She'd trained with endurance in mind since youth. She hoped they wouldn't need it today.

The man at the gate looked in their direction. His body jerked upward, rigid. He ducked through the gate right before a bell started ringing.

Shanti felt the minds, slow to start, but rapidly turning frantic. Chaos bubbled within the walls, and people ran every which way in confusion and fear. A more analytical mind sparked. That had to be the officer.

With no time to lose, Shanti clutched at all the Inkna minds, low in power and mostly useless. She lashed out, *striking* with a piercing blow into their brain mass. Two shields went up, a feeble attempt to push her away. A surge of power answered them, Cayan's *Gift* unfurling from containment with hard, raw force.

Minds near the walls became focused; they were probably nocking arrows and getting ready to shoot. Shanti *slashed*, taking them down as she drew closer. She threw her leg over the saddle and jumped, knowing her people would do better on foot. Hard ground punched her as she hit and rolled, bouncing up a moment later. Rohnan joined her, running. The rest fell in behind.

She took the gate at a sprint and *gouged* the minds waiting in the entryway. Their screaming greeted her as she barged through. Their bodies crumpled to the ground.

The city opened up into a dirty courtyard with grime covering the cracked and broken cobblestone. A haphazard gathering of men hastened to form a line, some only half dressed. Shanti sprinted into their number, stabbing one through the gut before any of them had even raised a blade. Rohnan's staff slashed a chest and Kallon's sword took out another.

Shanti flicked away a weak thrust before running the man through with her sword. She grabbed the front of his shirt and ripped him away as he died. Charging forward, she unlocked their *Gifts* from hers, still connected for communication, but now with everyone acting independently. Like arrows firing, the *Warring*

Gifts unleashed, *striking* and *cutting* minds as they fought through. When the line was dead, they caught up to her, jogging through the city.

Dirt and grime covered walls. Weeds grew between the cracks. Garbage littered the ground. Shanti felt a group of men coming her way. She ignored the female in the house to the left, and kept her eyes moving.

A man in a wrinkled black uniform with a single slash at the breast turned the corner up ahead. Two more joined him of the same rank. Shanti hefted a knife and threw, sticking it in his chest. Another appeared in the man beside him, dropping the Graygual to his knees. Rohnan reached the third with his staff and cut through the vulnerable neck. The man had barely struck out with his sword before he was sinking into a puddle of death.

"I see no signs of a large host," Kallon said above the din. A man ran at him from a side alley. He turned and thrust his sword through the Graygual's gut with quick economy. The man issued a high-pitched scream and fell away.

"No. They must be here to keep the city occupied." Shanti *struck* someone running to meet them. A shrill scream echoed against the walls.

More screams erupted behind them, a group of Graygual trying to run at their backs, but the Shumas didn't even turn to take them out.

Shanti felt Cayan's frustration and Sanders' boredom. They worked toward the northwest, the largest populated area.

Shanti turned a corner. A black back was running away from them, his sword nowhere to be seen. His back arched as he screamed before tumbling to the ground.

"Their minds are weak," Kallon said.

"They don't have the *Gift*. How would they block you?" Shanti turned left, confused by the strange layout of streets within the city. She felt minds running toward them, and some running in Cayan's direction, all originating from the same area. Shanti and Cayan's target area.

She turned left again then slowed to a stop, scowling at a house that closed off the street. "Were they drunk when they laid out this town?" She went back in the other direction and attempted to work her way around.

"Where townspeople?" Sayas asked from behind them.

"Those that survived the attack on Cayan's city obviously didn't survive the Graygual attack. Or they left." Shanti tried a left turn again, sighing in relief when the street was mostly straight, leading to a large, square building. In front of double doors stood a line of Graygual with straight backs and sloppy poses.

She shook her head. "These aren't army. What's the

point of them?"

Kallon sheathed his sword and unslung his bow from his back. "They are a good thing to toss at the enemy in order to see what he does." He yanked an arrow from his back and nocked it in a smooth movement. A moment later the arrow struck a Graygual in the chest. Another arrow flew, Sayas following suit. Mela was right after. Bodies fell, leaving gaping holes in front of the building.

"Stop!" Cayan's horse clattered through the grimy street, followed closely by Sonson.

The line in front of the building started to wobble. Graygual huddled close together, and then drifted apart again, the desire to run so strong a few had dropped their swords in anticipation. But there was nowhere for them to go.

"Where do you hail from?" Cayan asked, holding his palm up to the archers.

The lead Graygual stared up at Cayan with wide, terrified eyes. "Further north, sir."

"What happened to the Mugdock that occupied this land?"

The Graygual shook his head a fraction and glanced to the side. The next man shrugged while the others continued to stare with blank looks. Their minds were equally as empty. Xandre wasn't risking any sharp army men in this endeavor.

"How long have you been here?" Shanti tried, stepped closer.

The lead man's fearful gaze swung her way. "J-just a couple months. Oh—you're the violet-eyed girl!"

A flash of opportunity flared from the man on the end. His sword swung upward as he lunged forward. Shanti threw up her weapon to block. The blow never landed. A blast of power so ferocious that Shanti staggered backward crashed into the man. He barely had time to shriek before his limp body tumbled to the ground. Next to him, caught in the line of fire, the others screamed and clutched at their chests before sinking to their knees.

"Cayan! You have to choose who you affect with the power—you can't just blast everyone in the way!" Shanti shook herself out, and then smiled as Kallon bent to rest his hands on his knees. She pounded him on the back. "And just think, you have yet to carry out the challenge."

"He would benefit from some training," Sayas said with a white face.

Shanti started forward as Cayan jumped down from his horse. She stepped around the fallen bodies. "Usually I am his control, but…well, he reacts faster than he thinks, sometimes."

"Remind me to stay behind him in a fight." Sayas rubbed his chest. *"His power feels strange."*

"I am interested to see what he can do when let off the leash," Mela said.

"Has this city always been so dirty?" Shanti asked Cayan as she pushed her *Gift* behind the thick double doors. She ran her hand along the peeling paint and watched white flakes flutter to the ground.

"I have always heard it was, yes." Cayan turned back to those still on their horses. "Dismount. There are about a dozen in here that we know of."

"Were the Mugdock evacuated before this lot was moved in, or did they leave of their own accord after the battle…" Shanti sheathed her sword and took out two throwing knives. Fear and apprehension rolled and spiraled inside the room. Unease drifted from those behind her.

"Or did they join the army and forsake the women?" Cayan bristled. "They weren't an honorable people."

"Some of them might have been, but the loudest voices are the ones people hear most often." Shanti took a deep breath. "There is no way Xandre is in this room. Nor his prized inner circle. There is zero chance, but…" She licked her lips and squeezed the handles of her throwing knives. "If he is, he is protected from the *Gift* and will have half a dozen excellent fighters surrounding him. Maybe we should wait for Sanders."

Cayan surveyed the Shumas waiting patiently behind them, their limbs loose and shoulders relaxed. Shanti knew he could feel their turmoil through the merge, even if he couldn't see the fire burning brightly in their eyes.

"Sanders would pale in comparison to what we'll be taking in there with us," Cayan said with absolute conviction.

Kallon straightened a little. The movement was small, but spoke volumes. He approved of Cayan's validation.

"Enough stalling," Shanti said to herself. She stepped back, giving Cayan room. With a show of might, his foot smashed the door by the handle at the same time as his *Gift* surged out, flooding the room beyond. The door broke with a series of splintered *cracks*. The top hinge ripped from the wood.

Cayan shouldered through, with Shanti following close behind. The room opened up around her. Shapes hunkered to the ground at the other end, cringing from the pain Cayan was still pumping into them. A quick sweep of her gaze told her what she'd hoped and feared at the same time—no one else occupied this room.

She let a breath tumble out of her mouth as Rohnan and Mela ran in a moment later, bows in hand. Sayas and Kallon were right behind them with throwing knives.

Cayan's *Gift* withered away as his battle zeal quieted. He walked toward the enemy with sure steps, alert in case anyone should jump out of a cupboard or from behind the sagging couches. The men on the ground unfurled like flowers in spring and staggered upward. The first to recover looked around with dazed eyes. Then he burst into action. He jumped forward with sword outstretched, hacking toward Cayan with barely trained gusto. Cayan knocked the blade to the side and struck, piercing the man in the gut. Another man jumped up and charged. An arrow stabbed him like a pincushion. He faltered and lost the strength in his legs before tumbling to the ground.

One by one the enemy recovered and advanced. Wild-eyed and hopeless, they swung their swords or tried to throw their knives, defiant to the last in a land they had stolen.

She *slapped* her *Gift* onto their minds even as one of the enemy reached her with a battle cry. *Sucking in,* she drank in all his energy and life force, sapping him of strength and power. Confusion stole over his expression, and then a flash of fear, before he sank to the ground.

"There's your officer," she said as she jumped back, avoiding his thrust. The others behind him fell as well, some clawing toward her with determination not common in enlisted men. They must've been the Graygual flunkies, only useful for occupation and dying.

"What were these men promised in order to fight through their fear?" Cayan asked.

Rohnan backed away toward the door, as far away from those on the ground as possible. "They were manic. Their emotions weren't right. Corroded, almost."

"One wonders how long they have been kept in this place." Kallon checked the pulse of the Graygual at Shanti's feet. "He lives. That is a useful trick."

"It's a dirty trick when used how I was taught it. It came from the Inkna." Shanti put away her throwing knives and spread her *Gift* out. She felt her people, a few females that were probably prostitutes, and a couple of hiding enemy that the Shadow were making their way toward. No cunning intellect of a higher officer or inner-circle member. It didn't mean they weren't there. If last night had taught her anything, it was that Xandre wasn't showing his entire arsenal, and he wasn't going after her. He was waiting, and watching. Learning. When he did move, it would be with intelligence and purpose.

"How many cities like this does he have?" Shanti asked with a flash of rage. She faced her people. "How many in this land are his puppets, hoping for handouts and willing to lay down their lives for a cause they barely know? He can hide forever, sending disposable troops at us until he organizes a well-trained horde to take us down. It disgusts me how callous he is with human life."

"Which is why we are going to kill him." Kallon's stormy eyes flashed. "It is why we will avenge our people, and those who suffer by his hand. This is our destiny."

"It's why we are going to hit him where it hurts the most." Cayan dragged a piece of fabric over his blood-smeared blade. "In his pocket." He gestured Shanti toward the door with a last look at those on the ground. "Let's clear out the rest of the city. I want to make sure there's no one hiding in here with us, waiting for the cover of darkness."

CHAPTER 10

"Sir, I am pretty sure there is someone in there..." Gracas looked at the door to the dilapidated house with wide eyes.

Sanders gritted his teeth in an effort to maintain calm. The grinding sound gave him away. "Private, speak only when you can *add* to the situation."

"Yes, sir." Gracas shifted his weight from one foot to the other, then back again. "But do you want me to go in there, sir?"

Sanders stepped forward and grabbed the idiot by the back of his collar. He gave a mighty heave, smashing Gracas into the door. The door burst open, spilling Gracas into the dark space beyond. Sanders stepped in a moment later, and saw the woman Denessa had said was in there. Just as Denessa said, the woman wasn't armed, nor hostile. She sat at the edge of the bed with a patient air and a dead man lying beside her.

"Did he forget to tip?" Sanders peered behind a dresser into the shadowed corner, making sure there was no one intending to pop out unannounced.

"He scum, like them all." The prostitute heaved her girth up off the bed and adjusted her bodice. Her large chest wiggled, drawing more than one set of eyes.

"What happened to the people who used to live here?" Sanders asked, checking the closet. "They try to pay you, too?"

The woman sauntered forward with confidence. "Graygual move in, the others move out. Into graves. All dead."

Sanders motioned for the others to evacuate the small room. "You saw this?"

"No. I hear. I came after."

"You came of your own volition?"

The woman's brow scrunched up for a moment. "Your big words don't make your dick grow."

Sanders huffed out a laugh. "Too bad, ay? You come here on your own, or did the Graygual move you in?"

"Graygual come, we come. We work. We wait."

"For what?"

"For Wanderer. We help." The woman gestured down at the dead man. She didn't seem to notice the droplets of blood puddled on the floor and reaching toward her heeled shoe.

"We need all the help we can get." Sanders turned toward the door. To those waiting for him, he said, "Check in with all the women in the houses. Make sure they know the skirmish is over and they are free to go."

"We always been free to go." The woman, who had followed Sanders out, put her hands to her ample hips.

Sanders gritted his teeth again. What was it about him that invited women to speak their minds? Would nothing in his life be easy? "Tell the men that these women have a habit of killing their clients." He stalked toward his horse.

"You think anyone in here has that mind mask like last night?" Tomous asked as Sanders neared the horses.

"That's what we're trying to figure out, aren't we?" Sanders said. "Let's get this wrapped up and get gone. If we don't find them in here, we'll find them on the journey."

"You think they'll follow us?" Tomous climbed onto his horse.

Sanders waited for everyone to saddle up. They needed to spread their eyes around the city. If any with the mind mask were in there, Denessa wouldn't be any help to find them. It was time to do things the right way—with hard work and army know-how. "Whoever found us last night didn't do so by chance. The enemy wants eyes on us, and he found someone that Shanti couldn't see with her head. Just so happens I got eyes. They won't hide from me for long."

"An invisible enemy is hard to take down. Even for someone with eyes," Denessa said in a level tone.

"I'm no greenie, let's get that right. Butt out." Sanders clicked his tongue to get his horse walking.

"But…out…" Denessa gave him a confused frown. "I do not know that term."

"It means fuck off." Sanders spurred his animal. "C'mon. We got shadows to find."

※

ALENA WAITED WITH Leilius in barely suppressed nervousness at the front gate of the city. The other warriors were supposed to be flushing people out the back gate, into the waiting jaws of Lucius and the archers, but that didn't mean someone wouldn't accidentally run this way. With a sword.

The warm wood felt sturdy in her grip.

She'd just have to take them down before they got too close. It was doable. She had time.

An image of the Graygual from the previous night drifted through her mind. Specifically of him flicking his sword and batting away Maggie's fire-crusted arrow.

Alena's horse stomped, probably feeling her worry.

She really hoped those men had all been killed. And if not, that they hadn't followed the army into the city walls.

"I hope no one comes this way," Leilius said softly, as if hearing her thoughts. "I'm not used to this kind of thing. I still want to vomit when I stab someone. I don't like the sight of blood."

"Then why are you still in the army?" Alena took a deep breath and shifted, trying to loosen herself up. If she was too stiff, it would affect her aim. That might lead to the death of one of them.

"Because S'am needs me. She has to kill that Supreme man, and she needs help."

"But if you don't like killing people, how are you much help? I mean…" She swatted at a fly. "They put us out here, out of the way. Everyone else is helping tie everything up in there."

"I can get information. That's what I'm good at." A sickly expression crossed his face. "I can protect the city if need be, and sneak up on an enemy and stick a knife in him if I have to, but S'am is training me to be the eyes and ears in enemy territory. I'm good at that."

Alena rolled her shoulders as a strange feeling itched between her shoulder blades. Her body erupted in goosebumps. It almost felt like someone was lightly poking her.

She glanced at the broken gate. The scant trees beyond twisted and reached like dead things clawing at life, giving the city a haunted feel. "This is an ugly land."

"It's not so different from ours, it's just the Mugdock cut down a bunch of trees close to the city. They should've spread out the cutting if they needed wood, like we do. That way it wouldn't look so dead."

"Regardless of the reason, it's ugly." Alena shook

her shoulders. "I don't like the open area at my back."

Leilius glanced behind him. A frown crossed his face. "Something up?"

She shivered, feeling the press of eyes.

She guided her horse to the right, partially shielded from the land outside. "I just don't like putting my back to the unknown."

They passed a moment in silence as Alena felt that weird sensation again. It was almost as if a finger was tapping her on the shoulder.

Alena bent forward to look out of the gate. A blur of a black shape slid behind a tree up on the hillside.

Frowning, Alena walked her horse forward a couple steps so she could see.

A tall reed waggled in the breeze. Nothing else moved.

"Are the cats out?" she asked into the hush.

"Out there somewhere, I think. Why? Did you see something?"

Alena stared at that tree so hard it started looking distorted. Nothing moved, save the brittle leaves hanging desperately from the trees. "Nah."

"Are you sure?" Leilius clicked his tongue, having his horse walking forward to even up to her. He looked out the gate. "You should never second-guess yourself."

"I thought I saw a black shape, but…"

"And you think it was the cat?"

Alena shook her head, feeling that weird itch between her shoulder blades subside. "No, I don't think so. I'm just jumpy, I think."

"Okay…" The word was drawn out in a wishy-washy sort of voice. Leilius shrugged with one shoulder. "But if you think we should check it out…"

"*We'd* check it out?" An image of the man fighting Shanti last night flared in her memory. His sleek movements and inhuman speed paired with the glimmer on his blade. She sat back farther in her saddle. "It was probably nothing."

A shout sounded somewhere in front of them, and then was answered off to the right.

Alena glanced back out through the gate. A man, his face half covered in black, stood next to the tree. Staring at her.

A zing of adrenaline zipped through her body. Her hair follicles tingled in fear. "Oh no!" Her hands jerked to the right of their own accord. Dragging her horse's head toward him. *Why?* "Leilius. Quick. Help!"

"What? What's happening?" Leilius spurred his horse and brought up his knife. "Where?"

The man took off at a run, immediately masked by the wall.

"There's someone out there. One of those men!" Alena spurred her horse to the gate, but then stopped. "Should we follow? What should we do?"

The blood drained from Leilius' face. "Not follow!" Fear coated each syllable. "Let's get S'am."

"What about the people watching the rear exit? They are completely exposed!"

Indecision froze Leilius' movements. He stared at Alena with wide, fear-soaked eyes. Then his expression hardened up and his brow settled low. "We have to warn them. Let's go!"

"What about S'am?" Alena said, spurring her horse forward.

"We don't have time."

"We're supposed to *think* to communicate, remember?" Alena dug her heels into the horse's sides.

"Don't worry. I'm terrified. I'm communicating enough for the both of us."

❧

Lucius' horse neighed. It shook its head, its ears flattening. A black shape slid under cover like a phantom. He sat forward in his saddle, focusing hard on that area. His hand held his sword in a painful grip.

A feline tail flicked before disappearing.

Leilius heaved a silent sigh.

He shook his head and walked his horse forward, hoping some distance from the predators would calm it. "We shouldn't have those things around the horses in battle."

Timken, a man Lucius had come to know quite well when the Graygual had taken over the city, squinted as he looked at the rear gate. They sat on the hillside overlooking this side of the city, taking down anyone trying to escape from within. "It's hard to say. They were handy last night. They took down two men that would've escaped."

"They're useful, don't get me wrong, but they don't work well with the horses. The last thing you want is to be thrown before you even reach the battle."

Timken spat. One of the women in front of him glanced back with a scowl.

Horses off to the right started neighing and stamping their feet. One danced left, having its relatively inexperienced rider clutching her reins. Lucius clicked, getting the horse walking. He made his way down the back of the line as two Graygual sprinted through the open gate. The archers were ready. Two arrows were loosed immediately, followed by three more. Four arrows stuck in the man closest, and one went wide, barely glancing the leg of the other. The first man sank to his knees as the other faltered, his hand going for his thigh. Two more arrows flew, sticking in his side and his arm. He stumbled, dropping to all fours, before rolling to his unharmed side.

"Should we go finish him off, sir?" Abigail, a middle-aged woman who Lucius had incorrectly assumed was shy and reserved, fingered her knives.

"He's dying already, I think." Lucius' horse pranced and stomped the ground.

A black shape shook the foliage on the hill above them.

Lucius turned with his bow held up, waiting. The horse blew out a breath and pawed the ground.

A speck of black zipped further down the hillside but to the right, this cat moving off with the other.

Lucius sighed again, this time more audibly. He didn't know what was worse—the cats or skilled Graygual. Both were unpredictable and deadly.

"You ladies need better communication," Timken was saying, unaware of the danger behind him. "If you are this still and close, call out your man. Then hit your mark. There is no sense wasting all our arrows on the same man, or getting one but missing the other."

Another man fled the city through the gate. His sword was out but it didn't look like he had much of an idea of what to do with it.

"Mine!" "Mine!" "*Mine!*" "I'll get him!"

A slew of arrows flew out, all of them hitting their mark. Timken's chest deflated as he shook his head.

Another blur of black caught Lucius' eye away up left. The third cat, following the others.

He squinted into the glare of the sun as he passed out of a shadow and stared at that area. Wanting to be sure.

A Graygual burst from the city gate, followed by three more.

"Right!" "Left!" "On...the—" Arrows flew before the women could work their mouths to tell which man they had chosen. Enemy screeched and stumbled. One guy staggered into the wall and slid down, a line of red streaking the grime. More arrows flew, crashing into the falling Graygual. One arrow hit someone already dead.

"In a battle, this would waste arrows," Timken boomed. "You need to think first."

"Sorry, sir," one of the women drawled.

Timken braced his hand on his thigh and spat, earning another *look*.

Lucius glanced out to the right, looking for the retreating feline, when the thunder of hooves came around the city.

"Hold your fire," Timken said, staring off toward them.

Lucius scanned the trees again, not seeing any movement, before turning to the newcomers. He put up his hand to block the sun, realizing it was Leilius and Alena, pushing their horses hard. One of Alena's arms came up and did an arc above her head. She waved it furiously.

"She's yelling something." The woman at the end of the line sat forward on her horse, as if that small lean would solve the problem of distance. "Can anyone hear her?"

Lucius found himself leaning, too, before doing a quick glance at the gate. No one emerged.

"Attack?" Trise cupped her ear. "It sounded like she said attack…"

Lucius kicked his horse forward, feeling a growing unease as the two galloped toward him. Another flash of movement caught his eye, another black blur. Unlike with the cats, his horse ignored it.

Warning washed over him. The world slowed down as implications froze his blood. He turned in time to see a knife flipping end over end. It stuck into the side of Timken's neck with a moist *smack*. Surprise lit up his friend's face. The next moment he was falling.

"Get down!" Lucius screamed, kicking his horse toward the thrower.

Another knife flew. Its blade glimmered in salute before digging itself into Anabell's back.

"Move!" Lucius yelled in panic, slapping a horse on the butt as he passed. The animal whinnied and started forward, carrying the rider away.

A man in black popped out from behind a tree, knife at the ready. Lucius spurred his horse on, ready to try and deflect. The man's arm went up.

"Mine!"

"I'll get him!"

An arrow stuck the tree by the man's shoulder. He turned sideways as another flew by, barely missing. The Graygual straightened to throw again, his body positioning and technique perfect. An arrow zipped by his arm, catching his tunic. The throw went wide.

"Up there!" Alena raced into their midst with her bow raised and ready. She reached back and pulled an arrow from her quiver, nocked, and sighted, all in a smooth, practiced movement. She released.

Bushes shook high on the hill as someone ran. The man in front of Lucius followed suit, leaving a smudge of blood on the bark as he bumped past.

"Haw!" Lucius shouted, kicking his horse to run. A glimpse of black emerged ahead, and disappeared just as quickly, the man running through a tangle of brush. Lucius was there a moment later, stomping down the foliage.

"Did you see where they went?" Alena called, out of breath.

Lucius hopped down off his horse. He heard the tread of hooves coming in his direction.

"Make sure that gate is covered," he yelled, bending to the ground. No tracks marred the ground leading from this location.

"Mine!" someone shouted below.

Knife in hand, Lucius squinted into the trees, willing movement. Wanting to know which direction he should expect an attack from.

A horse crashed through the brush with Leilius on top, his knife out. "I don't see anyone, sir."

"That doesn't mean they aren't there." Lucius scanned the area.

"If they cut trees like we did, thinning them out, this wouldn't be so dense."

Lucius spared a glance for the kid. It was an odd comment to make at that moment. He let it go. "Did Shanti send you to warn us?"

"No. Alena saw someone head this way. We didn't have time to tell S'am." Leilius' expression fell. "We didn't make it in time, either."

"That wasn't your fault." Lucius backed down the hill, motioning Leilius away. "You head down and cover the others. I'll—"

"Mine!"

"Don't shoot!"

"Hold up!"

"Oops, shit!"

A blast of needles raked across Lucius' mind, making his legs go weak and his hands numb. Women screamed and Leilius moaned. Lucius clenched his jaw and fought back the pain, bracing for the Inkna.

The feeling cleared a moment later. "Watch that way," he instructed Leilius.

"What have you found?" Shanti's voice sounded like

a bell.

"Up here," Lucius hollered.

A moment later a black shape zipped from the right. Adrenaline spiked as Lucius lifted his bow. A feline head appeared above a tangle of brush. A rush of relief washed through him.

The feeling was short-lived.

The animal homed in. Its head dropped slowly before it moved in his direction. Like it was stalking its prey, the animal kept Lucius in its sights. More movement, from the other side, announced a second cat, crawling forward with the same slow stealth. They snarled, showing long white teeth.

"Shanti!" Lucius called, putting his hands out to the side to make himself seem bigger. The urge to run raced through him, something that didn't even happen with the enemy.

A swear announced Shanti jogging toward him. The cats, as if verbally called off, stopped in their advance. Their teeth disappeared, but they didn't relax.

"They're after the wrong person," Lucius said to Shanti, his hands still spread out wide. He followed her back down the hill, still not showing his back to the hillside.

"What happened here?" Shanti asked, her gaze taking in the two of their company who lay dead before looking at Alena, trying to steer a crying woman away from the carnage. The rest of the women, their faces white and eyes tense, stared at the enemy gate. They didn't plan on leaving their station.

"I saw two of them wearing the same garb as we saw last night." Lucius sucked in lungfuls of air, shaking with the pent-up adrenaline.

Shanti blew out a breath, glancing at the cats before turning her gaze up the hill. "I'm concerned with these numbers. Is Xandre close, or is he entrusting this task with those he deems worthy?"

"Or both…" Lucius bent, feeling for a pulse in Timken. Nothing. "He's had a lot of time to train. Surely he'll be able to spare a few by now."

Shanti was quiet for a moment, glancing over the fallen. Rohnan wandered closer with his staff in one hand. He put a palm on Shanti's shoulder.

"You need to teach those cats to follow a scent," Lucius said.

"They know how to follow a scent, but they'll only do it when they feel like it." Shanti gave a small shake of her head and looked at the city. "Pull everyone inside. Quickly."

"His knife throwing was perfect," Lucius said as he helped lift the fallen.

"They are the absolute best this land has to offer." Shanti scanned the hillside again.

"Let's hope not the *absolute* best."

"Let's hope." She looked behind her. "We'll be staying here for the night and planning out the next steps. I don't think our new friends will be going anywhere."

"They'll pick us off one by one."

Shanti's eyes flashed. "Only if they survive the night. I'll be inviting them to a hunting party."

"But they can sense your mind power. They'll know exactly where you are, right?"

"Yes, they will. It's a good time to see if they will engage. Xandre isn't the only one prepared to lay some bait and make assumptions based on the results."

Lucius' stomach flipped with her implications. "Does the Captain know about this plan?"

"No. It'll be a lovely surprise, don't you think?"

CHAPTER 11

"Cayan, we can't both go." The knives felt tight against Shanti's leg. Tingles worked down her spine in anticipation of what awaited her outside the walls.

Cayan looked up at the black sky where the slivered moon and glimmering stars provided very little light by which to navigate the wild hillside. "You need someone to watch your back. I'm going."

Rohnan shifted in the corner where he sat cross-legged. He put one hand on the double bladed staff lying in front of him. "He is trying to be rational, *Chulan*. Soon he'll just get pushy." Rohnan hefted his staff before standing. "The night is growing old. We should go."

Shanti offered them both a weary sigh. "The two of you try my patience."

"Likewise." Cayan touched his sword before stalking to the door. He spared a glance for the three cats curled into each other at the opposite end of the modest room. "We should bring the cats."

Shanti hesitated. "The cats will stay by our sides and either keep the enemy away, or get a blade in the gut if the enemy comes close. The enemy will have noticed them last night. They will expect them, and be ready."

Cayan's frustration sullied the air. "Daniels was dead set against this plan."

"It is a wonder you are going along with it." Rohnan headed toward the door. Shanti followed, thinking exactly the same thing. Cayan usually dug in his heels against a plan as admittedly harebrained as this. That he was going along with it made her nervous.

Because Daniels was right. This wasn't the best of ideas. The problem was that there was no other way. She said as much as they made their way to the Honor Guard where Sanders waited, as rigid as she'd ever seen him.

"Are we ready?" Shanti asked quietly, feeling the press of the unknown from beyond that wall. She knew they were out there, waiting. Watching.

"Where is everyone else, S'am?" Gracas asked.

"They are spread around the wall of the city," Marc replied, hunched over with a knife in hand. "Didn't you see them when you were on your way here?"

"So it's just us going?" Leilius' eyes were large in his narrow face.

"A few from each group will head out as we do," Shanti replied.

"Let's go over the plan one more time," Cayan said in his deep and confident voice. He was trying to sell this to the others as a good idea.

Judging by the doubt plain on his face, Sanders wasn't buying it.

"There are at least two Graygual out there," Shanti said, itching to feel the weight of her sword in her hand. "We don't care about the Graygual. We care about the *Gifted* with the Graygual. He's the one we need to capture or kill." Shanti eyed everyone, masking the holes in her plan with Cayan's level of confidence. "These Graygual have never been beaten before. Without our *Gifts,* the challenge of Cayan and I must be alluring to them. I wager they'll want to pit their strength against us. They will want to prove their dominance."

"But will they? That's the question," Sanders said.

"My feeling is, they will." Anticipation filled Shanti. She had that same desire, but for bigger results. She wanted to send a message to Xandre: she was still the best. And she was still alive.

Not only that, but she was going for him.

"And when they do engage, they'll bring their *Gifted* closer," Cayan said. "That's when you guys make the grab."

"Unless this Burson-like character can also track and fight, sir," Sanders growled.

"Inkna are not trained to fight. They are too valuable to lose, and most aren't coordinated anyway. This one won't be any different," Shanti said.

"This plan is ludicrous." Sanders yanked out a knife. "But if we're doing it, there's no time like the present. I want to get some sleep sometime tonight. We'll have a long road ahead of us tomorrow."

"That is what I love about this army," Rohnan said in a whimsical voice. "They never think about failure. Their confidence is infallible."

"Or stupid." Shanti motioned them forward. To Sanders she said, "You will wait for the signal from Kallon before you leave the city. Once it's given, get across the open landscape and into deep cover as fast as you can. From there…let your intuition guide you and keep your eyes open."

Sanders looked at the Captain for a beat. Not getting any kind of response, he shook his head. "How will we know when to come back?"

"Someone will find you and tell you." Shanti waited by the gate, knowing that there was enough light for the enemy to kill them with arrows as they ran out into the night. She only hoped the range of their *Gifted* wasn't strong enough to pick up their movements inside the city.

Failing that, she hoped they were still adopting a "wait and see" kind of mentality.

Steeling her courage, she let her mind meld with the darkness, feeling the cool night on the inside of her eyelids and the small hairs around her head disturbed in the breeze.

The soft sounds of distant crickets drifted on the breeze, no gap in their music. The stillness relaxed her and let her use her senses in a way impossible when relying totally on the *Gift*. The training in the Shadow Lands came back to her.

With that thought, she felt Sonson by the other gate with Boas, the two best Shadow at hunting in the dark. They would excel in this. She hoped that would also keep them alive.

"Okay." Deep breath. Everyone had to make it back from this, and this *had* to work, or the Graygual would just pick them off one by one in the days ahead. Shanti knew it. They all did. "Let's go."

Shanti ran from the gate, feeling and listening for anything that might announce an attack. Leaves rustled, making her flinch, but no arrows came.

Their feet pounded across the hard ground, loud despite their light feet. A bush wiggled on their right. Shanti's heart leapt.

Nothing came.

Breath coming quickly, they slipped into the cover of trees, each pausing beside a large trunk. Listening.

The night's soft sounds greeted them again, competing with the beating of her heart. Crickets sang, uninterrupted by them or anyone else.

Sighing, Shanti led the way until they found a thick grouping of trees and bushes. She crouched down and felt Cayan's hand rest on her shoulder for a moment. The peace and tranquility in his touch, and radiating through his mind, stilled her. They had made it, safely. So far so good.

Their *Gift* roamed and searched, finding nothing but animals and friends.

Quietly, utterly still, they waited. Patient.

Across the city, Kallon and Tanna ran out, finding the trees as easily as Shanti's group had. They walked for a while, and then stopped as well. Their minds settled. Finally Sonson slipped out of the side gate. Shanti touched the minds around the wall, spaced according to Cayan's instructions, checking in. This would be the optimum time for the Graygual to sneak into the city if they could avoid the bait.

A stray thought passed through Shanti's mind: *That was easy.*

Too easy?

The sound of crickets deadened to their right. Like a large black patch in the blanket of glittering stars above, the absence rang out louder than a shout. Louder still was the lack of living things in that area. Minds of animals and humans were silent.

The *Gifted* was there.

Slowly, consistently, a path of deadened sound headed their way.

A moment later, without warning, her *Gift* was stripped away.

The Graygual were taking the bait.

CHAPTER 12

"KALLON JUST MIND-GOUGED me. That's the signal. You boys know what to do?"

Marc stared at Sanders with the familiar feeling of acid burning his throat. A fleeting thought of the doctor, left at home, no doubt warm in his bed, came to him. As soon as that man retired, Marc had a viable *out* of the army business.

A hard finger prodded his chest, jolting him out of his reverie.

"*Well?*" Sanders leaned toward him just enough to convey the impatience in his crazy eyes. "Do you know what to do, Dorothy?"

Dorothy?

"Yes, sir." Marc tapped his knives, and then touched his sword, making sure. Alena's swallow was audible. Leilius shifted from one foot to the other.

Sanders nodded, scowled at Leilius, and then stared at Xavier for a beat. "Keep the doctor alive. You have the second most important job of this outfit. You got that?"

"What's the most important job?" Leilius asked in a quivering voice. He didn't seem any better at dealing with this sort of thing than Marc, despite having had plenty of practice.

"Killing those Graygual," Gracas answered.

"Keeping the Shoo-lan alive, you nincompoop. Without her, we're all dead. Which is why this hare-brained plan is a bad idea." Sanders cocked his head. The pop and cracks of the Commander's neck made Marc's teeth clench. "Why we are letting Shanti call the shots on this is beyond me." Sanders turned and stared out at the night before his gaze swung left suddenly. His whole body bristled.

He turned around and started pushing everyone back into the city. "Get away from that gate. They're out there."

"Who? The Graygual?" Rachie asked in a hush, backing up quickly. Marc was right behind him.

"They are going after the Shoo-lan. I'll be damned." Sanders started hustling everyone to the left, shoving and pushing them through the streets. "We need to get behind them."

"How do you know?" Xavier asked, helping to get everyone moving.

"The crickets went quiet." Sanders started jogging, yanking Leilius along with him. "On the trade route, you know there is a predator in the midst if crickets go quiet or birds scream. Same thing applies here."

"How do we know they are both there?" Marc asked, hustling along with everyone else as sweat dripped down his back. It was a clear sign he was headed into danger.

"We know they are close, or whoever wasn't protected would already be dead." Sanders stopped by the next gate. Marc hated how small the city was. "Okay, shut up."

Listening for the sound of crickets, Marc closed his eyes and drank in the sound, remembering how fast they moved and how terrified Leilius was of being face to face with one of them again.

This was a bad idea.

"Let's go." Sanders jogged out with his body bent and his head looking all around. Gracas and Rachie went immediately after. Leilius waited for Alena, and headed out next, leaving Marc and Xavier.

"C'mon," Xavier whispered furiously, grabbing Marc's arm. "You do this better than anyone else."

"I hate that fact." Marc swallowed, matching Alena for sound, and jogged out of the safety of the city.

As the walls fell away, the big, bare night reached out and grabbed him, offering nowhere to hide. Space stretched out to the sides, putting their flight across the open completely on display. Ahead, crouching in the darkness, lay protruding stumps and discarded branches, trying to catch their feet and slow them down.

This was the absolute worst gate to leave through, which was why no one was planned to. Here they were, completely exposed to anyone with a bow in hand.

Marc put on a burst of speed, running in front of Alena and Leilius and forcing Xavier to hustle to catch up. Then he overtook Sanders and nearly dove into the trees, so desperate to be under cover he couldn't think straight. Once there, he huddled down and caught his breath, fighting his fear with the need to survive.

Sanders jabbed him in the shoulder before pointing to the right and then up. He did the same to Xavier. Xavier nodded and plucked at Marc's shirt.

Marc shook his head. His panic hadn't quite overcome the fear. He was still mostly frozen solid.

Sanders' big, heavy hand slapped down on Marc's shoulder.

"You have this in you, boy," Sanders said. "Keep your wits and use your intuition. Xavier will prevent anyone from sticking a knife in your gut."

Marc winced again from the heavy, manly slaps. When it ended, he took a deep breath and refused to think about what he was doing, and how stupid it was to be outside the walls with the Graygual. Instead, he focused on remaining as quiet as possible as he wound his way up and over, probably above S'am on the hillside. His foot fell softly and precisely, the effort slow and tedious. Xavier didn't complain, just kept pace and stayed silent. They didn't need to voice that their life depended on not being detected.

After a while, the music of the night surrounded them. Marc closed his eyes and listened, thinking he could hear a couple patches where the sound was dead. Chances were that he was mistaken, but he couldn't worry about that now. Instead, he sat there. He'd never been able to sneak up on S'am, even in the Shadow Lands when she didn't have her mental power. She could hear him, or sense him, and often see him.

But that one time he had refused to play her game and just sat? She'd been annoyed and come to him. She'd had to get really close before she sensed him, and if she had been the enemy, he could've had her. Maybe. Hopefully, because that was the strategy he was employing. And if they never crossed his path? So much the better.

Xavier plucked at his sleeve. Marc shrugged him away. Xavier plucked again, a little more insistently. Marc slapped his hand.

Something skittered in the brush. A rock being kicked down.

Animals didn't kick rocks.

The breath caught in Marc's throat. Xavier went rigid beside him. The crickets all around them had fallen silent.

Something was above them. *Oh shit.*

Breathing deeply and evenly, Marc did not move. Not a single muscle. Not even a twitch. Xavier, thank all that was holy, did the same, relying on Marc to lead with his fear. A presence pushed at Marc's back.

His muscles started to quiver, the urge to run almost overcoming him. A tiny sound reached his ears. No more than a single blade of grass rubbing against a pant leg.

His breathing started to get shallow. He held his knife in a tightly gripping fist. The presence drew nearer, but still he did not move. Xavier next to him, his breath soft even in contrast to Marc's, hopefully knew what was coming, and planned to attack.

The presence stopped just above them. This was it. Now or never.

⁂

Deadness soaked up the air around them, the animals sensing the top of the food chain in their midst. They'd already become used to Shanti and Cayan sitting there. This was someone else.

A sensation niggled at her awareness. Something out in the night caught her attention. Like a bright light in a deep cave, she felt the presence nearing her. Death seethed, something lethal stalking closer, utterly silent.

Breath, deep and even, entered and left her body.

Emptiness crouched around them—no *Gift,* no sound. Full of danger. The grasses and brush felt scratchy against her body. She soaked in Cayan's heat and Rohnan's supportive warmth, and let the awareness and anxiety of that skilled Graygual enter her consciousness, then flow back out. She was at one.

A rush of movement had her on her feet with sword in hand before she knew what was happening. Arms swung downward with a sword hilt between them. The blade caught the pale glimmer of the moon. She threw her sword up to block. Cayan, on his feet at the same time as she was, sliced down at a man in black. Someone bore down from behind. A sword fell toward Rohnan's head. Shanti didn't even have time to call out.

CHAPTER 13

The crack of metal on metal robbed Marc of his focus for just a moment. Somewhere below him, in the trees, S'am was fighting.

Marc bit down on his lip with the urge to jump up and rush down to help her. He tightened his hand on his knife and continued to wait, hoping the person above him would continue moving. A yell pierced the night. Someone ran out of the gate and stared up at the hill.

She needs help, you idiot! Go!

A rustling sounded ten feet away, running back up the hill. Without warning, Xavier popped up like a groundhog, spun, threw something, and then started charging up the hill.

"Oh shit!" Marc jumped up after him, taking the blade of the knife and readying to throw.

Xavier dove into a group of trees. A grunt and sounds of fighting competed with the clashing of metal below. Marc sprinted up the hill. His foot hit a root then caught in weeds, making him stagger. He righted himself and charged onward, reaching Xavier as he punched someone beneath him.

"Here, I'll get him!" Marc changed the position of the knife and tried to get around the two men as they rolled around the brush. "Here!"

Marc bobbed and then weaved, seeing an opportunity to stick his blade in the enemy's side. He dropped to the ground and readied the attack when Xavier's hammy fist came up and knocked him in the ear.

The world swam for a moment as Marc spun. He landed on his face on the mulch-covered ground. After wiping away a small stone that had stuck in his cheek, he crawled back up and searched for the dropped knife. Unable to find it, he yanked out another and scrambled toward Xavier, ready for another go.

"Hurry, help me!" Xavier said frantically, pinning the man to the ground with his knee in the center of the man's back.

"Holy crap, you got him!" Elation filled Marc as he put his knife away and braced his hands on the man's legs.

"No, you idiot—tie his hands behind his back."

Marc took the small ties from Xavier and worked around to get the unconscious man's wrists next to each other behind his back. He looped the rope around a little tighter than necessary and tied it off. "Should I do his feet?"

"Yeah. I'll carry him."

Marc worked at the legs, getting them squared away before standing up and trying to catch his breath. Xavier bent forward and placed two fingers on the man's neck. When he straightened, he braced his hands on his hips and looked in the direction of the swordfighting. "Why are they still fighting? This should be the guy."

"Which guy?" Marc bent to peer at the man's face, still feeling the pull of S'am in trouble and needing help.

"The mental worker. I assume he is, anyway. He's too scrawny to be a Graygual."

"Is he wearing all black?" Marc squinted down at the dark clothes against the dark ground.

"No way of telling. But who else would it be?"

"A Mugdock?"

Xavier turned and faced Marc. His face dipped toward the ground. "Oh crap. Quick, help me check. The mental worker might still be out there."

⁂

CAYAN'S SWORD BLOCKED the strike before his body pushed the Graygual to the side, letting Rohnan duck out of the way.

In a rush of sweet sensation, the blanket covering Shanti's *Gift* ripped off her mind. The cunning mind of the Graygual in front of her sparked to life, cool and intent, but also curious. The Graygual behind was perplexed. Somewhere above her, Marc and Xavier were active, worried, and eager.

"Uh oh," Shanti said with a grin, circling the Graygual. "Your trip to the afterlife has just been guaranteed."

"It was always guaranteed. It will just come a little sooner. Will you hide behind your power, or will you fight?" The Graygual's sword slashed out, fast and precise.

She blocked his thrust and countered with one of her own, hacking at him before backing off then using a smooth strike. He flicked her thrust away and countered, the same precise style in nearly the same thrust. He was trained to within an inch of his life, she had no doubt, but his style showed little variety.

She had learned during her travels. She'd become better.

She stepped forward, skipping inside his reach, and hacked again, fast and brutal. He moved to the side, and she moved with him, expecting the counter and then receiving it. She kicked out, connecting her foot to his side before slashing back down. He staggered but blocked before spinning around. His thrust was almost unexpected.

That was a new trick. She'd have to adopt that.

She stepped forward and thrust as a blade swiped

the air behind the Graygual. It hooked in the back of his neck and raked across.

"No, Rohnan!" Shanti stabbed forward, getting her blade in his gut before the Graygual crumpled to the ground. "Blast it. He was mine."

"He registered his defeat. He knew you would win."

"So? I wanted the victory, you thief."

"You would've played with him, and we don't have time." Rohnan cleaned his blade before bending to check the body.

"I would have learned more about his fighting style to make it easier to take down his kind the next time." Disappointed, Shanti moved so she could see Cayan fighting the other one. He hadn't used his *Gift* either, probably thinking like she had. Or maybe relishing the challenge.

He moved forward to attack, fast and powerful. His thrust was vicious and quick. The Graygual knocked it away and pivoted. Cayan was ready with the next attack, battering at him. The Graygual turned again, and again, slower than Cayan and knowing it.

"He knows he has lost, as well. He is surprised that a man can best him." Rohnan moved forward with his staff.

"Don't do it, Rohnan!" Shanti spread her arm across Rohnan's chest to hold him back. "Let him learn from this Graygual. It'll make him better."

Cayan slashed through the other's arm, a deep cut that might've sliced close to the bone. The Graygual didn't so much as grunt. Arm dangling, he stepped forward with another thrust, slowed with pain. Cayan batted the strike away, met the advance with his own, and ran his blade through the other's gut.

"He'll head-butt—"

As if on cue, the Graygual bent forward. Cayan arched back to evade but didn't move in time. The man's head crashed into Cayan's jaw. A blast of power rocked out from Cayan, *scorching* the man in front of him. He convulsed then went slack. His body slid limply to the ground.

Cayan glanced down at the man before turning to survey Shanti. She couldn't see his eyes, but she knew his gaze was scouring her body, making sure she was okay. That done, he bent to the man and used the fabric to wipe his blade.

"This one used the same style of fighting as the one last night," Shanti said. "As the one you fought."

"They were trained in the same place. That stands to reason." Cayan straightened and wiped his brow. His *Gift* spread wider, checking everyone it touched. Shanti didn't tell him that she'd already done it. He needed to check in on his people.

"You and Sanders were trained in the same place, but your styles are so different it's laughable. And

Lucius isn't like either of you, yet you are all good. These fighters are *exactly* the same."

Cayan faced her then, wheels turning in his head. He didn't say anything. Instead, he looked in the direction of Marc and Xavier, who were relieved but carried a burden. Shanti had no doubt they had found the *Gifted*.

"For all he complains of his fear, and of his incompetence, Marc is one of the best," Rohnan said.

"He is like you." Shanti followed Cayan in that direction.

"How so?"

"He hates his role by my side as much as he loves it. He hates the anticipation of battle as much as he craves the thrill of the win."

"No." Sad amusement drifted from Rohnan. "He hates the violence of his role, but will do anything for his love of you. And in that, he *is* like me."

Cayan watched as three cats ran out of the gate, followed by Lucius and six other warriors. Lucius must've seen the fight and wanted the cats to help, like they had the night before. Thankfully, Cayan already had what he needed.

With a last look at the fallen at his feet, he made his way up the hill to where he felt Marc and Xavier in some sort of disorder.

"What are your thoughts?" Shanti asked, following close behind.

Cayan thought back to that battle. The Graygual had been skilled beyond anything he'd experienced, apart from Shanti. His movements were practiced and perfect, his speed lightning fast, and the strength behind the strikes noteworthy. He moved like a fast-flowing stream. And he'd been surprised by the challenge, which meant he hadn't experienced others in his travels that posed the same sort of opposition.

He was the top tier of Graygual, and Cayan had beaten him.

"This is doable," he said as he drew within sight of Xavier and Marc, arguing. Cayan stopped and faced Shanti. "It won't be easy, but we can win this war. We are better than their best Inkna, and better than their best Graygual. We will win."

Shanti's eyes turned solemn. "We are better, but also few. It has always been a fool's errand."

"You thought that claiming the Shadow was a fool's errand," Rohnan said in his musical, supportive voice. It was the voice he used when Shanti's thoughts turned dark.

Cayan took her hand and fed her a shot of determination as Rohnan continued. "You made the journey you didn't expect to make, claimed the people you didn't expect to claim, and reunited with your people, who you never thought you'd see again. And now you are here, about to capture one of Xandre's assets, having just killed his treasured fighters. You will go all the way to the end, and when you get there, you will finally make your grandfather smile."

Shanti snorted. "Even sitting among the Elders, that man will not smile. It would probably be physically painful."

Cayan squeezed Shanti's hand, bringing her eyes back up to his. For all her coarse tone and seeming disregard for Rohnan's speech, he could feel her heart swimming with emotion. Her pairing with Rohnan must've been Fate. He was the keeper of her faith; Cayan saw that now.

"He has a bigger army, but they are now too spread out," Cayan said softly. "They have left a great many holes. All we have to do is slip through. This is manageable, *mesasha*. We can win this, I *feel* it."

Shanti shrugged. "We just have to find the holes, then."

"Find, or create. Like now."

Shanti barely nodded. "We'd better get up to the boys. They are about to come to blows, by the feel of it."

Cayan smiled before running his thumb over her lips. Tonight had cemented in his mind that she was their most important asset. She needed those around her to accomplish her duty, but she was integral to creating the opportunities. Like tonight—this shouldn't have worked. None of this. The enemy should've attacked the city, or shot them with arrows. If nothing else, no one should've been able to find the *Gifted*. Yet two vicious enemies were dead, possibly a third, depending on if they had followed the directive and left the man alive.

Cayan started back up the hill, shaking his head. It was madness.

A burst of fear from the two boys had Cayan breaking into a jog. He cut through some brush and came upon Xavier and Marc, backing up against a body. In front of them, standing still with a lowered head, were both of Cayan's cats.

"Leave it," Cayan said before wading through the snarling feline bodies. These cats had no appreciation for new friends. He nudged the male aside with his knee and then reached down to push away the female. "Go on!"

"They don't listen." Shanti waded through next.

"Where's yours, S'am?" Marc asked with wide eyes, still staring down at the cats.

"Who knows? He does whatever he pleases." Shanti put her hand on Marc's shoulder before moving him to the side. She crouched down to the body, reaching out to brace two fingers on his neck.

"Is he an Inkna?" Cayan asked.

"He's dressed like one, but…" She leaned back and looked up at the sky. "I don't have enough light to see for sure, but his features don't make him look like he was born to the Inkna. His body is bigger. Broader." She ran a hand up the back of the man's shirt, then pulled back and squeezed his butt. "He has some muscle tone. I'd bet he was or is a fighter."

"He was really quiet," Marc said, backing up so he was nearer Shanti. "He was as quiet as those Graygual. Almost. He panicked, though. He took off running. That's what gave him away. Or he just never learned to run quietly."

"So he has training of some kind." Shanti motioned Rohnan forward. "Carry him into the city. We need a better look at him."

"I *told* you," Marc said sullenly.

"All I was saying was that we should wait for S'am!" Xavier moved around to the captive's feet.

"It's dangerous to keep him alive." Cayan turned toward Sanders and gave a long, loud whistle.

"I said that about you," Shanti said.

"I can handle this guy." Xavier hoisted the body up and over his shoulder.

"It is better to fight with large men. It makes laziness easier." Rohnan followed behind Xavier.

"He can cut off our power, making us susceptible to

Inkna," Cayan said. "We won't be able to feel what's coming or what's ahead."

"We can keep him unconscious."

"You can also keep him at the back of the line with a guard," Rohnan suggested. "Your range will be greater than his."

"We can't always keep him at a distance." They got to the city. Men rushed forward to relieve Xavier of his burden. "Keep him secure. Work with Marc and Ruisa to come up with something that will keep him unconscious."

"Who got him?" Sanders asked.

When Cayan was sure his orders would be followed, he directed Shanti and Sanders toward Daniels' tent. The man didn't want to take residence, even temporarily, in one of the hovels in the city. "Marc and Xavier."

"Do we think there are any others?"

"Doubtful," Shanti said as Cayan reached the flap of the tent and held it open. The soft glow of the lantern illuminated her beautiful face as she smiled at him before ducking into the tent ahead of him. He motioned Sanders through after her.

"Don't expect a smile from me," Sanders growled. "I'm not that kinda lady."

Cayan smirked as he waited for Rohnan.

"I will wait out here." Rohnan stepped to the side and gracefully fell into a cross-legged position.

Cayan knew better than to question him. Instead, he followed his grumpy Commander through. Daniels stood in front of a map, trailing a finger across and down. He glanced up as everyone came in.

"How did it go?" the older man asked. Creases lined his face and circled his eyes. He was under a lot of pressure to find a way that would minimize casualties while still ensuring victory. It wasn't an easy task.

"We took down two Graygual and captured a third man who we think is *Gifted*," Cayan said as he came to a stop at the map.

"Why would it be doubtful that there are others?" Sanders asked Shanti. "There's no telling what else that Being Supreme has under his hat."

"There would have to be another *Gifted* who can block power for there to be others," Shanti said. "And while that is probably true, he is only the second I have come across, which means they must be rare. Rarer than our *Gifts*."

"I agree." Cayan scanned the way before them on the map. "If Xandre has another, he wouldn't assign them to the same task. What would be the point? The chances of that *Gifted* being captured were minute. I am still amazed that we were able to do it."

Sanders pointed at Shanti. "Her harebrained ideas work more often than they don't, but when they don't, they *really* don't."

"Yes, thank you, Sanders," Shanti said dryly. "Enlightening."

"What do you think?" Cayan asked Daniels.

Daniels straightened up with a grimace. "We should get word to the Shadow Lord. She and Portolmous are waiting in the east. They don't want to push through the Graygual until they know where they're needed most."

"And when, exactly, do we mean to go?" Shanti asked, peering between Sanders and Cayan at the map. Her eyes went wide. "*That* city?"

Cayan looked at the sprawling interior laid out before him. "Yes. That city. I mean to make a statement."

"Do you mean for us to live through it?" Doubt colored her words.

Cayan leaned against the table as certainty and confidence filled his center. "I'm not just making a statement to Xandre—I'm making one to this whole land. People need to see that Xandre isn't invincible. They need to see that he *can* be stood up to, and he *can* be beaten."

"Well, it'll be good practice." Sanders crossed his arms over his chest. "I sure hope you can pull some magic out of your ass, Daniels, because we're going to need it."

Daniels' eyebrows lowered. For a moment it seemed as though he would ignore Sanders. A moment later, his chin rose slightly. "I have gone over all the possible scenarios and chosen one I think will work with our limited forces. The Shadow will meet us there from the other side. The hardest part will be coordinating the two forces."

"How many Inkna are in that city?" Sanders asked.

"From the reports we've received, there are a great many Inkna," Cayan said, refusing to acknowledge the tiny kernel of doubt. "There are far more Graygual. They are complacent, though. They have run that city for years. They have their system down and have not received any pushback for a long time. They won't expect to be attacked."

Shanti wandered toward the door. "If they know we are coming, they'll prepare. We should hurry." She stopped by the tent flap and glanced at Cayan. The spicy feeling of their *Joining* rose up, overwhelming his senses. "I'll see you later."

With a tiny smile, she left, her confidence surging. Confidence in him and this plan. It could only mean this was the best, or maybe the only, way.

"She's right," Cayan said to Daniels. "We need to leave tomorrow and waste no time. We'll take a direct route. Hopefully we'll have the city taken before news of our whereabouts reaches Xandre."

"With his spies disengaged, I'm sure of it." Daniels wiped some dirt off the corner.

"We can't be sure of anything." Sanders took a step

away and shook his head. "What are we going to do with the captive?"

"We need information," Cayan said. "We'll talk to him first and see how he came by his post. Hopefully he'll cooperate."

"And if he doesn't?"

Cayan clenched his jaw. "We'll see what happens. Hopefully it won't have to get messy."

"Don't let the Shadow at him, then." Sanders took a step toward the door. "Something tells me they don't play nice."

"And you assume the Shumas do?" Cayan nodded in farewell to Daniels and followed Sanders out of the tent.

"You should think about the kind of statement you want to make, sir," Sanders said, his voice deep with warning. "This land won't want to trade one tyrant for another. We need the Shadow brutality for battle, and something tells me the Shumas will make that brutality pale in comparison to the rage they have stored up, but people shouldn't see that side of them. We should hide them."

Cayan shook his head. "I'd do the opposite with the Shumas. I'd put them on display. I want people to see the desecration and sorrow in their eyes, and I want people to see that they are fighting back. That they have not been beaten. People need someone to rally around.

That someone will be Shanti."

Sanders sighed. "To speak plainly, sir, I hope you know what you're doing."

"So do I." Cayan scanned the land with his mind again, making sure no one waited in the woods. What he had planned could go horribly wrong. In fact, there were very few ways it could succeed. But they had to try. There were no other options.

CHAPTER 14

SHANTI RODE IN silence, staring next to her at an ugly man with a few wicked scars on his face and arms. It looked like someone had taken to him with a sword and then left him for dead, not expecting him to get up and keep going. He reminded her of Tomous. And of Rohnan. And herself.

His shoulders were pushed back and the set of his jaw was defiant as he looked straight ahead, his icy blue eyes unfocused. His fists occasionally clenched behind his back, and Shanti suspected he was pulling at the rope binding his wrists. Her *Gift* was smothered.

"So you were hacked at by the Graygual, and you thought, 'I know what I'll do, I'll join up with those bastards and help kill people just like me,' huh?" Sanders, riding on the man's other side, spat. "That makes a lot of sense. No explanation necessary."

Ahead of them walked a line of horses and men, following Cayan and Lucius, who led to their next destination and hopefully not their death. They had been right about this man's range. It was less than half of Cayan and Shanti's. Cayan was beyond his influence and made sure Shanti rode as close to the middle of the line of fighters as possible. He was too overprotective for his own good.

They'd been at this for a couple hours now, Sanders doing most of the talking. So far, they'd gotten very little out of the man, but what they had gotten was informative.

"So what's next, then?" Sanders asked. "You hang out with us, hoping for the best, until you can escape and go back to a tyrant who made you look like a cut-up slab of meat?"

The man gritted his teeth. "I have never killed anyone. I make it so no one else can kill with the mind power."

Sanders braced a hand on his knee in indignation. "Do you actually believe this horse shit?" He shook his head and looked toward the front. "For the first time, I wish that twin of Shanti's could use his mind magic."

"You killed the men I was with. How are you any better than the so-called tyrant?" The man's hand flexed and released.

"Or maybe you're just dumb." Sanders' face went red, an early indication that he was close to losing his temper. "They were trying to kill us, you shit for brains. That's what it means when scary people sneak up on sleeping people in the middle of the night with a big sword. What would you have done in our shoes? Oh, that's right, you would've rolled over, played dead, and then sashayed right into the enemy's hands so you could help rule the land."

The man swung his eyes toward Sanders. His whole upper body flexed, showing an array of muscle along his back definitely denoting the ability to fight. His hands were tightly clenched, clearly fighting his own temper. Shanti couldn't see either of their faces with this man in the way, but judging by the silence, and the duration of the stare, she bet they were trying to kill each other with their eyes.

"Marc, go get Tomous," Shanti instructed.

Marc lethargically looked back at her and stared for a moment with dazed, tired eyes. He blinked a couple of times. "Sure. I mean, yes, S'am." He took a deep breath and turned his horse out of the line before riding to the end.

"You don't like the truth, huh?" Sanders prodded, anger in his voice.

The man had returned to staring straight ahead, apparently trying to ignore Sanders. Sanders was doing an excellent job of getting under his skin. He was a hard man to shrug off. Poor Junice.

"How long have you been in the army?" Sanders asked.

Silence answered Sanders' question.

"How many kids did the Graygual kill? Or don't you care about trivial things like that?"

Muscles flared and fired along the man's shoulders. The veins in his neck stood out. He was struggling with something, and Shanti bet it was memories.

"Yes, S'am?" Tomous moved his horse in behind her. There wasn't enough room for more than two horses and one Bloody Bastard to walk side by side on the road. The Bastard didn't like other animals in his horse bubble.

"Our friend here was taken down by the Graygual, similar to you." She jerked her head at the man. "Similar to me."

The man jerked as if he had been poked in the backside. He didn't turn her way.

"I wondered, if you were chopped down, what would make you join their army?" Shanti asked, always watching the man. Trying to learn from his body and reactions what he wouldn't reveal with his voice.

Tomous took a moment before he answered. When he did, his voice was dripping with a hatred so intense that Shanti barely kept herself from looking back. "Never. There is nothing that would make me fight by their side. Nothing that would make me help them destroy someone else's life as they destroyed mine. Anyone who does should die a slow and agonizing death. I'm on hand if you need that done, S'am. Let me know. I don't mind getting my hands dirty to rid the land of filth like this."

"You'll have to get in line, Tomous, but thank you." Shanti saw the man's shoulders droop just a bit. A moment later, his muscles flared again. He'd had a moment of sadness, she'd bet on it. He was trying to stay hard and strong, but he had a war of emotion that he could barely contain or cover up. He wasn't like a Graygual officer in character, and he certainly wasn't trained like them.

"Deprive him of sleep," she said to Sanders. "And by all means, continue to torture him with your personality. He'll break sooner or later."

"He'll get brained with a rock sooner rather than later if he doesn't start answering some of my questions," Sanders growled.

Shanti made a clicking sound with her tongue. Her horse launched forward, throwing her back in the saddle. "Damn it!" She clutched at the saddle and pulled herself forward as the horse picked up speed. "Slow down, you filthy animal!" She pulled on the reins, tugging the horse's head back. "Slow...*down* or I will put spikes in your mouth next time!"

The Bastard whinnied and half jumped, digging in his hooves on landing before hopping forward to slow. Shanti clutched with her legs and steadied her balance, breathing heavily.

"You'll wind up as dinner if you keep this up," she warned. She lightly tapped her heels to his sides. Thankfully, he started walking.

"Your horse is feeling better, huh?" Sonson asked with a grin. He was riding at the front of his Shadow, keeping everyone together. The Shumas were right behind them, all just out of the Graygual's range and working on communicating through the *Gift*.

"Unfortunately, yes." Shanti scowled down at her animal. "I doubt he'll be any less surly, though."

"Just like his rider." A peal of laughter rang up from both the Shadow and Shumas.

"I'm really getting tired of that joke." Shanti prodded her horse to go a little faster, wanting to get up to Cayan without making her horse sprint to do it.

"It's not a joke," Sonson yelled after her.

As she neared the front of the line, Cayan glanced back. Those beautiful blue eyes were a pleasant change from the icy ones filled with pain at the back. "Lucius," he said. "Fall back."

Lucius glanced over his shoulder at the Bastard before pulling back gently on the reins. Very obediently, his horse slowed to allow Shanti access to the Captain.

"I miss the boring horse I rode out of your city," Shanti muttered.

"What have you found out?" Cayan asked.

A male skittered by the edges of Shanti's awareness.

Judging by the road they were on, others she had felt, and the fact that it was a single person, it was probably a bandit. He wouldn't get close enough to be trouble.

"He's hiding something." Shanti thought over the lengthy and stilted conversation. "He wouldn't say much, but with Sanders constantly annoying him, he made some admissions early on, one of those being that his village was cut down by the Graygual. He'd been confused at first when people around him were falling from the Inkna's abilities, but he hadn't felt anything. As soon as he figured out Sanders' methods for extracting information—probably much different from the Graygual method of using pain—he stopped saying much of anything. He's smart. And determined."

"So the enemy grabbed him?"

Shanti furrowed her brow, considering his tone and words carefully, trying to make sure she pieced together the correct story. "I don't think so. He was cut down, thought he'd die, but didn't. It was when he was recovering that the Inkna approached him. I'm not certain, but I think it was some time later. I don't know. He's healed now, and showed confusion when I asked various training methods. I don't think he's been with the Graygual that long. So what was he doing between nearly dying, and joining the Graygual, if not being trained?"

"I don't like it. He doesn't fit."

"No, he doesn't, but we have no idea how. Or why. He must've met Xandre. *Had* to have, right? How else could he have ended up with the inner circle?"

"There could've been a go-between, but he would certainly know something. He has information we need, whether he knows if it's useful or not."

Shanti sighed and looked out at the trees. The Bastard did that weird noise, halfway between a growl and a snarl, both not sounding like they should come from a horse. She yanked the reins left, trying to put more distance between him and Cayan's horse. The Bastard would pick a fight, and Cayan's horse would not back down.

"This accursed animal makes my life difficult," she said with another yank out of temper.

"Now you know how Sanders feels."

Shanti narrowed her eyes at the side of Cayan's face where that dimple was showing. The indentation smoothed over quickly as seriousness returned to Cayan's bearing. "You told Sanders to start sleep depravation after we stop?" Cayan asked.

"Yes. He's tough, but he's not cunning. I'm sure he'll let more slip when his brain becomes foggy with fatigue."

Shanti's *Gift* rolled over a female far out to the left. A moment later she felt a few more people of both sexes idle. She glanced up at the sun, high at its zenith. "What should we expect from this land? It's farther south than I have been."

Cayan half shrugged, unconcerned. He glanced around him. "Not much. Smaller traders and travelers use this route. The weak get picked on and stolen from, sometimes worse. The strong are left alone. We won't encounter any problems."

"Do you know this from experience, or is that what Sanders told you?"

Cayan gave her a confused look. "What's the difference?"

Shanti snorted. "Sanders is in a league of his own. Crazy. No one is messing with him. The people out there might very well attack someone like Leilius or Marc."

"Let's hope they attack Maggie. She'll get to spread her wings."

"We are going to have to stop eventually. If the"—she didn't want to call him an Inkna—"*stranger* is awake, it means we'll be blind. Any outliers could get attacked."

Cayan chuckled, his big shoulders shaking. She had no idea why. "Even our weaker warriors would stick a knife in an attacker's rib if surprised by a bandit. They might be shocked if they did so, but they'll be fine. Marc can sense danger—he's done it in the dark twice now—and he is *the* weakest fighter we have, if you don't count some of the women. And I don't, because they will be looked after."

"You'll look after the women but not poor Marc?"

"Marc is part of the Honor Guard and under your command. It is you that will not look after poor Marc."

"Ah." Shanti couldn't help a smile. "As Rachie would say, you got me there."

"That was a hint, you know. We need our doctor."

"Don't tell me how to do my job." Shanti looked away to hide a smile from him.

"Later I'll tell you some other things I'd like to have done. To me."

"Sanders would make a comment about married people in the army." Lucius' voice drifted up. "He would wonder what this world had come to. I might think the same."

"We aren't married and Sanders needs to butt out," Shanti said.

"Not technically married, you mean." Cayan's voice was light, but she could feel his gravity. He was trying to stay light during the peaceful times. They were few and far between.

CHAPTER 15

"Hold up." Sanders held his fist in the air so those out of earshot knew to stop. The Captain and Shanti sat rigid, one looking out to the right, one staring straight ahead. They were using their mental power.

He glanced behind him and saw the line three horses wide extend back and around the bend. Lucius was with the prisoner near the back of the line.

"What's here?" Sanders asked Daniels.

Daniels glanced down at his empty lap where the map usually was. He put his hand on top of his saddlebag before scrunching up his brow in thought. "Small town up ahead, I believe. It's the only town between here and our destination. Apart from that, there are smaller camps and trading outposts, like we've seen already. None of those will bother with a force as large as ours."

Sanders glanced behind him again. He remembered when he'd been taken by the Graygual and Inkna. The Graygual weren't an honorable sort, but they protected the things they valued, and only an idiot wouldn't value someone that blocked out mental power. They needed more people around that prisoner if the Graygual were going to make a play to recover him.

"Sanders."

Sanders' head snapped around at the implied order from the Captain. He directed his horse around the others and walked until he was next to the Captain's large stallion. "Yes, sir."

The Captain's eyes were unfocused. "There is a host of watchful minds up ahead. We think they're guarding the town. Within those there is one that bespeaks Graygual officer."

"How high a rank, sir?" Sanders asked.

"He's high," Shanti said. "Intelligent and cunning. Not as high as the Hunter, but he'll have skill and speed. He'll have a few good officers under him, and he'll be a good leader. This may be speculation, but…the Graygual aren't known for their creativity in training."

Sanders remembered what the Captain and Shanti had said about the inner-circle warrior. They weren't original, but they didn't need to be. They were excellent.

"What's our move?" Sanders asked. "Go around?"

Shanti shook her head and looked as if she was holding something back. The Captain stared at the back of her head for a while before heaving a sigh and looking down at the head of his stallion. He seemed to be fighting with something, but Sanders had no idea what. With that woman, Sanders imagined the littlest of things became ten times more complicated.

"We're going straight through," the Captain said in a strong and sure voice. Sanders knew him well enough to hear the resignation in the words. "We'll hit them hard and fast. No sneaking."

"Sir." Sanders braced his hand on his leg and tried not to shift uncomfortably. "All due respect, but that city is not our play. If we go through, it'll act like a warning for the Graygual. They'll know we're coming, killing any chance of surprise."

"Do you think a horde this big can go around without being noticed?" Shanti asked in irritation. She didn't look back at him. It sounded like a repeated argument. "They'll see us, or feel us. This isn't like that Mugdock town. These Graygual are trained. They don't miss much. In the time it takes us to go around, we'll be spotted, and we'll have an army waiting for us."

Sanders gritted his teeth. "If you don't mind me saying, sir." He glanced at the silent Captain before returning his gaze to Shanti. "But there is a chance we won't get noticed with you and the Captain running interference."

"The interference will be noticed, as will our tracks." Shanti shook her head. "We came this way, so we need to commit to this way. If we blaze through that town, killing or maiming everyone we can, we can be through and onward in no time."

"The townspeople will help," Kallon said, now directly behind them. "They are scared to act now, but when the balance is restored, they will rise up. We've seen this time and again. I agree with *Chulan*."

"If the Captain had time to get to that challenge between you two, you wouldn't be so sure," Sanders growled.

"He's right," Rohnan said in that damn placating voice.

Is this what had happened to the Captain? He'd been browbeaten into this decision by the most stubborn people alive? Well, Sanders wasn't so easy to sway. "What do you know about it, gorgeous?"

"I am not so mistrusting as you—"

"That's enough." The Captain shifted forward in his saddle and then sat back, his shoulders straight and broad. He'd made his decision and was gearing up.

Sanders shook his head. "I strongly urge you to reconsider, sir."

"We should give the townspeople a chance to win back their freedom," Sonson said, moving his horse closer. "We cannot do this alone. It sounds like it's time to make our situation known."

"I had wanted to keep that a secret a little longer, but it cannot be helped." The Captain turned to Sanders with authority. "This situation is much like the one in the Mugdock lands. Prepare to attack."

Sonson nodded at Sanders and turned his horse. Sanders turned his horse, too. *This situation is much like the one in the Mugdock lands.* The Captain had been referring to taking the city. He was talking about when they snuck onto the hillside in the dark to catch a predator without a net. It had been a fool's errand, but had worked out exactly as Shanti had guessed.

The Captain was letting her off the leash again, and this time, all her people and the Shadow would be beside her. God help them all.

A COUPLE OF hours later, Shanti sat in the middle of the lane astride her horse with Cayan and the rest of the mental workers around her. The spicy simmer deep in her body heated up, growing into life. Electricity crackled as her power built, answering the deep well of energy boiling within Cayan. The Shadow came in next, spinning the power and morphing it, making it pulse around them. Then the Shumas boosted it, making it grow into a living thing. Like in the trials all that time ago, the power took on a life of its own, surging but playful. Flirty and dangerous.

"Unleash the fury!" Cayan yelled for everyone to hear. "Let's free these people from tyranny!"

A cry went up from his men. The Shadow and Shumas hardened up, silent. Ready.

Shanti threw up her hand. "Let's—" Her body jerked backward as the Bloody Bastard took off running. She heard a pounding of hooves beside her, and the thundering of the whole army behind. "Ruined my moment," Shanti muttered through gritted teeth.

The ground jiggled in her vision before she shifted and braced. Her body merged with that of her horse, matching the movement and finding balance within his stride.

Feeling out in front of them, she gripped the mind of the first Inkna sentry, and the few after, in preparation. They flew around a soft bend. She *speared* the sentries as the Bastard sprinted down the lane, the ground even and smooth. Their minds winked out, only of moderate strength and no match for the might at her disposal.

A surge of power went up from the town, only a couple of hundred yards away now. The enemy had felt the sentries die and knew danger was drawing near. *Here we go!*

"Haw!" She dug her heels into the Bastard's side and gave a grunt when he put on a burst of speed. He took off like an arrow.

The town came into view. Townspeople were running for cover. Shanti spared a small part of her power and touched as many minds as she could, layering them with feelings of relief, joy, and ease. She envisioned wrapping them up in blankets of safety, making them welcome the people bearing down on their town. Finally, she injected a shot of courage. It would not diminish their fear, but it would bolster their natural inner strength. It was time for them to fight.

A line of black ran toward the edge of the town. The Graygual response time was impressive.

She *searched*, combing through the town for the *Gifted*. She found them, many in a state of urgency, some waiting anxiously. About a dozen—they were of moderate power and experience, but a shiver of fear worked through their minds as she *clutched*. Clearly they could feel the power on their doorstep. There was only one force it could be.

The Chosen.

Hating to disappoint them, she *struck*. Her power thrust out of her, slicing into soft brain matter. Agony flared before half the minds blinked out, dead. The others held on, clawing through the pain.

The gates loomed. Graygual stood in front, holding shining blades and experienced poses. Shanti ripped out her blade as an arrow whipped out from the side. Heads popped up over the walls. Bows came up.

Bursts of power flared around her now as the Shadow and Shumas were in range. Their attacks fell on the archers. Screams rent the air. A wave of arrows took to flight anyway, few of them well aimed. Someone groaned in the cluster of Cayan's army. A gasp preceded the sound of a body hitting the ground.

"Steady!" Cayan yelled, throwing his voice over the noise.

The Bastard gave his equine war cry, unlike any other horse she'd ever heard, followed by a loud whinny as he reached the line of Graygual. He barreled through, knocking his way into the city before flinging out a foot behind to catch someone in the head. The blow cracked the Graygual skull like a melon.

Shanti slashed down with her sword as power slapped her. She shielded as the Bastard reared, having her tipping in her saddle. She threw a leg over without thinking, and jumped. She hit the hard ground and rolled, coming to a stop at a Graygual's feet. She kicked out, catching his knee. His leg bent sideways. He screamed and fell. Still on the ground, she struck toward his chest. Misjudging, she missed. Her blade rammed through his throat. *Happy accident.*

She hopped up. A sword swung through the air, right for her head. She ducked as a blast of power smacked into her. The remaining Inkna were getting annoying.

Without warning, Cayan's huge undertow of power bubbled up and overflowed. It rolled through her and then surged out, shaking the ground as it ripped through the battle. Pain hammered through the Graygual, making them shriek. Her power swirled higher, filling the void between them with electricity.

"Blast it, Cayan," she swore, slashing through a Graygual and running deeper into the city. He was right beside her, moving so fast she could barely see the tip of his sword. "You have to aim!"

"I reacted. Quit nearly getting your head lopped off!" he yelled back. He blocked a thrust and then kicked out to the side, catching another Graygual in the jaw. He cut through the man in front of him before ripping him out of the way, too impatient to wait for him to sink to the ground in death.

Shanti took out a knife and threw it at a Graygual who was running around a house toward her. Another knife hit the next man before Rohnan appeared by her side, his staff whirling.

"Take out the Inkna," Rohnan yelled over the din.

"Give me a minute, would you? I'm leading the attack here!" She caught a sword strike, stepped back, and looped her sword around. The Graygual blade went flying. She stabbed him as she *searched* for the Inkna again. They weren't hard to find. They were clustered together at the back of the city, scattering their efforts. They were outnumbered, perhaps for the first time in their lives.

Her power surged, then felt the growl of Cayan's might and spiraled higher. Electricity crackled. Her *Gift* grew and expanded, swirling out. A low-level *boom* shook the foundations of the city. A huge explosion of power ripped out of Cayan, bringing the crowd of Graygual to their knees. Shanti's power frizzed into white-hot points of light, raining down on the Inkna like a lightning storm. There was nowhere to hide and no hope of blocking. It pierced their consciousness and shattered their minds. The Inkna minds winked out almost as one as the Graygual before them writhed, clutching their chests and screaming in agony.

Shanti felt minds bent on violence in the sky. She glanced up at the rooftops before sending out mental warning. She pointed upward and yelled, "Archers!"

Arrows rained down before Shanti and the army could move. A slice of agony seared her arm, the arrow ripping flesh but not sticking.

Bursts of power flared, but not before answering arrows flew from the army.

"Mine!"

"I got left!"

"I'm shooting anyone I can!"

An arrow stuck into a Graygual chest, followed by two more. He fell to the ground as more arrows struck those around him, this time coming from the sides.

"The townspeople!" someone shouted behind her.

Shanti blasted the town with a surge of pride before *searching* out more Graygual.

"Back of the city," Cayan yelled, doing the same thing.

He led the charge with her right behind. The Shadow and Shumas spread out, trying to fill the area with power in case anyone else popped out.

"Are the Graygual running?" Sanders yelled up.

"No. Not cowering, either. Waiting." A surge of adrenaline rose up in Cayan. She suspected it was a trap.

Shanti thought of the Hunter.

Townspeople emerged from houses along the lane. These were mostly men but included a few women; they had angry or determined expressions, with tattered clothes and rusty swords. One carried a shovel. They were prepared to do whatever they had to.

"This way!" Shanti yelled, directing them to follow.

"What are you doing?" Sanders asked.

"They need to win back their town, and we are going to help them do it." They ran through a building and met a middle-aged man. He held his sword like a lover, standing on slightly bent knees and looking at a large house at the end of the lane.

"*Well met*," Shanti said in the traders' language.

The man met her eyes in confusion. He shook his head and said something Shanti couldn't understand.

Sanders rattled off an answer, or an insult—there

was no telling, really—and nodded. "He says the Graygual officer is in that house surrounded by Inkna."

"The Inkna are dead and the officer is waiting for death," Cayan said in a flat voice. He glanced at Shanti, letting her take the reins again. This new leaf he'd turned over regarding her rash decision-making was a pleasant change. It was also terrifying. Didn't he realize that sometimes she needed to be reined in?

"Let us clear the way, and you will have your vengeance," Shanti said to the man.

Sanders translated in a voice that sounded like a threat.

"We're on the same team," Shanti told Sanders.

"That's why he isn't dead. Hurry up." Sanders motioned her on.

"Give the man a little power…" Shanti jogged toward the building with her *Gift* spread wide. For Sanders' benefit, she said, "There are a few more Graygual throughout the town, and a couple more trying to run, but the Shadow and Shumas are taking care of that."

"I wish you'd left a few Inkna alive…" Sanders growled.

She doubted that her smile reached her eyes. "Next time." At the door of the house, she felt a thick arm come across her chest and force her back.

"No." Cayan stepped in front of her, and gestured

Sanders to his side.

She should've known that making decisions only went so far.

Shanti *clutched* the Graygual mind, ready for what was going to come.

Cayan braced to kick the door down, but the man from the town quickly stepped forward and put his hand on Cayan's arm. He said something and waited. Sanders translated, "He says he should've protected his town in the first place. He should do this."

Cayan clenched his jaw. His power bubbled within him, barely kept under control. He stepped away.

Shanti felt more minds gather, watching. Women and men both crowded around as the man from the town stepped up to the door and grabbed the handle. He turned and threw the door wide.

"Should've checked to see if it was locked," Shanti muttered to Cayan.

The Graygual sat at the table in a large, well-appointed dining room. Judging by the familiarity with which the man moved through this house, checking hiding places, and his sorrow, it was probably his.

"Tell him the Graygual is the only one alive here," Cayan told Sanders.

A moment later the man turned to Sanders, and then narrowed his eyes at Cayan. It wasn't until he met Shanti's eyes that his face drained of color and his eyes started to shine with moisture. He uttered something as his knuckles drained of white on his sword handle. Shanti could feel his gratitude mixing with his profound hope.

Sanders didn't translate.

"I bet you would've told me what he said if he was cursing me," Shanti muttered as the man kissed the back of her hand.

"Yup." Sanders jerked his chin toward the silent and patiently waiting Graygual. "He wants you to do the honors in killing the scum."

"No, *Chulan*," Rohnan said with urgency. "He needs to do this, and the townspeople need to see him do it. They *need* this, *Chulan*."

Shanti gave the man a deep bow, and gestured him on instead. "Tell him I have done my job so that he can do his."

"No," Cayan said softly before Sanders could utter the words. "Tell him to claim his freedom."

After Sanders relayed the message, the man paused. He turned his attention to Cayan. For a moment the two men stared at each other in a silent exchange, before the man's grip tightened on his sword again and determination coated his features. He turned toward the Graygual.

"*You will make a wonderful pet,*" the Graygual said to Shanti in his home tongue. "*The Being Supreme has great plans for you.*"

The man from town wasted no time. He slashed down at the Graygual's neck, cleaving it almost clean off. For a moment, he just stared down with rage masking his expression. That dripped away, though, and in its place was intense, gut-wrenching sorrow.

"I must go, *Chulan*," Rohnan said, backing out of the door. "I suspect the Graygual took his family from him."

Shanti nodded and backed out as well, leaving the man to his grief.

"That was the right thing," Sanders said when he met Shanti outside. "Letting him do it. That was the right thing to do."

"It seems so." Shanti looked into the breeze, letting the air dry her eyes.

"The Captain said to do whatever you wanted as long as you were with Rohnan." Sanders stepped back toward the door.

"What are you doing?"

"I need to translate for him. He's got to get this city organized before we can move on."

"We need to speak to some of these people, *Chulan*," Rohnan said softly. "They have the same pain we do. They have lost a lot of people."

"How are we going to talk with them? Do any of us know this language?"

"One of us must. Your grandfather was thorough."

Shanti chose a path to Sayas. He was the biggest busybody of them all, so he'd probably know who knew what. As she made her way, she thought of their upcoming battle. This town was small, with nothing more than the spillover of the larger city up the road. But even so, those archers surprised them, and the Inkna had posed a bigger problem than they should've done. It didn't bode well. Even using *all* their resources in the next city, unless they did something different, they wouldn't live to take Xandre down.

CHAPTER 16

"SANDERS, WHERE DO we stand?" Cayan wiped his hands on a rag as he came to a stop next to his commander.

Sanders straightened up slowly and then stretched with a grunt before putting his hand to his lower back. "The people are rallying, sir."

Cayan glanced up at the sun, finding it closer to the horizon than he might've liked, and then blew out a breath as he surveyed the small town. Starved and bedraggled, the people here had been through much hardship. The Graygual officer in charge of this city wasn't as firm in his control as the Hunter, and it showed. Lower-ranked men had taken advantage where they could, fighting, killing, stealing, and whatever else. Those who protested were run through with the sword or left the town, saying they would return with help. In many cases, their bodies were found hanging in a tree, or their heads showed up outside the walls on a spike. The town had been cowed through fear for themselves or their families, and they'd given in. Of course they had—they didn't have anyone strong enough to stick up for them. Not against the Graygual with the Inkna at their backs.

Cayan felt Shanti before he saw her. She came around the bend with blood dripping down one arm and dirt smearing her face. That graze must've hurt, but she hadn't let Marc stop her long enough to bandage it. With Tanna, the Shumas that had been taught this region's dialect, at her side and Rohnan at her back, she wandered through the town, hearing stories and woes. With most people she nodded and touched them somehow, often with a supportive hand on their shoulder. Sometimes she gave a slap, and once she punched a man. He fell back like a sack of potatoes. When he got up, fire lit his eyes and courage straightened his back.

Cayan had no idea how she knew what each person needed, but she seemed to heal them with nothing more than a listening ear and a reaction.

As she drew closer, she glanced his way. Sorrow pulled down her features and a gut-wrenching devastation churned her thoughts. She was thinking about the destruction of her own people, Cayan knew. She was reliving the horrible destruction that had befallen her way of life, and it was eating away at her.

"Sometimes I wish I'd never met her," Sanders said as he followed Cayan's gaze. "An ignorant part of me pretends that if we'd let her die in the burnt lands we wouldn't have suffered any of this. We wouldn't have had to voyage to the Shadow Lands and we wouldn't have lost people to the Hunter's men. The women would be safe behind our walls, not out fighting beside us. Tobias would still be by my side, taking care of the things I missed… I pretend she is the cause of it all, sometimes. And I hate her for it. It's easier than dealing with the destruction she heralds."

Cayan felt a flash of rage, but he said nothing. Just waited.

"But then I remember the Inkna-inspired Mugdock attack," Sanders said. "We would've beaten them without her, but we would've lost people. *More* people, I should say. Many more. I still would've been taken, but there was no way you could've got me back. Then the Inkna would've moved in to our lands, and it would've turned into this. The loss, the horror—we didn't succumb to this because of her. Pulling her out of the burnt lands was our salvation, just in time. And I would fight forever by her side to prevent this from happening again, or to save those who didn't have a Shanti to turn the tide. I suspect everyone she meets, and everyone she saves, will feel the same. I don't know about this Wanderer tale, but if it was a person, like Burson says, it is her. For all I want to punch her in the face, she has a *way* about her. She is the backbone of our survival."

"You feel better, getting that off your chest?" Cayan resisted the urge to slouch in fatigue. He needed to stand straight and tall at all times, to give these people a pillar of strength to look toward. Shanti would heal their hearts, and he would direct their swords.

"Excuse me, sir. I had to vent. And I *would* punch her in the face, but she always feels me sneaking up on her." Sanders looked back at a fallen beam, part of the destruction and decay from the Graygual occupation.

"Noted." Cayan looked around, seeing the townspeople start the work to fix their homes or rebuild their shops. "They lead with a form of hierarchy, and only one man is standing from that. They have a Women's Circle, but only three women are still alive. They are trying to reestablish."

"What about their army? Any survivors?"

Cayan tilted his head for a brief moment and turned to look out at the opposite way. "The Hunter kept our people alive because he wanted to trade them for Shanti. This Graygual officer had no reason to spare troublemakers. Their army is in tatters."

"They will fight." Kallon walked toward them with a face made of stone and eyes as stormy as the sky before it crashed down on the land. His shoulders were back, straight and proud, but his emotions were in a turbulent state. "This is not the worst I have seen. In those towns I passed, or helped, I did not spend half the time on their broken villages that you are. Yet still they banded together."

"You saying we should just fuck off and leave them to their misery?" Sanders asked, bristling.

Kallon cocked his head. He gave a frustrated shake of his head and muttered a curse word before whatever confused him dropped away. His eyes turned piercing before he directed his gaze back at Cayan. "You have plans, somewhere to be. You didn't want to come this way, and you didn't want to help because of the overall goal. Even though you bent your will for the *Chulan,* you still stay and fix the lives of these people instead of rushing on." His chin raised a fraction. He shifted his weight, a barely perceptible move. "I always rushed on. I never stayed." His hands clenched. "You are the better man for it. The better leader." Kallon clenched and unclenched his jaw. "To keep my honor, I must admit that you deserve the *Chulan.* Her grandfather never thought a mortal man would. She is touched by the Elders, and speaks on their behalf. It seems she has found a refuge in you that our people find in her. For that, I will welcome you into our people when she decides to mate you."

He stared straight into Cayan's eyes, causing a shot of adrenaline to race up Cayan's spine. War raged in that look. Pain. "This does not negate my challenge," Kallon said, finally.

With that, he turned and glided away, much too graceful to match the sullen mood that swarmed around him.

"Well I'll be damned," Sanders said softly.

Cayan's fingers tingled as he watched the other man. His *Gift* bubbled and boiled, desperate to be used. He glanced in Shanti's direction. She was looking at him with a half-smile on her face.

"Her people are crazy," Sanders said. "I like them."

"Our Women's Circle want to overturn the unspoken rule that nakedness isn't allowed outdoors." Cayan blew out a breath in a laugh, trying to work out the rush of Kallon's renewed interest in a challenge.

"What the bloody hell?" Sanders stared at him, shocked. "If they think I am going to turn the other way when a man comes dangling along on the walkway, they have another thing coming. I don't care that they can make my life hell; I will not bend on that point. I don't need to see a bunch of dicks swinging around! And do you know what Junice would do to me if I glanced—*glanced!*—at a naked woman? I might as well look for a new house, because she wouldn't let me stay with her, that's for certain. What has gotten into their heads? It's bad enough women are throwing on pants and marching into the army, but now they want to watch naked men wander around the place? No way, sir, if you don't mind me saying. That cannot happen. Think of the children!"

Cayan laughed, blindsided by Sanders' sudden shift in mood. Townspeople looked at him, shocked and confused. He couldn't help it, though. The chuckles built, the misery from seeing these townspeople turning into hysteria. Guffaws erupted, consuming his body and making him double over.

"You need to get a handle on yourself, sir," Sanders said in a low voice. "If these people see you cracking up, it'll undo everything you've done."

Cayan laughed just a bit harder at the absurdity of all this, at the madness of thinking he could bring down a tyrant like Xandre with their tiny force. They'd lost five people today, and this was only a small town. They'd lost two taking the Mugdock city, and that should've been nothing. There was no way they could win. No way this could work out to their benefit. What were they doing?

"Hey." Shanti's warm hand touched his shoulder. Her feminine scent, mixed with that of battle and victory, wrapped around his head.

Without thinking, he scooped her up into his arms and carried her away, out of the town and into the nearby trees. There he laid her down in a rush of need before stripping off her pants and pushing down his own. Fighting the uncertainty of what was going to come, and the overwhelming odds, he lost himself in her body. He thrust into her, power and dominance. He took solace in her arms wrapped around his shoulders and her thighs squeezing him tight, and he pushed into her over and over, hard and brutal. Her *Gift* wrapped around his, coaxing it higher. The control he'd barely held on to with Kallon fell away. His power gushed out and blasted through the town. It didn't carry an attack. This time it carried Shanti's essence—pure and soft. Loving and supportive. The soul she tried to hide filtered among the people and soaked into them. His *Gift* pulsed with her heart, feeding courage and replacing their misery with hope.

"We can do this," Shanti said in a low voice, her lips on his. "Don't lose faith."

He grabbed the back of her neck and pumped his hips, focusing on her body wrapped around his. Her faith in him. Another explosion of his power matched his climax. He emptied into her as his *Gift* blanketed the town in his renewed faith. In courage.

SANDERS PAUSED AS he hefted the beam. A wash of tingles covered him before infusing his mood. His heart started to thump and his desire to rule the world made him drop the beam and straighten up. He looked around in confusion. A soft feeling warmed his middle and flipped his stomach before a rush of emotion surged.

"What the hell is this?" He put his hands on his hips and realized the townspeople were also looking around in wonder, dumb smiles plastered on their weary faces. Alena stopped sweeping up glass and hugged a random townsperson. Leilius was smiling like a fool at the man beside him. Marc had his arms crossed and was hunched against the wall, looking surly.

It was Marc's mood that made reality dawn.

This was that mind power. It wasn't real.

Sanders grimaced and looked back in the direction the Captain had taken Shanti. "This just isn't natural."

"But it put in good mood, yes?" Sayas grinned at him as he walked by.

"There's work to be done," Sanders yelled at him. "Don't go starting an orgy!"

Shaking his head, Sanders gave up on the beam. He'd wanted to work out a little frustration with manual labor, but things were starting to crack. The Captain was using logic in an almost hopeless situation, Shanti was calling the shots, and he'd turned soft. Something had to be done or they'd all fall apart.

"Wrap it up," Sanders called. He made a circle in the air with his finger. A few people looked at him, apparently trying to make sense of his words. As they were his people, who spoke his language, this was just another part of the problem.

He looked left and right, then felt a crushing blow when he remembered there was no Tobias to get things moving. A flash of agony welled up. He grasped for rage to replace it. Without thinking, he took a few rapid steps and grabbed Leilius by the collar. "Let's go!" He shoved the boy forward before glaring at Marc. "We're moving out."

Marc hopped forward, not fazed by the Captain and Shanti's mind voodoo. Sanders looked at Xavier, the first competent person he saw. "Get everyone moving. Let's gather on the east side of the town and set up camp. We move out tomorrow, dawn."

Xavier stared at him dumbly for a second. He glanced around him, clearly wondering if Sanders was talking to someone else despite the direct stare.

"Is that a problem, Senior Staff Officer?" Sanders barked.

Xavier's eyes rounded. "N-no, sir. I'll get it done, sir."

Sanders walked on. He'd just given the kid a promotion. Xavier was a little young for it, but he'd been in more battles than some of the veterans, and had benefited by learning the battle strategies of three different peoples. He'd rise to the challenge if anyone would. Sanders needed someone he could trust.

Outside the city, Sanders made his way past the Shadow sentry sitting in plain sight. He paused then turned to the man. In the traders' language, he asked, *"Did you see any action?"*

"Yes." The Shadow pointed off into the distance. *"Graygual were trying to get away. I killed them."*

Sanders looked where he was pointing. He saw one body facedown with an arrow in his back. *"More than one Graygual?"*

"The others I killed with my Therma.*"* The Shadow tapped his temple. *"I was told not to leave my post."*

Sanders nodded. *"Good work. We're meeting on the other side of the city. We'll leave tomorrow at dawn."*

"Should leave after dark." The Shadow grabbed his bow from the ground and stood in a smooth movement. *"I only killed the Graygual I felt. My range is not great. Some will have gotten away."*

Sanders shifted, thinking over what he knew of the Graygual. *"They don't seem to surrender. If they run, they'll just be killed by the higher officers. So they wouldn't check in with one of those."*

The Shadow grinned. It was a predatory expression. *"Not all of these are from the Graygual land. The army is also made up of normal men who don't know the customs. They don't know what they've gotten themselves into. They will sing like canaries before they are done away with."*

Sanders gave a nod before turning. His first foot hadn't hit the ground before the Shadow said, *"I've heard of you, you know. The Inkna hate you more than the Chosen. You withstood their torture and killed them all."*

Sanders scoffed. *"I didn't kill anyone."* Why lie? Not like it was a big secret. *"I shat my pants while a girl rescued me."*

The Shadow laughed. *"I have never heard of anyone escaping torture. I heard you mocked them."* The Shadow hefted his bow, preparing to head to the meeting place. *"People talk. The Graygual will hear of us before we get there, unless we hurry."*

Sanders watched him walk away for a moment. He snatched a piece of grass from the ground, sniffed it to make sure it hadn't been pissed on, peeled the end, and stuck it in his mouth. He needed something to chew on.

"Daniels," Sanders barked as he approached the hiding place. One of the women rose from some brush not far from where he stopped. He hadn't even noticed her. "Good work. Head to the east side of town."

"Thank you, sir. Yes, sir." She took off at a jog.

He might actually get used to the women after all. When they got it in their heads to follow commands, they did it without the need for violence. It was just getting through their thick heads that was the problem.

"What news?" Daniels asked, his hand on the shoulder of the prisoner. Tomous walked out behind, his face a mask of disdain.

"We're heading to the east side. Town is still in disarray but they are getting their leadership in order. Once that's done, and their army is in some sort of shape, we'll make a plan. Not long now."

Daniels glanced at Tomous. "Take the prisoner."

"With pleasure, sir." Tomous roughly grabbed the prisoner's arm and pushed him ahead.

"He'd better arrive alive," Sanders ordered.

"Yes, sir," Tomous said. Sanders caught a hint of frustration.

When they were out of earshot, Sanders said, "There's some question of when we leave."

"We will be on our way at dawn, I thought. That is what the Captain said when he checked in after the victory."

Sanders grabbed his wrist behind his back and studied the ground as he walked. He relayed what the Shadow had said.

"You didn't kill anyone. You were mostly dead."

The sound of grinding teeth wasn't healthy. Sanders spat out the mangled stalk of grass while he squeezed his wrist harder. "Yes, Daniels, I pointed out the flaw in the story. My point was regarding to how fast word travels."

"Ah yes, I see your point, muddled as it is." Daniels stroked the stubble on his chin. "This Shadow makes a valid argument, but we are a day away. The men are tired from battle, and traveling at night is treacherous." Daniels' brow furrowed. "I will need to speak to the Captain and Shanti about this. We need to know how fast the Graygual can prepare a large force for battle."

CHAPTER 17

After an exhausting night and morning of traveling at a breakneck pace, Shanti crouched with a small force behind a hedge of a farmhouse, staring ahead at a tall stone wall with very few handholds or areas to climb. At the top stood a sentry, only his head visible. Beside him the wall dipped for a place to fire arrows, and then rose again for cover. The crenulations lined the whole of the wall, perfect for defense. Way off to the right, guarded from above by four Graygual, sat a large archway, currently open to travelers. Spikes of a gate barely showed below the arch, and thick wooden doors were pulled wide behind.

"All that structure, and they still have a moat." Rohnan was looking at the deep and wide water-filled channel running around the city.

"It's basically a fortress," Xavier said dismally. "How are we supposed to sneak into that?"

Shanti turned around and sat on her butt. She brought out the map Daniels had given her—he'd stayed behind with Cayan, Sanders, and most of their people, intending to travel at dawn. It was all part of an elaborate plan that could go wrong in so many ways. The first of which was sheer size of the city in front of her.

"This is madness," she muttered, shaking her head. "We can sneak in, but…"

"*What of the Shadow?*" Sayas asked Sonson with a grim face in the Shadow's language.

"*They are making their way here, as far as I know.*" Sonson made a half-circle with his finger. "*They are aiming to meet with the Captain's army. Daniels has been sending instructions.*" Sonson shook his head. "*A lot can go wrong, but even if that works out, it won't do any good. Even if we had twice the number of warriors they have, triple, this city was built with defense in mind. If they raise that drawbridge, we're as good as done. Even if they keep it down, all they have to do is lower that gate and we're out. It would take a huge force to pry them out of that city.*"

"There is a back way." Leilius scuttled forward and pointed at the area at the top of the map. "Shouldn't we check out the back way? It's bound to be smaller, right?"

Shanti felt pressure on her chest as doubt crept into her. While she could probably climb that wall and sneak in that way, after swimming through a disgusting moat, only a couple of others could as well. Despite how far they'd come, the Honor Guard wouldn't make it. Not even some of the Shadow and Shumas would.

Sneaking in the front? How? Even if they had good enough disguises to mask their lightness of hair and feature, their power would flare like a bonfire in the middle of night. Inkna would pick them out immediately. The back way wouldn't be any better. Not even the cover of darkness could help them—not that it was an option anyway. If they waited that long, they'd delay the rest of the plan. That would leave a large army just over the hillside, trying to hide in bushes while Shanti tried to find a way in.

Shanti watched a horse and cart amble up the road not far from their hiding place. The farmer, rail thin and hunched on his seat at the front of the cart, whipped his starved horse to go faster. The horse bobbed its head, but didn't increase its speed. They both looked like they were a few months away from an unmarked grave.

After a few minutes of trudging, the farmer stopped at the gate and stared straight ahead as a Graygual poured through the cart's contents. He moved items and opened bags. After that, he peered at the farmer, before waving him through.

"Whoever's in charge runs a tight ship," Shanti said as that weight grew. "We should call this off. Hit another city. This is a bad idea."

Sonson stared at her for a moment before turning

back to the city with a thoughtful scowl on his face. "No. There has to be a way. Can we put the gatekeepers to sleep, or black them out, while we run through?"

"They will have Inkna monitoring. They'll know an enemy is in their midst." Shanti looked at the sky, pleading for guidance.

"I can get in." Leilius poked the map at the back gate. "I can get in, and I bet I can get this open. Daniels only has two guards marked. Though how he knew, I would love to know."

"It won't stay open long enough to bring any amount of army through," Shanti said.

Leilius rose up in indignation. Xavier dragged him back down behind the hedge, but the indignation didn't leave his voice. "But I can get it open long enough to get you guys through, and then we can figure out what to do next."

"If you use violence, that will raise suspicion," Sonson said, moving closer on his knees. Determination colored his tone.

"We don't need violence," Maggie said. Ruisa nodded and put her hand to a pouch at her belt.

"I can get in." Alena was staring at the road where a forlorn woman was making her way along. A large basket balanced on her head. "I can figure out how to carry a basket like that."

"We can pay some of these farmers for their stuff."

Xavier looked at Shanti earnestly. "We'll pay them, and send them on their way. They'll be glad to leave, and it probably won't take much gold. Then we can get in that way."

"This will work, *Chulan*," Rohnan said with a hand on her thigh. "Have faith in those around you. It is their turn to make miracles."

"Get out of my head, Rohnan." Shanti slapped his hand away.

"We are too different from this land to sneak." Mela spread her arms and looked down at her body. "Even if we colored our hair, we would raise suspicion. We need to let the boys and girls go, *Chulan,* and get us in back."

"We not climb you." Sayas looked at the wall.

"Not with the Captain guarding you as he does, anyway." Mela winked at Shanti. Seriousness then took over her expression. "But he's right. We can't climb the wall. *I* can't, anyway. Send the boy in. He is invisible when he wants to be."

"I'm not a boy," Leilius muttered.

"I bet they have prostitutes in there." Alena shrugged. "Once I get in, I can get close to the guards that way, I'm sure. They won't expect me to slip something in their drink."

Shanti glanced around the group. Confident eyes and eager expressions looked back. They didn't want to give up or turn back. They didn't want to pick another city that gave them some realistic chance at survival. They wanted to reach for the unattainable, and find a way.

Emotion punched her. Helplessness, fear, anxiety—the likelihood of losing everyone to this venture was so real. She couldn't bring herself to give the direction and lose more of those she loved to the Graygual.

Without warning, a palm slapped across her face. Her cheek burnt as her head swung to the side. When she looked back, Alena knelt in front of her with a hard expression. "Shake this off. You shake it off, S'am. There's work to be done." Alena sat back on her hindquarters, sounding amazingly like Molly, the nursemaid from the Westwood Lands, for a second. "Now. What's next?"

"I WOULD RATHER have gone as a rich merchant," Leilius murmured as he shuffled down the lane toward the gate of the city. "Hunch more, Xavier. They're going to know you're not downtrodden."

Xavier bent his spine and tried to look straight ahead of him regardless. Not only did it look funny, but it would not fool any intelligent person.

"Like you have shit on your face, idiot!" Leilius elbowed him. "Like S'am just punched you in the ballsac."

The toe of a woman's boot came up between Xavier's legs. It smacked into his crotch before disappearing again. Xavier grunted painfully and collapsed, dropping his sack of grain and clutching his balls. He curled up with his face in the dirt.

"Maybe that was a little too hard," Maggie said. She didn't sound sorry.

Leilius took a couple of steps away. She was turning into the female equivalent of Sanders.

"C'mon, up you go." Maggie hoisted Xavier up. "I just wanted to make sure you didn't get us all killed. You'll be fine. Walk it off."

Xavier wheezed out unintelligible words. His face was strained and bright red.

"So...let's have Alena walk up front with Ruisa and I, then." Leilius motioned her forward.

They changed positions before Leilius felt a hard mental prod. The feeling weakened his knees for just a moment. The others winced. S'am was telling them to get going.

Trying not to look back toward the hedge where everyone had returned to watch, Leilius picked up Xavier's pack and handed it to him. Each of them had sorry and holey-looking garments that were a few sizes too big. Stains and rips marred the threadbare fabric. In their sacks was miserable grain from soil that had been stripped of nutrients. At least, that was what the Shadow and Shumas had both agreed on. They'd overworked the land, not rotating it as they should have to keep fertility in their fields. They hadn't been able to produce enough to satisfy the Graygual, so they pushed the land harder, until it was near the end of any production at all. Judging by the look of them, and the constant wailing of their too-thin baby girl, famine was not far away.

Leilius blew out a breath. "It is a sad day when one gold piece would buy all this." He started walking.

"Very sad." Rage tinged Maggie's voice instead of sadness.

"It's going to raise suspicion, though, what S'am did," Xavier said in a rough voice that was filled with pain.

"Rohnan was positive the family would share with their village people." Alena adjusted her shawl and then resituated her pack.

"Rohnan can't tell the future," Xavier said. "Why share with their townspeople when a sackful of gold will buy them an entirely new life? Away from the Graygual. They'll have their kids to think about. No, she should've just given them one gold piece like they asked." He groaned. "God, Maggie, did you really need to put so much weight behind that kick?"

"By now they'll know that there *is* nowhere away from the Graygual," Maggie said.

"Shut up!" Leilius lifted his eyes enough to see the drawbridge not far away. The boards were weathered and discolored, sturdy enough for holding people, but a battering ram would take it down easily. Of course, getting a battering ram over a twenty-foot gap wouldn't be easy.

A Graygual from the wall looked down on them for a brief moment as they stepped onto the boards leading over a swampy mess of water. Their feet made dull thuds as they crossed into enemy domain. A beady-eyed Graygual looked Leilius over before moving on to the others. He grabbed Leilius' sack and pulled it open. A moment later he checked out the others, yanking the edge of the fabric harshly. When he reached Xavier, the guard paused, his eyes scanning Xavier's width of shoulder. Without warning, he gave Xavier a solid shove.

The knife burnt on Leilius' hip, itching to be brought out of hiding and stuck in that guard. Blood pounded in his ears, fear gearing his body to run.

Xavier staggered and hit the wall, groaning. The large man cowered for a moment, catching his breath. He'd never been a good actor, so this proved that Maggie had indeed kicked him a little too hard. Good thing for it.

The guard barked a couple of words and threw his thumb over his shoulder. It stupidly occurred to Leilius that none of them spoke the common language in this land, nor did they speak Graygual. How the hell would they communicate?

Before Leilius could glance back to make sure everyone was accounted for, the *clomp, clomp* of hooves on cobblestone caught his attention. Coming their way were two large, shiny stallions pulling a grandiose coach. The coach driver sat primly, dressed in tailored silks.

The driver yelled something, his harsh voice hinting at vulgarity rather than high class. His scowl had Leilius moving to the side and hunching. Alena bumped into him a moment later, muttering an apology and scurrying to his other side.

"They have dirt-poor farmers feeding the nobility. Disgusting." Maggie's eyes flashed.

"Welcome to the real world." Xavier's stiff walk perfectly toned down his large frame. "That's how things work in places like this."

"The Captain will sort it out. C'mon." Leilius motioned them away from the crowd and into a large street. He skirted to the side quickly, slinking into darker patches beside buildings. "Let's get to cover and we'll figure out what to do next."

People of all types wandered the streets, from the downtrodden, bringing in their meager wares to try and get a day's bread, to the hard-eyed merchants looking to fatten their purses. Occasionally men in tailored clothes walked ahead of fine ladies and men, pushing and shoving people to make room for the rich folk. Their eyes were vicious and their manners coarse, much like the driver they'd just seen. Those in their path quickly scurried out of the way or were subject to a rap on the head and tossed to the side.

One such man, his fat stomach pulling at the seams of his bright blue garment, yelled at an older woman in his way. The woman, a frail thing leaning heavily on a cane, gave a start and immediately tried to shuffle toward the wall. Other people had already made the move, however. She hesitated, looking around her, trying to escape.

He yelled again before baring his teeth.

"We have to help her." Xavier took a hasty step toward her.

"They'd report us!" Ruisa punched Xavier to stop him as the servant in blue bore down on the old woman.

In a fit of violence, the servant swung the back of his hand across her face. The force whipped her head around. Her body crumpled. Her cane skittered across the street, and under the feet of the crowd hurrying by.

The servant walked on with a sour look. A lady dressed in the same blue, with a dress that billowed out in a show of tailored excellence, altered her course by three steps in order to avoid the downed woman. Her hem barely brushed the still figure lying in the street. The rich woman neither slowed nor looked down.

Leilius felt a push, only then realizing he'd stopped and was staring at the limp woman lying in the road. The breath was trapped in his chest as unexplainable emotion tugged at him. That could've been his nana. It could've been her who hadn't gotten out of the way in time, and had been shoved aside.

"Move!" a gruff man said in the traders' language.

Without thinking, Leilius turned toward the man and dug two hard punches into his ribs. He brought his elbow across the man's face, smashing into his jaw and knocking him to the ground.

With defiant eyes, he stared down another man pushing into him, begging him to make a move. When the man didn't, Leilius shoved Ruisa out of the way and glared at Maggie, daring her to say something, and stopping the flow of people in the street. He bent to the old woman before placing two fingers on her neck. A feeble pulse pushed back.

"C'mon," he said in Shanti's hacked-up language. His accent wasn't great—he hadn't been learning long—and she probably wouldn't understand him, but he didn't care. It felt right. "Me help."

Her rags moved and twisted as he lifted. Soft whimpers left her lips. She was as light as a bag of bones.

"*Are you okay?*" Leilius asked in the traders' language.

The woman, head naturally shaking in the way of the old, looked up at him in wonder. Tears rolled and fell down her wrinkled cheeks. "*You must go. You'll get in trouble.*"

"*Are you hurt?*"

A shaking hand touched her hip, making her wince. "*I don't think it's broken…*"

Leilius dug into his pants. He pressed a gold coin to her palm before curling her fingers around it. "*Get yourself healed, get some food, and then get out of the city. The Wanderer is coming.*"

A flash of hope shone in her eyes. Her fist tightened before another tear slipped down her cheek. "*Go,*" she said softly. "*Go. You are not safe here.*"

Leilius patted her hand before grabbing the nearest person. A ruddy-faced woman with thin lips pressed together stared up at him with awe and fear mixed together.

"*Help her home,*" Leilius said in a rough voice he barely recognized as his own. "*See to her.*"

"*Yes, sir.*" The woman called a teenage boy with a flare of defiance in his eyes to her. His brow lowered and his jaw clenched. He gave Leilius that open look Leilius had seen a million times before from the Honor Guard each time S'am taught them something new.

That was when Leilius felt all the eyes on him. A busy street in a large city had stopped to watch Leilius see to an old woman. This was the opposite of all he'd been trained to do.

"Let's go. Quick." Leilius tried to slink into the crowd. Instead, it parted for him, allowing him to pass through easily. More eyes were on him now. Curious eyes.

"Hurry!" Leilius yelled behind him, half running now.

"This way." Xavier swatted him, pushing him right.

"Xavier!" Ruisa called.

"Leilius, wait!"

Leilius tried to stop and turn around, but bodies were all around him. He'd created a huge bog of congestion with his bleeding heart. Hands pushed at his body.

"Ow!" Leilius swam through sweaty chests and bony elbows. He reached the side and flattened himself against a rough wall. The crowd moved slowly and people either tried to peer over their neighbor to see what the hold-up was, or stared ahead lifelessly and stooped, half-dead and complacent.

A curly head followed by Xavier's face bobbed above the people for a moment. Then again. He was jumping to try and find Leilius.

Taking note of his location and the speed of the

crowd, Leilius threaded into the bodies once again, squeezing through cracks and shoving through barriers. "Xavier!" he yelled.

"Here!"

A boot came down on his foot. Leilius threw an elbow as punishment. He slipped by a man in silk with a big gut and couldn't resist. Stumbling, he bumped into the man. Leather slid across his fingers as Leilius reached into his pocket. A grunt later, he'd unhooked the purse then staggered into someone else. A lean bag of coin jingled in his palm before he could tuck it away close to his body.

"Here!"

Leilius ducked around a woman in a wool dress and shot out a hand. His fingers clutched threadbare rags covering a heavily muscled body. A fist came down and smashed into Leilius' forearm.

"Ow! Damn it!" Cradling the injured arm to his chest, he elbowed Xavier.

"Sorry. I didn't know that was you." Xavier patted his shoulder. "The girls have gone. I lost them."

Leilius put his hand to Xavier's back and applied pressure, trying to get the big lug off to the side. "We won't find anyone while we're in the thick of things."

"You created this, you know. Not that I blame you." Xavier tried squeezing in between two women, but he didn't squeeze so well. Instead, he jostled them out of the way. "Sorry."

"Don't say anything. You'll give yourself away."

"What are you doing, then?"

Leilius gritted his teeth. Suddenly the game where they tried to steal things without talking made a whole lot of sense.

Breathing heavily, they made it to the side then slid along the wall. As they reached a corner, a wave of blistering pain tore through their minds. Like acid poured down his skin, fire and agony blanked out Leilius' thoughts. He looked down in panic, but all he saw was his clothes, perfectly intact.

"Inkna," Xavier whispered painfully.

Everyone in the road groaned or cried out and sank to the ground. Children started screaming. Loud wailing sounded up the street in the way they'd come.

"We did this." Xavier squeezed his eyes shut. "This is what happens when someone defies them."

Leilius took a deep breath and let the pain consume him. He felt it tear through his body and drip down his middle, becoming a part of him. He gave a moment for total surrender before taking another deep breath, tolerating the agony.

Xavier stared at him with pain-soaked eyes, in the same frame of mind. Sanders' training had come in handy.

"Let's go." Staying low, making sure not to raise any

part of him above the cowering crowd, Leilius half crawled around the corner and away from that main street. The crowd immediately thinned and the pain subsided enough to where he was no longer in survival mode. Another deep breath and they were around another corner, into a narrower lane with broken-down shops and shabby buildings.

"That Inkna seemed pretty strong," Xavier said, lifting a pant leg to check his skin.

"All Inkna seem strong to us. Let's hope he doesn't seem strong to S'am."

"What do they do with female Inkna?" Xavier wondered as they straightened up to the height of those around them. Lowered brows over eyes tight with fear scanned the way ahead as people slowed in their progress. More than one person looked at Leilius and Xavier, clearly wondering what was happening up ahead.

"*Go around*," Leilius said, shaking his head. He motioned away left in case they didn't speak the traders' language. "Inkna."

A man's eyes widened briefly. He glanced at the woman next to him, who was staring in shock. The man looped his arm around her shoulders and directed her away, both of them hunching as if they were walking in a hailstorm.

"I think Inkna women are breeders," Leilius said as

he took a small-scaled map out of his pants. He hunched against the wall. "And we probably shouldn't talk to anyone from now on. These people don't seem that friendly."

"Big city."

"Huh?" Leilius glanced up.

Xavier fished a small brown sack from inside his pants. He jiggled it and grinned. "Big city. People aren't as friendly. Look what I stole."

Leilius shook his head. "That was risky. You shouldn't be trying to rob people. You'll get caught."

"You're just mad because you can't do two things at once."

"Oh, you mean like find you in a crowd, make my way to you, rob someone of a bigger bag of coin than that, get us away again, and now plan our day? Yes, Xavier, you are a true marvel." Leilius shook his head and pointed at their rough location on the map. He traced it back to where the girls separated. "Should we try to find them?"

The grin melted off Xavier's face. "We planned to separate anyway. We have different tasks. Now is as good a time as any. My only worry is them getting caught. We might need to make sure they get away."

"They didn't get caught." Leilius straightened and slipped the map back in his baggy clothes. "You don't know Maggie. Seriously. That woman is crazy. No wonder she came up with that exploding thing—she is probably going insane after all these years without a proper way of working out her violence. Can you imagine what S'am would be like if she was a stay-at-home wife?"

"Maggie wasn't married."

"Exactly. She didn't even have a man to distract her. No, she'll be fine, trust me."

Xavier rolled back on his heels as he looked down at his toes. "I hope they're together."

Leilius thought of Ruisa and Alena. Ruisa might be able to handle being alone as she had been through the Shadow Lands. She at least had some experience. Alena, though…

"I do too," he said.

CHAPTER 18

"ARE THEY IN?" Rohnan asked, facing the gate, watching the various comings and goings.

Shanti kept her eyes closed, her face pointing at the dying sun, lightly monitoring the most inexperienced members of their group. She barely connected with Xavier and Leilius, their minds whirling with determination. Ruisa and Maggie revealed a completely different swirl of emotions. Fear, anxiety, and worry pulsed out of them.

"Something has gone wrong." Shanti prevented herself from tensing up. It wouldn't help the situation. She needed all her focus to maintain an extremely light mental touch within those walls. If even one Inkna got a whiff of her power, the whole city would clamp down.

She found Alena away from the others, drifting out to the east of the city. It felt like she was alternating between fear, uncertainty, and steadfastness.

"Whatever triggered the compassion from Leilius acted as a catalyst. The group remained stationary for a moment, and then drifted apart. Each of them holds some kind of fear." Shanti considered using a fraction more power in order to lay a supportive blanket over Alena's mind. It would help her confidence and decision-making, but too much and she might grow too adventurous. In that city, *adventurous* might get her killed. "There are three groups now. Alena is on her own."

Kallon stiffened. "Do we go in after them?"

Shanti shook her head and repeated her calming technique, trying to keep Kallon's turbulent emotions from building on her own uncertainty. "We will wait and see what they do. Judging by the feel of them, they aren't in immediate danger."

"Here comes the coach." Sonson straightened enough to move toward the hedge near the road.

"Did you see why they stop?" Mela asked. "I not watch."

"They were adjusting their baggage, I believe." Sonson took out a knife. "Does anyone want to walk around the city as a noble?"

"Yes." Mela laughed. "Why not?"

"You would stick out," Tanna said offhandedly.

"I wouldn't even know how a noble from this place might walk?" Denessa said as she fingered a knife.

"That is an idea." Shanti lifted until she could just see over the hedge. Well-bred horses walked up the lane, pulling a gorgeous coach with all the finery and embellishments that money had to offer. "That will be a Graygual. No one else would have that much wealth in this place."

"Well, then, using their clothes or not, I say we kill them." Sonson took out another knife, one for each hand. "I'd hate not to pay them back for what they did to my people."

"Cayan has always wanted to dress me like a doll. Maybe I'll see if the way of life fits me…" Shanti pushed forward, excitement at the prospect of actually doing something surging within her. "The question is, even if we wear those clothes, won't the Graygual still notice us?"

"Maybe. We can work that out later." Sonson peered over the hedge.

Shanti moved in beside him, careful to keep her body away from the dead holes in the foliage. "I can't condone killing those who have not killed, no matter where they came from."

"Then we'll take their money, their horses, and their clothes," Denessa said. "They can sit in the cold, naked and tied up, until we can figure out what to do with them."

"Good compromise." Shanti took out her knives and moved along the hedge. When the others had taken their positions near one or more gaping holes from dying plants, they waited.

The coach ambled along the way. The driver stared straight ahead with a stiff back and arms. He was playing a part, even though no one could see him from inside the closed carriage behind him.

Shanti felt the minds inside, not at all surprised to feel a *Gifted* among them. She met Sonson's eyes after the discovery, making sure he had reached the same conclusion. His nod was slight as the coach came up alongside the empty farmhouse. It didn't slow, and the mind within didn't reach out to search. They were comfortable in their superiority.

A rush of irritation had Shanti rising just a little, ready to engage. As the horses passed, she plowed through the foliage and *wrenched* the horses' minds. Their eyes rolled before they screamed. Hooves flashed out as Shadow and Shumas burst from the side.

The driver recoiled, half cowering. A moment later he reached toward his feet, coming back with an ornate blade.

"That's enough for me," Shanti said. She threw her knife. The blade stuck in his gut as Denessa jumped up onto his bench. She raked her knife across his throat and pushed him out of the way. She grabbed the reins and pulled back to steady them while Sonson ripped open the coach door. A hard blast of mental power *singed* him before filtering through their merge. The power was sucked in and fought, Sonson easily putting down the attack.

A moment later, two men and a woman were torn from the coach interior. They wore stern expressions and more wealth than Shanti had ever seen on a person.

"*Bandits don't fare well in this part of the land,*" the lady said with an air of superiority.

It took Shanti a moment to realize she was speaking in the traders' dialect.

"*Neither do Graygual,*" Shanti said in the woman's native tongue.

The woman sneered and haughtily looked at the man standing beside her. "*They learn a new language and think they can rule the land.*"

"*You are not afraid of dying?*" Shanti asked, walking closer.

The woman sniffed, refusing to look directly at any of her captors. "*Why, because you have a wilder among you?*" She laughed. "*You have already committed yourself to a public hanging. Do you also want your family, your children, your friends, and your entire town burnt alive?*" The woman sneered before finally meeting Shanti's gaze. Her face froze as she formed her next word. Her body became rigid and all the blood drained from her face.

"*You have already killed my family, my friends, and burnt my entire town. And, as I am sure you know by now, we are not wilders.*" Rage boiled within Shanti, who realized that this was one of the social elite among the Graygual. She had thrown lavish parties for officers to celebrate their victories. She had probably dined at the same table as the Hunter, and maybe even bowed and gushed over meeting Xandre. She was filth, and disgusting, but she didn't have blood on her hands. Not directly.

"You are right, though. I am not going to kill you." Shanti slowly put away her blade. *"But I am going to strip you of everything you hold dear. And no, I am not so stupid as to think you care for anything that breathes."*

She glanced at Sonson. "Do as we planned. Take their money, clothes, and horses. Tie them up and put them in the farmer's house. I imagine he'll come back before we leave. If not…maybe he never will. We'll just have to hope he can read."

"Why is that?" Sonson asked.

She frowned at him. "Because we're going to leave a note." Shanti ran her hand along the horse to quiet him before looking over the coach. At the opened door, she saw the lush leather seats and the dead Inkna in the corner. At the back, she fingered the locked trunk before tracing along its seams. "Let's see what's in this."

"What are you thinking?" Kallon asked.

"Besides the wealth in this carriage that will be distributed to the poor people in this land?" She grinned, standing back and looking at the carriage again. "This is an entry ticket right to the highest officer of this city. The question is, how can we best use it to our advantage?"

⁓

"Wait!" Ruisa yanked on Maggie's arm and dragged her to the ground. Crouching behind three barrels outside an inn, she retrieved the map from the pouch tied around her neck. "We need to get our bearings."

Maggie, breathing heavily from exertion, hunkered down beside Ruisa.

"Alena's not an idiot," Ruisa said, tapping the rear gate. "She'll know to head there."

"She's never been in a big city before. She'll probably get lost."

"You haven't either. What makes you better than her?"

"I'm with you." Maggie wiped her hair off her forehead. "But you're right. There's nothing for it now. There's no way we're going to figure out which way she ran."

"Bloody Inkna," Ruisa murmured, looking over the barrel at the back door of the inn. A small engraved wooden sign read, *Honey Beaver*. "Oh ew, this isn't an inn. It's a brothel."

Maggie pushed up to glance at the sign before leaning toward her and the map. "We'll probably run into the boys if we stay here…"

Ruisa snorted despite the situation. "Probably not Xavier. He has no trouble getting girls. Leilius, though…" She paused to take a deep breath "Okay, I think we should stick to the sidelines. We don't want anyone recognizing us."

"Or raping us."

"Trying to, anyway. I don't know where we could hide dead bodies." Ruisa slid her finger over the paper, tracing out a few options. When she found one that might work, she folded the map in half to just show the section she needed to work with, then put it away. Next she took out a mixing vial and a couple of other bottles. "What do you think we should do? Poison the food, or…?"

Maggie looked inside the pouch and checked Ruisa's stores. She tapped on a clear bottle with a green top. "Just put them to sleep. We need to get hold of some alcohol."

"The guards will probably have alcohol."

"I doubt the Graygual would let that sort of behavior fly. Not in this kind of place. There is a lot of money tied up here."

Ruisa rolled her eyes. "You think the Captain lets that sort of behavior fly? But what will you find in most crow's nests, hmm? A drop of whisky, that's what."

Maggie tilted her head in acknowledgement. "So

now we just need better clothes."

"Or nudity…" Ruisa opened her neckline down to her cleavage and then let the garment hang off her shoulder.

"You're a virgin, I take it," Maggie said dryly. "Men aren't going to want to drink alcohol if you're offering sex right from the get-go."

"Well…that's our whole plan, I thought…"

"We need to party first." Maggie drummed on the barrel. Then she leaned forward and bumped her forehead against it. "Looks like a brothel might be right up our alley."

Ruisa's stomach flip-flopped. She sighed. "Men never have to resort to this kind of thing."

"Or we could see if we can snatch something from a clothesline. Or steal from a shop. That was my original plan."

"I wish that had been an inn." Ruisa put away her map. "C'mon, let's go see if we can trade for something."

"Why not just buy it?"

"I don't know that flashing money around while wearing rags is really the best approach in our situation." Ruisa stood and moved out from behind the barrel.

"Now I know what Alena was talking about," Maggie whispered.

"What's that?"

"She's the oldest of the Honor Guard, but feels like the youngest half the time. You guys are savvier than the normal army men. They just follow orders and try to stick pointy things in people. You guys…have more skills."

"And we're in danger constantly. That's S'am for you."

Maggie was silent for a moment as they walked around the building. Then she said, "I wonder if they'll take a transfer…"

A cart trundled by, hauled by two horses with clearly defined ribs. Passersby hurried along, rarely looking anywhere but directly in front of them. A woman on the opposite side of the street had her child's hand firmly in her own, hitching up her skirt for speed. Based on her appearance, she was somewhere within the middle class, with enough money to eat and dress herself, but without extravagance. Still she hustled along, clearly not wanting to be out on the street.

"It's late afternoon," Ruisa muttered, aware of the bright splotches of sunlight in between the elongated shadows. "I'd understand why people would want to get home after dark in a busy city, but while it's still bright? Doesn't make sense."

Maggie shook her head slowly, a troubled expression on her face. "We had a curfew when the Hunter ruled our city. Maybe that."

"Did that stop you from looking at each other, though?"

"Mostly, yes. But that was because we didn't want to give anything away. These people might be strangers. It's a huge place."

Butterflies fluttered through Ruisa's stomach. "Maybe. I guess we'll find out soon enough." Careful to hunch like Leilius would, Ruisa skulked down the sidewalk toward the entrance of the brothel.

"I don't know that women walk like that," Maggie whispered.

"I'm acting poor."

"You look like you're saddlesore. Girls like you wouldn't have a horse, which means you've been riding something else all night…"

"For an unmarried woman, you sure have a lot of knowledge about this stuff." Ruisa looked back with a quirked eyebrow.

Maggie shrugged. "A girl has needs."

Heat rushed to Ruisa's cheeks as a grin pulled her lips. She shrugged and looked up at the sign. Then the busy street in what looked like a well-kept part of the city. She frowned. "Maybe this *is* an inn."

"They need a name change if it is." Maggie ran her finger in a decorative groove in the door. "Sure is nice for a brothel, though. Not that I have a lot of experience…"

In a sudden panic, Ruisa patted herself and looked around her feet. "Crap, what did we do with our sacks?"

Guilt passed over Maggie's expression. She looked back the way they had come. "I have no idea. I forgot about it. Should I go check by the barrels?"

"We are terrible at this." Ruisa blew her bangs up in irritation, trying to remember if they'd even had the sacks when they were at the barrels. A man passed, keeping his eyes on the ground. "If this turns out to be an inn, we'll go back. If it's a brothel, I doubt they'd want it anyway. C'mon, I think we need to hurry."

Ruisa pushed open the door and was greeted with a lovely floral scent. A wide staircase curled around from the entrance with a finely turned wood banister. Just off the entryway stood what looked like a parlor, decked out in velvet chairs mostly occupied by lounging ladies wearing skimpy clothing or extravagant nightgowns revealing everything from nipples to their lady wares. One woman sat completely naked, scratching a small board across her manicured nails.

"Brothel," Ruisa said.

Stiffer than a man with a hard-on, Ruisa continued forward to a tall, round table bearing a pink feather in a glass vase. A moment later a stocky woman with a pronounced bust sauntered through the doorway on the right. Her gaze swept Ruisa and then Maggie before shooting to the entryway beyond them. She stopped at the table and leaned a pudgy elbow against the surface.

The woman said something that Ruisa couldn't comprehend. She shook her head. "*Do you speak the trades?*"

"*We all full up. We don't need no more girls,*" the woman said with a bored expression.

Ruisa's face started to burn. "*We were just wondering if you would maybe trade for our clothes?*" She plucked at her rags.

The woman's brow creased.

"*I paid,*" Maggie said in the most hacked-up rendition of the language possible. It was all too clear that she'd just started to learn it.

"*She said we can pay.*" Ruisa prevented herself from tapping her sack of coins. That jingle would send the wrong message.

The woman's gaze slid over Ruisa's body, pausing on her arms and resting on her hands. "*Where you from?*"

Ruisa fisted her hands. The woman's gaze flashed to her eyes, and then to Maggie, giving her the same scrutiny.

"*We don't want a job,*" Ruisa rushed to say, feeling the urge to cover up her body. "*Just clothes.*"

"*You once a pretty girl. What happened to you face, eh?*" The woman leaned toward Maggie.

Behind them the door opened with a gust of foul-smelling air. Ruisa hadn't noticed that the city smelled so bad until she'd stepped inside this parlor. A man stalked in with a stained shirt and dirty boots. His grizzled face held a sneer and his lustful stare was directed toward the parlor.

"*You wait here, eh?*" The woman walked around the table with a sway to her hips that denoted her trade. She spoke and caught the man's attention.

"I wonder if she sizes everyone up like that," Ruisa said, not sure if the stare had made her uncomfortable, or just added to how the establishment was making her feel.

The man stared into the parlor where giggling and sultry voices drifted out. He then glanced toward Maggie and Ruisa, surveying them.

"This was a bad idea," Ruisa muttered.

He jerked his chin in their direction, followed by a point at Ruisa. Lust sparked in his eyes as he asked something that sounded like a question.

The woman glanced back, shook her head, and then placed a hand on his arm, trying to steer him toward the workingwomen. He shrugged her off, stalking toward Ruisa with fire burning in his gaze.

Cold tingles spread down her skin as that slimy gaze oozed over her body. Her hand jerked toward the sheathed knife hidden in her bosom. She half hoped the boys would burst in, because this felt more like an attack than anything she'd experienced before.

He stopped too close to her, his size dominating her small frame. His eyes dipped to her bust. He licked his lips and said something that seemed to be directed to the hostess.

"*He thinks you new, eh?*" the woman said, moving to his side. "*You virgin?*"

"*I'm not here for that,*" Ruisa said through a tight throat. "*I just want something else to wear. I can pay. I don't need money.*"

"*He make big offer,*" the woman persisted with a fist on her hip. Her eyes flashed, but not out of greed. "*You pretty girl and pure. He want you bad.*"

"What are they saying?" Maggie asked.

"He wants to buy me." A weight had settled on Ruisa's chest as the man continued to survey her body. He spoke again.

"*He just raised offer. He probably be gentle. He might make offer to save you for just him. That big money, girl. That big dream.*" The woman shifted again. The glimmer in her eyes said she was having fun.

Ruisa's body tightened up as a strange kind of fear worked through her. "*Please tell him to go away.*"

"You need to stay strong, Ruisa," Maggie muttered. "Harden up. You look vulnerable. This kind of guy is going to thrive on that."

As if he heard Maggie's comment, the man grabbed Ruisa's arm and yanked her toward him. His breath, a mixture of stale alcohol and vomit, coated her face. She gagged and panicked, struggling against that strong grip and the hardness pressing through his pants and into her stomach.

The woman made a comment to the man. He smirked, and then jerked Ruisa's arm as he turned. His grip tightened as he pulled her toward the staircase.

"*I said no!*" Ruisa yelled out, tears coming to her eyes.

"Do you want me to kill him or are you going to do it?" Maggie asked, following. "Say the word, Ruisa."

"*No one miss that man,*" the woman said, stepping to the side to watch the progression. "*No one be looking for him.*"

The man shoved Ruisa toward the stairs as the woman's words soaked into her. Gritting her teeth, fighting a fear like she'd never known, she ripped out her knife and spun, sinking it into the side of his fat neck.

The woman rushed forward, yelling. She reached the door and threw the bolt, locking it. Women of all nudity levels rushed out of the parlor.

"*Leave in the knife!*" the woman called as she dragged a piece of black material from the parlor.

Ruisa paused in shock of what she had done without

meaning to, before jerking her hand. The knife came out just a little, but slid back in, following the woman's commands.

Maggie stood in the center of the hallway with a knife in each hand, her eyes on fire. She was ready to kill anyone who came at her.

The man gurgled as his knees gave away.

"*Grab him!*" the woman called.

Two women rushed up, one to each side, and directed his convulsing body toward the black fabric now spread out in the entryway. He hit the ground face first as the gurgles died away. Red seeped from the wound and pooled, a glimmering, deep red.

"*Sloppy. Now we have to strain our backs.*" The woman rolled her eyes and waved her finger at a few of the girls. "*You know what to do.*"

A woman with exposed breasts sighed expressively, showing with her whole body how annoyed she was, before slipping out of her silk garment. The others stripped too, revealing well-maintained hair around their lady bits. Working together, they heaved the man up while two other girls pulled on the black fabric, moving it until just his boots were off the fabric.

The handle on the door jiggled.

"*Hurry up, girls!*" the woman said.

Maggie jumped out of the way as a barrel rolled out of a back room. A girl wearing a sheer red negligee followed behind, directing it to the entryway. Once there, she popped off the top and turned it, maneuvering the opening toward the man. "*He's not going to fit.*"

The woman put her hands on her hips as the door jiggled again. Someone knocked.

"*Quick, get him in the back. We might need to cut something off.*" The woman got down on her knees and cut the fabric. She flipped the roll, tightening the loose fabric, then pushed it to the side. Two of the women grabbed it and dragged it back into the parlor. Two more women grabbed the man, each taking a hand, and tugged toward Maggie. She jumped out of the way in bewilderment. A thick line of blood followed the progress of the body as it disappeared from sight.

A harder knock sounded at the door.

"*Let's go, ladies!*" the woman clapped as a woman with a mop splashed water down. Two other women spread what looked like oil on their bare skin. As the mopper was moving out of the way, the two women stepped into the entryway and embraced.

"What the hell is happening?" Maggie asked with a slack jaw.

The mopper ducked out of sight, leaving behind her a floor slick with red-tinted water. As other women knelt with towels and rags, the lips of the two women in the middle met. One of their tongues came out, then the next, and they engaged in the raunchiest form of kissing

Ruisa had ever seen.

The head woman opened the door, out of breath. Two men waited there, their faces painted with impatience. The woman said something in an apologetic tone, and then swept her hand toward the kissing women. As if on cue, one of them slid the palm of her hand over the breast of the other, and then on down, over her stomach and dipping in.

Ruisa's face started burning again. In a trance, she watched fingers dip in, and then start to pump in and out. The other woman gyrated her hips and moaned as their kissing became more impassioned.

The men's faces went slack before they walked into the room on uncertain legs. They didn't notice the blood-tinged puddles on the floor, nor the smear of red on the head woman's face, nor even that a few of the girls were wiping themselves down and getting dressed. They only had eyes for the show of female flesh going on in front of them.

The head woman spoke again. The kissers stopped what they were doing and grabbed hands. Ruisa ducked out of the way, allowing the women to lead the men up the stairs.

"I am way too naive for any of this," Ruisa admitted, feeling heat where she probably shouldn't.

"Me too, and I'm not naive." Maggie wiped her forehead.

"Come with me, you two." The head woman stepped around the standing water and through the rear door.

The dead man lay next to a tub, bleeding onto the thick fabric. Around him, stacked neatly against the back wall, were other barrels. A worktable crouched in front of those, with paper spread over it in messy stacks.

The woman led them around the body to a table and chairs. She barked orders to a scantily clad woman, then reached down and snatched the knife from the man's neck. Without so much as a grimace, she settled her girth into one of the chairs and tossed the dripping knife onto the table. *"Who are you, eh? And no lie to me. I cannot help you if I get lies."*

Ruisa looked at Maggie. "She wants to know who we are. She said she can't help if we lie."

For the first time Ruisa could remember in her entire life of knowing Maggie, the woman looked utterly and completely lost. She shook her head and shrugged at the same time.

The memory of prostitutes helping them in the Shadow Lands flicked through Ruisa's head. Then of those in the old Mugdock city. This woman's words, and her lack of concern regarding the dead man, struck a chord.

She leaned back in her chair. This could be a really, *really* bad idea. *"We travel with the Chosen."*

The woman surveyed Ruisa for a long moment before nodding once. "*I heard of Chosen. Some man, yeah? What you do for this Chosen?*"

"No, he's… It's two people. The Chosen. It started as one woman, but in the Shadow Lands—"

The woman sat forward suddenly. Elbow braced on the table, she put her hand out to stall the conversation. Gaze pinned to Ruisa, she said, very slowly, "*Tell me about this woman.*"

Something flashed in the woman's eyes. It wasn't just hope. This was familiarity. Almost. A knowing gleam. With S'am, that could be a very bad thing.

"*Why?*" Ruisa asked. Her eyes briefly dipped to the knife. "*What do you know about that woman?*"

"What's happening?" Maggie whispered as her hand dropped to her knife.

"*Look.*" The woman put her hands up and tilted her head. "*You kill man, yes?*" She stuck a hand out to the dead man. "*In this town, you get hanged for that. Maybe worse. Maybe they let officers relieve themselves with you first, eh? Maybe you get picked for top officers. They like young, pretty girls. Could be worse. But…*" She jerked her hands up and tilted her head again. "*I try tell on you, you kill me. I know you have more knife, eh?*" She made a circle in the air as she pointed at Ruisa. "*And I know this one is dangerous.*" She swung the hand toward Maggie. "*You girls know what you about. So what is point of these secrets, eh? Are you with violet-eyed woman, or no?"* She slammed hands down on the table and leaned forward. *"I am waiting for her all this time. Oshawn arranged meeting, then sent me here. I open shop, make living, and clean house where I can."* She gestured toward the barrels. *"I have network, even in city. In all cities. Beer come in, dead man go out, friend dispose, no one sees."* She shrugged. *"All while I wait. I be ready. But time slipping away."*

"What's happening?" Maggie whispered again, more urgently.

Ruisa shook her head, trying to make sense of all she'd heard. The woman spoke so fast and with a strange accent, so some of the words became garbled and lost. Ruisa had to piece the sentences together.

"She cannot come into the city yet because Inkna would feel her mind power. She has others. People from the Shadow Lands, and from her homeland. We were sent before her as we can get around the city without being discovered, and because we don't have any mind power." Ruisa touched her head. *"Soon we need to get her inside, though."*

The woman's eyes lost their twinkle. A small crease formed in her brow. *"This city is protected."* She blew out a breath. *"I thought Oshawn wrong to send me here. I should have known Wanderer make big statement. Maybe too big."*

"The Captain chose this place. He's her…fiancé."

The woman shook her head. "*Inkna do mental...*" She mimed holding a broom handle and sweeping. "*They check. Dangerous to bring her inside.*" She tapped her chin and glanced over at the table strewn with papers. "*What was plan?*"

"Did she say plan? Does she want to know what we're doing?" Maggie asked with alarm in her voice.

Ruisa flashed Maggie a scowl to keep her quiet. "*How do you know S'am? The Wanderer, I mean?*" Ruisa asked.

The woman pushed out a laugh. "*She ask me for clothes, just like you. You no look like her, but you muscled. You can fight—I see that. I know right away when you say that Oshawn sent you.*"

"Oh yeah? Is that why you tried to sell me to that filthy guy?"

She laughed harder. "*I no try to sell you. I tell him that he might have to trade life to get you upstairs. He no believe me. Now he dead.*"

"Time's wasting," Maggie said.

"*Look, I want to believe you. We need all the help we can get, but I can't tell you our plans. If you aren't who you say you are, everything will be foiled.*" Ruisa shook her head. "*Can we buy some revealing clothes off of you? Like...real clothes, just nicer than what we're wearing. Not as revealing as the girls in your parlor.*"

The humor dropped away from the woman. "*I am

Tauneya. I was in Hunter's camp. I give her clothes to get the Seer and the Ghost out. I am one who gave her map to escape. I have *spread word of her coming. My girls ready. All across land, they ready. The Wanderer Network be waiting. We all wait. For her. Now, tell me the plan, and I will help. Without me, you all die.*"

CHAPTER 19

"THROUGH HERE." LEILIUS motioned Xavier into an alleyway. Shadows clawed at the ground, eradicating any remaining sunshine. "We need to check out the front gate before the sun goes down."

"We still have a couple hours," Xavier whispered as he snuck in behind. They'd been all around the city, discovering that the map wasn't the most accurate thing they'd ever used. Alleyways often proved to be a dead end, making them turn back to try another way. They tried to keep to smaller streets, but occasionally someone pointed at Leilius, their expression turning to one of shock or delight. If people could point him out on the street, that meant that the city was talking about what he'd done. But *that* meant the Graygual would have their eyes open. He did not want to fall into their hands under any circumstances.

"Are you sure it goes all the way through?" Xavier asked as they neared the middle. A large canister was piled high with refuse and overflowing, its stink permeating the alley, and almost blocked their way. Leilius held his breath as he squeezed by it. He stepped over the body of a dead rat and made sure to stay away from the grimy wall at his back.

"No, but what choice do we have? If you'd start walking like a spy instead of a pretty boy, we might not be in this mess."

"We should change clothes."

Leilius rolled his eyes. "Waltzing in and buying new clothes wouldn't look suspicious at all, no. We dress in rags like the poor for fun. It's a style choice."

The shadows pooled on the ground up ahead. Beyond them stretched black. A wall.

Leilius let out his breath and stopped. "This is impossible. And I haven't seen one clothesline. We might have to wait for dark."

"There's a door, though." Xavier walked forward on light feet. "Might be the back of a shop. Think it's a clothes shop?"

"No. Our luck, it'd probably be a Graygual house or something. C'mon, let's go back."

They turned back only to stop suddenly. Leilius melded into the side of the alleyway immediately. Xavier was next to him a moment later, his heavy breath on the back of Leilius' head.

"Step away, idiot," Leilius hissed.

A group of five women had stopped just inside the alleyway. That wouldn't normally be cause for alarm, but these women seemed different. Shiny, skintight leather from head to toe, the curves of their bodies effectively on display. In many cases the neckline dipped way low, showing ample cleavage. One plummeted all the way to her belt, showing a strip of feminine body Leilius rarely saw.

"What are they holding?" Xavier whispered, his voice quivering in fear.

Leilius closed his eyes tight. He'd heard of these women. Occasionally men had been taken from trading routes. Young men, usually. Sometimes they turned up a while later with horrible stories and wounds to show for it. Sometimes they were gone forever. "Whips."

"No, I mean the one with metal. Is that a chain?"

"These are Mardis, Xavier." Leilius took out a knife.

"Naw. Are you sure?"

"How many women wear leather and carry whips? I haven't heard of very many."

"You also haven't been traveling all that long. This is a city. They wouldn't allow this type of thing here."

"Then why aren't you stepping out and saying hi?" Leilius asked sarcastically before realizing that the women had remained where they were, and were now staring at them. One of them called out.

"What language is that?" Xavier asked. "Shit. They're coming."

Leilius stepped into the middle of the alleyway with

his knife firmly in hand. The element of surprise was gone, so now he'd have to fight. There were more of them, but he hoped they weren't like Shanti. If that was the case, he should be able to barrel through.

"*We don't want to hurt anyone,*" Leilius called out, hoping they spoke the traders' language. "*We lost our way.*"

"*You found your way, you mean,*" one of the women said delightedly. "*You are at our back door. Some of us like when men come in our back door.*"

Xavier quickly stepped away from the wall.

"*Oooh. Look at you,*" one of them purred.

"*I claim that one,*" another said.

"*Ladies, we can all share. They are young. Lots of stamina.*" The chains rustled.

Leilius pulled on his collar, trying to get a little air to his suddenly hot neck. "I'm in over my head here…"

As the women drew closer, Leilius had a harder time feeling his fingers around his knife thanks to the pounding going on in other places. His eyes meant to look into other eyes, but he couldn't peel them away from half-exposed breasts. And the little crease between her thighs.

A *crack* made him jump, then he felt a horrible pain in his hand. He glanced down dumbly at his thumb, then the knife now lying at his feet.

"We should run," Xavier said in a wistful voice.

"Yeah," Leilius agreed. He really meant it to sound more convincing.

"Tell me true, were you looking for us?" One of them stopped in front of Leilius. Her red lips were curved in a smile. A pink tongue spread moisture across her bottom lip. Leilius stared, transfixed, as a cloth appeared from nowhere and covered his mouth and nose. He knew one moment of warning before he drifted into blackness.

***

ALENA FROZE MID-STEP. Her foot hovered above the footpath. Raucous laughter drifted out from around the corner. Her foot didn't make a sound when it landed, but the slide of her shoes against stone as she pivoted did.

She took a deep breath. The map crinkled as her grip tightened. Running would draw attention, but having a Graygual take notice of her while she was standing flatfooted would be much worse.

Chatter rode the dying laughter. A shout pierced the air. It sounded like drinking, carousing men.

Alena glanced around the clean streets and well-kept buildings. She'd found the nicer part of the city and discovered it was largely occupied by Graygual and rich people. Oftentimes those rich people were also Graygual. They rarely had the snowy or wheat-blond hair of Shanti's people, but it was clear they hailed from a colder climate where their skin wasn't used to the blazing heat of the middle-land or south. In contrast, Alena should've fitted in just fine. She had darker hair and nearly matched the sun-kissed skin tone. But in this part of the city, she stood out like an intruder. Locals weren't admitted, it seemed. They were a conquered people, best left to the slums and less reputable parts of the city.

Another shout echoed down the street, but the men weren't getting any closer. They had to be in an inn or some other gathering place.

Letting out the breath she hadn't realized she was holding, Alena brought the hastily duplicated map up again in a shaking hand. She *should* need to go right for a ways, take a left, and then another right. That should get her into the rear gate area, where she hoped to meet up with the other women.

She let her hand fall and surveyed the street in front of her. With the sun nearly set, and time slipping away with each passing second, she was way behind. She should jog the route and get the job done.

She walked slowly to the intersection and peered around the corner. The street was deserted.

Confused, she glanced the other way and found the same thing. It was way too early for a curfew. Wasn't it?

She bit her lip. Going down this street would paint a big target on her back. A poor local dressed in rags in the rich area? Yeah, right. String her up by her neck right now. They'd think she was here stealing.

She turned back the way she'd come. She'd have to find another route to take. The map she'd been given wasn't up to date, that was clear, and it was causing her to lose precious time.

She jogged back the way she'd come, hanging a left down an alley. A small amount of litter, most likely blown in from the wind unnoticed, lined the small gutters built into the road for rainwater. Crates lay off to her right. One had fallen off the stack and busted. Beyond that lay a closed door without a sign.

Alena slowed to a stop, feeling her heart sink at the blackness in front of her. Another wall. It wasn't even a building, just a big brick wall erected to sever the passageway. It had to be on purpose. The Graygual had been thoughtful with this city's protection. It didn't bode well for their cause.

Alena had about-faced and started walking out when a hollow thud announced a door being unlocked. She scurried to the side of the stack of crates, and the door swung open a moment later.

Fast and harsh-sounding syllables interrupted the hush of the alleyway. Heavy footsteps scraped against the ground. Between the cracks of the crates came a robust man in a white smock. A cook.

A boot scuffed before a crate squealed against the

ground. A gruff voice rang out. The boots, dull and black, came around to the front of the pile.

Alena yanked out her knife. If she killed someone, they'd never know it was her. In a city this big, it could be any street urchin. She'd just have to get out of there before anyone found her.

A hand reached across her line of sight. The fingers prodded a broken piece of wood in the fallen crate. The crate lifted away behind the others.

Heart thumping madly, Alena held her breath, waiting for him to walk away. A shock of adrenaline coursed through her as the man stepped out in front of her.

Shock smacked his face. Her hand jerked of its own accord, the point of her knife rising dangerously close to his chest. She couldn't commit, though, and she didn't know why.

His gaze dipped to the knife. A brief flash of fear crossed his features until his eyes darted to her clothes, her shaking arm, and finally her eyes. Something sparked in his gaze, but she couldn't say what. Finally, he raised his hands slowly. Words rode a soft and calm tone.

She shook her head, her brow furrowing. He said something else that almost sounded familiar. It was probably the speech the traders used. Everyone seemed to know it. Except her, obviously.

She gripped the hilt of the knife tighter and shook

her head. Trying to convey her desire, she took a step away. "I don't speak…" She shrugged.

"Wait!" he pleaded in a rough, barely intelligible accent, holding his hands higher but taking a step after her. "I help. Me help. You." He put fingers to his mouth, miming eating with his hands. "Hunger? Eat?"

Alena's stomach rumbled, selling her appearance. She put her hand to her stomach. "I'm okay. No thank you." She took another step away. "Don't follow me."

"Wait! I cook. Graygual." His hands made a shape of a ball in the air. "Many. Many food." He reached toward her, miming handing her a morsel. "Bit food. Eat." He showed her two palms and feathered them in her direction, telling her to wait. Then he held up one finger. *One moment.*

He half turned and gave her that one finger again, insisting that she stay put. He hurried back into the kitchen. Alena turned to run, but for a reason she couldn't explain, she thought of Kallon in that clearing. He'd taken the time to help her. He counted on her. They all did.

She hadn't graduated into the Honor Guard because she could fight with a sword a little, nor because she was great with a bow. If that were the case, she'd still be with the archers. She was in the Honor Guard because she had other traits to offer. Shanti had seen something in her that was not like the others, and, in realizing it, had given her large shoes to fill, like the others.

She stilled her mind and took one more breath. She let in the night, her surroundings, the sun retreating from the ground. The clank of dishes and sizzle of food on fire seduced her ears.

Alena drifted closer to the door, knife held tightly. Fighting her fear of discovery, she slunk toward the edge of the door and peered in. Steam rose from pots. Dirty pans and bowls were heaped near a washbasin. Cups and goblets of all shapes and sizes littered a table, also ready to be washed. More than a dozen people stood with sweat on their foreheads and stains on their clothes, making food that would be served to the enemy.

Alena fell back against the wall and looked at the sky. It was so clear. God had sent the Hunter to prepare them for this. All of them, including those who had only wanted to find a good husband and have a nice home, like her. Until the Hunter had barged into her life and made her understand the value of freedom, she hadn't seen the point in learning about the craft of mixing poisons. Such an antiquated practice, she'd thought. And here she stood, at the edge of a kitchen that fed the enemy, holding the knowledge of how to poison the whole lot of them without them being any the wiser until it was too late.

This was her destiny. Shanti's faith in her, and Kallon's, meant she had to step up, fight her fear, and fulfill her duty.

Alena blew out a breath. That inner pep talk didn't do much to rid her of the jitters.

The man hurried out of the kitchen and started when he found her so close to the door. He offered her a chunk of bread and a small portion of meat that had been cut into. It was probably a leftover portion of someone's plate. Alena grimaced and waved her hands to ward him away.

Not understanding, he pushed it toward her. "It okay. No…one know." He held it steady.

Alena looked past him at the kitchen, and took a chance. "Do you know the Chosen?"

The man's brow creased. He shook his head in confusion and pushed the food at her again.

"Wanderer?" she tried.

A flash of understanding crossed his face before warning lit in his eyes. Anger lowered his brow then. This time when he pushed the food at her, it was hostile. "Take. Go."

A surge of stubbornness accosted her. She was trying to fulfill her destiny, dang it. He was supposed to be the easy part.

She reached into her pants and drew out her small pouch. It jingled as she opened it and extracted one gold coin. She held it out. "The Wanderer is here. I need your help. I will pay for your silence."

She really hoped money would buy cooperation. With those farmers, it seemed to have gone a long way.

The man's eyes dipped to her hand. He stared for a moment before he shook his head in small jerks, frustration crossing his expression. "No, no. Go." He looked at the food in his hands, then the gold, and finally the pouch, unsure of what to do. Obviously she could buy ten meals with just one gold coin, let alone what might be in the pouch. "No."

"Please. Help. Here—"

A woman's voice screeched out of the door, making the man glance backward. He shook his head again, indecision staying his feet. She could see the desire on his face, both for the gold and something else. She had to believe he didn't like being ruled by the Graygual. He was just as trapped as she had been.

That gave her an idea. "The Wanderer, the Chosen, freed me. Saved me. I joined with her, with them, to help others. Let me help you."

The voice screeched again. The man turned back to it, but didn't commit. Not totally. He looked at Alena, his face troubled, before completing the turn and going back into the kitchen. He closed the door behind him.

"Dang it," she swore. She dropped her hands and stood there for a second. There was nothing for it—she'd have to hold them prisoner. Or wait until everyone had gone home for the night and sneak in…

Patting her pouch, which held more than just coins, she mulled over how to get back into that kitchen. They had a bar that they probably secured the door with after they went home. That would prove troublesome. Maybe the front of the building had glass, though. Maybe she could get in and find something to poison.

As she reached the crates, pondering where she would go to wait, the door slid open again. She turned back in both hope and fear, ready to run. The man stopped in the middle of the alley with the same troubled face. Beside him stood a middle-aged man who seemed vaguely familiar.

"Hello?" the man said hesitantly, his accent thick.

"Hi!" Alena stepped forward, feeling the smile pull up from her toes. "You understand me?"

A grin tweaked his lips. "Westwood Lands? Yes. I traded often in my youth. With a surly Commander who'd just been promoted…"

"Commander Sanders, must be."

"Did you have something you needed to translate?" he asked, his brow furrowing.

"Uh…yeah. Tell him that I'm with the Wanderer." She waited while the man repeated it. "And that the Wanderer is here with an army." She gave the basic gist, and then what she planned.

The man stared at her for a long beat. The cook

prodded him eagerly. Finally, still watching Alena, the man spoke to the cook.

"You can really do as you say?" the man said softly after he was done.

"Yes! Please. Let me help you. Or you help me. It really amounts to the same thing. Help me free this city."

The man shook his head as the cook bit his lip. Time flowed by, tensing Alena's shoulders.

"It's dangerous," the man said in a hush. "We could all be killed—"

The cook interrupted him in crisp tones. The man sagged. "He said he'll do it."

CHAPTER 20

Leilius' eyes came open slowly. His head swam, and he felt drowsy and stupid. Something pulled at his wrists. He soon realized it was rope tying him to a post. No, not a post, part of a bed. Wiggling, he felt the soft bed beneath him, large enough for two sleepers. He was sprawled out in the middle, his ankles tied as tightly as his wrists.

Warning bled into him as one more realization dawned. Rising up, he stared down at his naked body. His manhood lay to the side, out for the world to see.

He yanked at his hands as the scene in the alleyway came flooding back. Women. Leather. Skin. Whips. Oh fuck.

He yanked harder, pulling up his knees. The rope dug into his skin.

A door opened at the end of the room. With it came a soft breeze that brought gooseflesh to his skin. A woman walked in covered in leather except for her arms, her breasts, and a hole at the top of her thighs. Leilius shivered for a couple reasons, and one of those was fear. An excited kind of fear, but fear nonetheless.

"*Well, well, you're awake.*" The woman sauntered closer. Leilius tore his eyes away from her breasts, perky with pink buds of nipples, to what was in her hand. Unfortunately, the hand was by that other hole, and he'd never seen one of those before.

His chest grew tight and his mind swam with confusion. He was a prisoner, he was afraid, and yet there were things in this room he didn't mind seeing at all.

His body was not confused—it was reacting.

"*You like what you see, yes?*" That inviting patch of skin was so close, standing right beside the bed. It glistened. Was it supposed to glisten? "*My, my. Ready and eager. No wonder you came looking for us.*"

He shook his head and tried to speak through a suddenly dry mouth. "*Not looking. I swear. I wasn't—*"

A slap rang through the room. It took Leilius a moment to realize that it had to do with him, and another to feel the pain blossoming up from his stomach. "What—"

"*Oooh, I like your native tongue. Speak more of that.*"

Another slap. Pain blistered up through his ribs. Her breasts jiggled.

"*Speak!*" She whacked him again.

"You need to let me go. I have stuff to do. I don't know that I want to go, but I really should. I think this is one of those gray areas between duty and pleasure. And pain. I'm not really sure—Ow!"

With a laugh, she bent down and took one of his nipples into her mouth. His eyes rolled back in his head. *Ooooh my God, why do people not like this?*

As if hearing his thoughts, she said, "*You like this, don't you?*"

Or maybe she was just reading his body.

"I should go." He shook his head. "*I should go. I wasn't trying to find you, honest. And you are a lovely woman. Really, very beautiful. But—Ow!*"

The pain blossomed into other feelings that were starting to pound in extremely exposed parts of his body. "*Maybe just a few minutes. I can stay for just a little while.*"

She grabbed something off a nightstand and then clamped it onto his nipple. Leilius jolted in pain, and then couldn't help an embarrassing moan. Another metal thing clamped on his other nipple, and he repeated the display again.

One of her knees indented the bed beside his hip. Her other knee swung over him and landed on the other side. That distinctly feminine area hovered above his distinctly masculine area. All he could feel was the pounding and the rushing in his ears.

"*You're a bad boy, aren't you?*" Her finger disappeared between her candy-red lips.

"Not…really." His voice was way too high.

As that wet finger left her parted mouth, his heart clattered painfully against his ribcage.

"Yes, you are. You need to be punished." The finger circled a little nub near her lady parts. She moaned and dropped her head back as her hips moved in a circle.

"Okay. Yes, okay." He needed to remember that spot on a woman's body, because she really liked it. That would probably serve him well in the future. If he could just get rid of the buzzing in his head, and think straight, remembering any of this would be so much easier.

She reached further down and dipped a digit into herself. Leilius' throat issued a strange, strangled sound he had no control over. The sound got even weirder when that finger started to rub around his tip.

"Oh, this is good. I am so glad we were near that door." Her body lowered until his tip touched her warm wetness. "Oh God, this is happening. This is really happening. Oh thank God—"

The door burst open with a squeal of wood and hinges. The woman swung a leg away from him, turning in alarm at the sound.

"No!" Leilius shouted.

Xavier stood in the doorway, butt naked, with welts down his chest and blood dripping from a few tiny cuts. Eyes on fire, he held a knife in his hand and war in his bearing.

"Go away!" Leilius shouted, trying to motion with his tied hand. "I'm just fine. Come back in an hour."

Xavier threw the knife as rage lit his expression. The woman shrieked, trying to lift a leather paddle to block the throw. She was too late. The blade stuck in her shoulder. She fell back with a cry and clutched at the wound.

Leilius jerked upward, straining against the binding. "No, Xavier! She wasn't hurting me!"

Xavier glanced at him as he crossed the room to her. "You have welts all over and shit on your nipples. This bitch"—disgust mixed with the rage—"is messed up." He yanked the knife out of her shoulder and grabbed her hair with his other hand. He moved to swipe the blade across her neck.

"No!" Leilius screamed, thrashing against the bonds. A loud crack had the bed breaking. He pushed at Xavier's shoulder with his newly freed hand. "Xavier, no. Please. Just give us…"

Xavier paused, a look of incredulity on his face.

"Okay, sure, this isn't the time…" Leilius quickly let himself out of his bounds. "I'll go. Just leave her alone."

Xavier noticed the soldier at attention, the only thing in the room sticking up. "You took the serum?"

"What serum? Listen—" Leilius spread out his hands, trying to indicate everyone should just take it easy. "I'll get dressed, and we'll head out. No biggie. I would've liked to…but I understand the press for time. It's okay."

Xavier was looking at Leilius like he was a strange and new kind of bug. He blinked twice and glanced again at Leilius' wood, which was a little embarrassing, before leaning right down into the woman's face. He put the tip of the knife next to her eye. "*If I ever hear of you doing something like this again, or any of your* sisters, *as you call them, I will cut out your eye before I stick this knife in your heart. You got me?*"

The woman gave a soggy nod, those plump red lips trembling. Leilius' heart squished from seeing her in pain. He wanted to say something, but wasn't sure what. In the end he just opted for: "Sorry about him. He's prone to violence." It didn't really seem like the right thing, but it was something. It was all he had, anyway. All his blood flow was still directed toward a very hard part of his body.

Leilius jogged out of the room behind Xavier, moving stiffly, the chain connecting the nipple clamps bumping against his chest.

He probably should've taken them off…

The room next to his had the door thrown wide with two dead women lying almost naked on the floor. The headboard of the bed was in tatters, with what looked like chain ripped through the wood. Rope lay at the base where it had been left, the other ends still wrapped around Xavier's ankles.

"You got two?" Leilius asked in wonder. "And you wanted to get away?"

"What the hell is wrong with you?" Xavier demanded. He turned a corner and paused, waiting for an attack. The outer room was empty. "They probably went looking for more. Vile." Xavier ran to a pile of garments in the corner. Theirs was on top. Xavier didn't grab those. Instead, he sifted through and grabbed other items.

"What about our coin?" Leilius asked, hunched in the cold, wishing his body would calm down. Standing with another man while having a stiff member was embarrassing.

"Check over there." Xavier pointed behind him to a long table. Strewn along the table were a few papers, a plate with crumbs, and a box. After investigating, Leilius found three of their pouches inside that box. The fourth, one that they'd brought in themselves instead of stealing, was missing.

"They didn't go looking for more men—they went to spend our coin." Leilius palmed the other pouches. "Good thing we robbed some, then."

"Grab something to eat that we can take, and then we have to go. I hope we haven't blown our duty."

"Not like it was really our fault." Leilius snagged

some partially stale bread and a few pieces of jerky. That was all that was available.

"You could've fought a little harder," Xavier said dryly. "And I get it, I was stunned a little too, but..." Leilius handed over a lump of bread as Xavier held out some clothes. "I'm taking the pants that fit. I'll wear the threadbare shirt, and you can have this shirt and wear the patched-up pants. There aren't any other clothes that will fit us."

"I can wear the rags. I don't care."

"What the hell is wrong with you?" Xavier demanded again.

Leilius paused with a lump of bread in his cheek. "What?"

With an angry scowl, Xavier ripped the chain away from Leilius' chest. The nipple clamps tore away, drawing a shock of pain, followed by a rush of agony. "Damn—oh, that hurts. That does not feel good when you do it. Holy—" Leilius cupped his throbbing chest.

Xavier gave him an odd look, but said nothing. They dressed in silence. Leilius got the distinct impression most people didn't like a little pain with their pleasure. This was probably something he should keep quiet about.

He also wondered if Rohnan knew anything about it. That guy knew more about women and sex than anyone in the land. If he could talk to anyone, it would be him.

"C'mon," Xavier said in a rough voice. "Let's go before they come back. I wouldn't want you to be mad at me for killing sexual torturers."

Definitely something to keep quiet…

Xavier pulled open the door and peered outside. Twilight had fallen, tricking the eyes with half-light as shadows started blending into the night. Not a soul walked on the street, not even a Graygual.

"Must be a curfew," Leilius whispered.

Xavier nodded before stooping and jogging out along the wall. Why he stooped was a mystery, since it made him stand out even more for the oddity of it, but Leilius followed silently, trying to get a clear look at the street and all possible hiding places. They quietly ran until they hit an alleyway, and stepped inside out of plain sight. Leilius ripped out his map and checked their location.

A thought occurred to him. He looked up. No one ever remembered to look up. "I have an idea."

A hasty climb and a skinned knee later, they hoisted themselves onto the nearest rooftop. Shallowly pitched or completely flat, these roofs were perfect for getting around. With a last glance over the edge, he started jogging in the direction of the gate.

"I do not care for heights," Xavier said behind him.

Leilius didn't roll his eyes for fear of tripping and

rolling off the edge, but he really wanted to. Instead, he kept moving until they reached a gap between buildings.

"Now what?" Xavier leaned forward, trying to see the street below.

"Well…we could jump…" Leilius gauged the distance to be eight feet. "Although…we might not make it." He started moving along the edge until a small bridge of stone connected the buildings. It was one of the brick walls that had been erected to keep people from moving through the walkway. "How are you at walking in a straight line?"

"Shit. Isn't there another way?"

"Yeah. The street. But that would be way worse than falling on your head in privacy, I bet. The Graygual aren't as forgiving as the street."

"Fine. Go."

Leilius turned and crouched down to his hands and knees. He crawled backward down the slope and then dangled over the edge until his swinging toe touched brick. Lowering himself from the edge, he waited until he had his balance before letting go. The chilled breeze licked his outstretched fingers. The darkness mostly masked the small area to step.

"This should be interesting." Hoping for the best, not daring to look down, Leilius quickly crossed the top of the brick wall. Only once did his foot hit the corner, making him swing his arms dramatically to keep balance. At the far side, he let out a sigh of relief before looking back for Xavier.

The larger man had his arms stretched out to the sides. Every once in a while his head would turn just a bit, indicating he glanced at the ground. His arms would dip to one side, or windmill, as his body swayed.

"Don't look down!" Leilius said in a stage whisper. "It's throwing you off balance."

Xavier stilled, and then edged himself along, too slow for comfort. Leilius opened his mouth to say something, but thought better of it. He was making it. Slowly, but surely, he crossed the narrow bridge, until finally, Xavier braced a hand on Leilius' shoulder and issued the same sigh Leilius had.

"Did it. Okay." Leilius looked up at the ledge. "This is going to be tricky. Give me a boost."

Stepping on Xavier's threaded hands, Leilius hoisted himself up, then scrabbled at the straight edge of the building, not finding much purchase. With his fingers digging into the roof tiles, he finally clawed himself to the top. He then sat and dangled his legs over.

"What are you doing?" Xavier whispered up.

"Use my feet like a rope. I don't know how else to do it."

"I'll jump. Grab my shirt and help me get up."

"That might be a terrible idea," Leilius muttered

before glancing down at the dark ground far below. Stepping aside and mentally preparing for this friend to slide down the side and break something, he readied himself with legs bent and hands out. Xavier's head bobbed up a moment later. His big hands slapped the roof as he tried to find purchase, but almost immediately he started slipping.

"Crap," Leilius grunted, grabbing his shirt and straining everything in his body to keep Xavier from sliding. His feet slipped again and Xavier started to slide again, and this time, Leilius was going with him. "Do something!"

Xavier pushed himself up somehow, his big shoulders bunching under Leilius' arms. A knee came over the edge before the big kid was crawling up onto the roof.

"Wow." Leilius backed up and wiped his forehead with his sleeve. "Good job."

"Let's go." Xavier's chest heaved from exertion.

Off they went again, covering a huge area before they hit another gap larger then they could easily jump or hop over. Panting from fatigue, Leilius put his hands on his hips before he stared down at a unique-looking ladder. At the end the rope was connected to a little anchor-like thing in the roof.

"Looks like we're not the only ones who thought of getting around this way..." Leilius looked around the rooftops, but only saw chimneys and the encroaching night.

"Get down!"

Leilius' shirt tugged him downward until Xavier let go. "What?"

Following Xavier's pointed finger, he looked out over the edge of the building to the street. Walking down the middle were two men dressed in black. They were too far away to see if they were Inkna or Graygual.

"We'll just wait until—" A light prod touched Leilius' mind. It felt like a finger jabbing his brain. He barely had time for a shock of warning before a blast of needles tore through him. Spikes of hot metal pounded into his head while a meat cleaver chopped into his body. The pain made his jaw clench and body convulse. Blackness fizzled his thoughts, taking over him. He could barely breathe. He couldn't feel his limbs.

He was going to die.

A new burning filled his mouth and coated his throat. He coughed and swallowed, barely feeling a hand on his face. Weakly, he batted at a palm covering his nose and mouth until the pain started to recede. His body slowly went numb. He'd let S'am down.

CHAPTER 21

SHANTI SLOWLY DROPPED her hands, ignoring Rohnan's thrust. Their gentle sparring to pass the time suddenly forgotten, she turned toward the distant city as her heart started to hammer. Leilius' mind went blank. Xavier's did the same a moment later.

Breath catching in her throat, she took two fast steps and put more power into her touch. Nothing. There was an emptiness where their minds should have been.

"No," she breathed against the tears coming to her eyes. She felt the others, giving them a soft poke to make sure they were alive. Delight swirled up from Alena, cutting through her intense focus in the middle of the city, and relief came from the others who were making their way to the rear gate. Shanti didn't know what Alena was doing, but she was sure it would help their cause. Alena didn't do anything by halves. The others were right on target.

Trying to breathe through a tight chest, Shanti started pacing. She *searched* the area where they'd last been right before incredible pain took them. "I can't feel Xavier and Leilius," Shanti announced. "They're gone. Their brain paths are black."

Everyone stopped what they were doing and turned to her. Rohnan's comforting hand on her shoulder was welcomed.

"You said they'd had some pain earlier," Kallon said in a businesslike voice, purposefully showing no emotion, as was his job as her First Fighter. "Perhaps this is related and they have simply lost consciousness."

Shanti thought back, shaking her head. "Xavier fought that enemy away, I'd bet my life on it. He got Leilius out of whatever they'd landed in. This was…different. A different kind of pain. This was Inkna."

"The other wasn't?" Sonson asked.

"No. That was physical. No *Gift*." Tingles spread through Shanti's body as adrenaline keyed up. Rage started to simmer, feeding on the fear that she had lost two people so dear to her heart that they were family.

She would not lose any more of her family. "I'm going after them."

"No. Wait!" Rohnan's hand turned into a hindrance. "We must wait. It is not time."

"I don't care what fucking time it is, Rohnan. I will not lose those boys, do you hear me? Not them."

"Just to present all sides of the argument," Sonson

said with his hands out, "if they are already dead, going now might kill the rest of them, you, and this whole plan. If they are dead, there is no help you can give them."

Shanti slapped Rohnan's hand away and squared off with a straight-faced Sonson. "If they are dead, I will bring back their bodies so that we might give them a proper burial like they deserve. Alive or dead, I will not forsake them. I will not leave them in there to rot. I'll go alone if I have to. I am not asking you to follow me."

Sonson turned his palms toward the sky as a grin spread across his face. "Just making sure you thought this through. I'm ready."

"You're not alone, *Chulan*," Kallon said. "I will follow."

"If we wait a few hours, we will have nothing in our way," Rohnan said in his annoyingly calm voice.

"If they aren't dead, a few hours might be too late," Sonson said, checking his weapons. "Besides, that is a huge city. We can drag people into the shadows for hours and kill them before anyone would have a clue. Wake everyone up."

"This land is terrified of the Shadow." Denessa tightened her sword belt. "Let's show them why."

"*Chulan*, you are thinking with your emotions, not your—"

Shanti slapped Rohnan's hand off her shoulder

again and smashed her fist into his jaw. "You try to hold me back one more time, Rohnan, and I will break your jaw the next time, got that? I'm going in. Those boys saved my life, and more importantly, they saved my soul. I am indebted to them more than I can ever repay. I will sacrifice everything for them. Do you understand me?"

"Just like old times," Sayas said with a grin, standing by the road patiently.

Rohnan dropped his hand from his jaw and stared at her defiantly.

"Okay, then." Shanti checked everything over and started jogging toward the city. She didn't care who followed. She didn't care if she was completely alone. She would either save those boys, or tear down that city in vengeance.

To her surprise, everyone filed in without a word. Expectation ran around their group and the occasional vicious grin crossed faces. Every member of this collection of people had lost someone at the Graygual hand. They'd suffered, they'd bled, and now they were finally hitting the Graygual where it would hurt the most. They were all ready. This had been a long time coming.

Another surge of tingles washed over her as they made their way through the sparse trees, using the pooling shadows to mask their movement. Silence reigned around them, their footsteps not making a sound to disturb the night. Every one of them was a master at their skill set and deadly with their steel. The Graygual wouldn't know what hit them.

The girls were already near the gate when Shanti and the others moved into position. She could feel two other women with Ruisa and Maggie, along with three males.

"No Inkna at the gate, huh?" Sonson asked quietly, directly behind Shanti, masked only by a low cropping of bushes.

"They must be monitoring the guards," Shanti reasoned. "With this level of defense, the Graygual wouldn't get lax at the entrances to the city."

"Then putting the guards down doesn't seem like the best idea."

"We'll be through by the time someone comes to investigate." Shanti moved through the night, fast and stealthy. At a jog, she ran across the open space and to the rear drawbridge. She let her *Gift* descend more heavily now, feeling for anyone that would see her. The guards were not close, but someone lingered at the top of the wall.

She glanced up in time to see a startled Graygual lean more heavily over the stone, trying to get a better look.

"I got this," Sonson said with a rough voice.

With a shot of power, he drove a mental spike

through the guard's mind and then reversed somehow, quickly draining the man of energy until he was almost catatonic. The warning and pulse of anxiety from the guard diminished until he seemed dull. If she hadn't known better, she would assume he was no more than bored and idle.

"Fantastic trick," Shanti whispered as they reached the open gateway. Another guard, probably seeing the fall of the first, ran toward them.

"I learned that from an Inkna. They are ingenious in warfare. Had they been warriors, we might've had difficulty." Sonson took to the other guard, striking him down as quickly as the first.

"We haven't met those guarding Xandre yet." Shanti motioned the rest of the group toward them, bringing them at a dead run.

She slipped inside the walls and took in the battlements at a glance. Stairs led up to the walls on each side. Sonson waited for his people, and then motioned a couple up. *"Make those guards look lazy, and keep anyone else away,"* he instructed in the Shadow language.

"There are two leaders now, huh?" Shanti asked as she waited for the remainder of her people to pass through the gate and file around to the pools of black, out of sight.

Sonson turned to her. Shadows mostly masked his

grin. "Forgive me, *Chulan*. But we need revenge. I do not trust that you can live up to the terror of the land."

Shanti felt a zing through the connection as everyone, Rohnan included, made it through the gate and stood silent. Arousal and lust poured out of the guardhouse to the right. The urgency to find the boys called to her. "You are nothing but a tall tale. When they realize you are only men, you'll just be the enemy again. But us? We are dead men and women walking. We are ghosts and phantoms. We are back from the dead. Way scarier. And we've always been better."

"I accept that challenge. Go hunt for the boys, but kill as many as you can. We'll check in on Alena and kill as we go. Give us plenty of room. Whoever gets caught automatically loses."

"We'll all lose if someone gets caught," Shanti said as she stepped toward the guardhouse. Ruisa and Maggie were in there somewhere, disgusted.

"Not necessarily. Let's just hope the Captain shows up with my people at the right time."

Shanti touched her hand to her heart. "Stay alive."

Sonson touched his heart as well, before stepping forward and embracing her. "I'll see you take the city, or I'll see you in the next life." He kissed her cheek. "Happy hunting."

"CAPTAIN!"

Cayan turned on his horse without stopping. Whoever it was would catch up to him. He could barely feel Shanti's pulsing *Gift*, flaring and throbbing. If it hadn't been for the *Joining*, they'd be much too far away to feel anything. She was up to something, which meant she was no longer waiting for him. That meant something had gone wrong.

"Captain, Daniels has a message." Tomous pulled his horse out of the trot. "The prisoner claimed that Xandre would recover him. That it was only a matter of time."

Cayan's horse stumbled on an unseen rock in the road. If only the moon were a few more days into its cycle. Its light was meager and visibility was poor. "He is an incredible asset. We know that. Hopefully we'll be behind large walls before they come."

"Daniels also says that they should put him to sleep for the battle. Just in case."

Cayan nodded, bracing a hand on his thigh. The man was almost delirious with lack of sleep. It hadn't got him talking much, as they'd hoped. Right now, though, they couldn't do anything about it. Once this city was in their possession, they'd have more time to plan. That was when they'd need the information in that man's head.

"Anything else?" Cayan asked, without sparing another glance. A surge rose up from Shanti. He knew that collection of emotions, however faint they were. She'd just killed.

He sucked in a breath and leaned forward on his horse, wishing he could run the horse hard all the way to the battle. They wouldn't have long to go, but they'd arrive in the dead of night. They'd have to wait for dawn, when another large force of the Shadow were supposed to meet them. That was *if* the Shadow showed up at all. Daniels had not received a message from them. They might have their own battles to fight.

"He thought we might stop soon to rest the men and horses," Tomous said hesitantly. "Just half a night…"

Half a night might be too long for Shanti. "We continue."

Shanti shoved the Graygual into a closet and leaned against the door so it would latch. "Oops."

"Think anyone was monitoring that one?" Kallon asked, coming out of a room at the back.

"We'll find out soon enough."

Maggie followed Kallon with an annoyed expression. Ruisa stood next to the guard slumped at the table, adjusting the supplies in her pouch. A woman dressed like a prostitute swapped out the drugged whisky, making it look like the man had passed out. She undid his fly and tossed a pink undergarment on the ground.

It seemed Ruisa and Maggie had enlisted the help of professionals. How, Shanti did not know, but she couldn't hide her pride.

"We're good?" Shanti got a nod from both girls, and a blank stare from the helper. "What about the other girl?"

"She's adjusting the man in there." Maggie jerked her head back to the room. Her mouth twisted in an uncomfortable expression. "These girls…service the guards a lot, I guess. They get food and stuff." Maggie shrugged. "Anyway, they'll make their way back. The Inkna on patrol know to leave them be."

"Good. Let's go." Shanti directed the girls out of the door ahead of her.

"Why are you here so early?" Maggie asked quietly as they stepped out into the stillness of the night.

A surge of pain bled through Shanti's middle. Rohnan shifted to their right. "Xavier and Leilius lost consciousness. I need to find them."

Maggie's lips thinned. Ruisa's eyes went wide. Sorrow radiated from both of them, but neither of them said a word. It was as if they were afraid to ask what that might mean.

"You won't be able to understand our communication, so just keep on your toes," Shanti said, once again feeling the pull of urgency. "We'll tap, touch, push, or shove you to get you in position. We will rarely speak. Yes?"

"Yes, S'am," they both whispered.

"Sonson is headed toward Alena. We will go to where I last felt Xavier and Leilius. Do you know anything about this city that might help us?"

Maggie hooked a thumb at the prostitute coming out of the guardhouse. "She would. Ruisa can somewhat speak to her."

"She doesn't know the traders' language all that well," Ruisa said.

Shanti glanced at Tanna. Unless she was completely mistaken, this was the same dialect as the city they'd just come from.

Tanna stepped forward and said a few words. The woman answered, proving Shanti's theory correct.

"*Chulan.*" Rohnan's tone said that he was still sullen that she'd punched him. Some things had not changed since their youth. "Maggie and Ruisa haven't slept. They are both dead tired. We should give them at least a few hours."

Shanti nodded, feeling her own fatigue pulling at her limbs. She'd forced herself to sleep for a few hours while they had waited, but it hadn't been enough. Unfortunately, she didn't have time for more.

"I can handle it," Maggie said quickly.

"We'll need you tomorrow," Shanti said. "Can these women give you a place to rest?"

"We can go back with her, I guess. The Inkna didn't bother us on the way here. We just got a few disapproving looks."

Ruisa adjusted her top, trying to cover up a little more.

"Okay. Go. Let yourself be consumed with fear if something goes wrong. I'll find you near dawn if not before." Shanti touched Ruisa's shoulder, and then Maggie's. "I don't want to lose you girls. Be smart. And good work."

"Yes, S'am," Ruisa said with a small smile. Maggie nodded in acknowledgment.

Tanna turned back to them. *"Let's get further into the city and I'll fill you in. Their curfew is strict. We shouldn't see anyone but the enemy, and if we do, they won't notice us. They'll have their own terrors to escape."*

Shanti didn't bother voicing her acknowledgment. Instead, she reduced the spread of her *Gift* to the immediate area. An empty space greeted her, devoid of Graygual, Inkna, or anyone that might be out for the night. In a city this large, she should at least feel a stray cat prowling the night. But there was nothing.

She took off at a fast jog, not wanting to push her luck. When they reached the first building, she slunk into a small pocket and waited for everyone to make it across, then gave the signal for the rest to fan out. Some crossed the street quickly so they would line both sides. Picking up her pace again, she made a path to where she thought she had last felt the boys. From the different vantage point, she couldn't be absolutely sure, but she hoped that somewhere within the area there would be some clue.

Two blocks up and she felt someone coming. A sole figure with the *Gift,* moving slowly down the middle of the street. Inkna.

She blasted a small *warning*. They slinked off to the sides and folded into the darkest shadows to wait. The scuff of a boot echoed down the still and quiet street. A soft light glowed, getting brighter as the Inkna came closer. His crisp black shirt front ate away some of the radiance in front of him. His pale skin seemed to glow. Thankfully, he was an idiot, made obvious by such a bright light on a dark night. He wouldn't be able to see beyond that light with anything but his *Gift*. Soon he would be blind.

A surge rose from Sayas, informing her that he would take down the enemy.

Shanti felt a light poke to her brain. She left her shields down, inviting him to take a good look at the biggest monster prowling this night.

His foot stubbed against the ground. His light swung up near his face, showing her his frightened look, but doing nothing to help him see.

Sayas ran out behind the Inkna. His arm wrapped around the man's chest and his knife ripped across his throat. Mela arrived a moment later, grabbing the falling body and helping to drag it, still convulsing, into the deeper shadows.

Shanti was jogging before the feet disappeared from view.

Around a corner, another mind entered her awareness. This wasn't *Gifted*.

Shanti slowed and flattened, sliding up to the edge. A quick look told her it was a patrolling Graygual. He had the lantern, but no *Gift*.

A blast came from Mela this time. She was going to take knife duty.

Kallon and Sayas ran across the street, taking cover on the other side. A shout came from down the way, the Graygual having noticed the moving shadows. He didn't know what he'd gotten himself into until he'd turned the corner. His chest smacked into Kallon.

Faster than thought, Kallon had his hands on the sides of the man's face and twisted. The loud crack signaled the end of that Graygual.

Mela punched Kallon in the arm and flashed him a "what gives?" hand movement. Kallon shrugged in a "what was I supposed to do?" kind of way. She shook her head and helped hide the body.

Sayas held up two fingers to Shanti. They were taking Sonson's bet seriously.

Shanti rolled her eyes but kept on, disposing of two more Inkna before they reached their destination. Once there, she moved around the base of the building and continued down the street, calling up a mental map in her head and trying to pinpoint where they were.

She felt a tap on her shoulder. Rohnan pointed down the street where another guard was moving, still outside her tight circle of *Gift*. He stopped where he was, staring off to the right.

Hope flooded through her. She started moving that direction. Before she could take two steps, however, something jetted out. The altercation was over in a moment. The enemy's feet slid into the shadow.

Sayas put his hands on his hips. *"They're good, I'll give them that."*

"We're better," Mela said, glancing up.

Shanti felt it. A presence above them, hardly detectable. Someone was on the rooftops.

Confusion taking over her, she jogged to a decorative stone outcropping on the building and quickly scaled the side. A figure walked along the roof, holding its stomach. Almost as though it was a whiff of scent, Shanti could detect the maleness of the person.

"What *Gift* is this?" Rohnan asked quietly, standing up next to her.

The figure stopped suddenly and turned their way. For a moment, each party stared at each other. Then the man fled.

"Hurry!" Shanti yelled, running after him. She tried to clutch his mind, but it was like grasping a fish in freezing waters. She couldn't quite lock it down. Instead, she tried a light *stab,* hoping to knock him down so she could catch up.

Her power hit him and deflected, nothing more than a glancing blow. She tried again, but with more power. This deflect had the man staggering. Whatever was protecting him wasn't good enough.

She threw another shot at him, making him fall to his knees. She was on him a moment later, tackling him. They rolled, body over body, stopping on a steeper grade before sliding toward the edge. Shanti let go of him and pushed him away, not wanting to go over with him. The roof tore at her fingers as she clutched at it, sliding to a painful stop. The man flailed and pitched over the edge.

Rohnan was there just in time, lying down on the corner and grabbing downward. He grunted, pulled.

"Help, *Chulan!*"

She was with him a moment later, ready to cut the man's hand off to save her brother. It wasn't necessary. The man was as still as a stone, looking up at them with an imploring look on his face.

Shanti reached down with an open hand. The man put his knife between his teeth and swung his hand up, clutching Shanti's. Together, they pulled him up over the ledge and then dropped him, gasping, on the roof.

"*What language?*" Shanti asked in the traders' dialect.

"*This will work. Who are you?*"

"*What is over your mind that I can't use my Gift on you?*" Shanti asked.

"He is afraid and curious," Rohnan said in a low tone. "I can barely feel it."

Shanti couldn't feel it at all.

"*I recognize...are you a Shumas?*" the man asked, this time with wonder in his voice.

Shanti sat back quickly, out of the reach of his knife.

"*I do not recognize you... I have met your brethren.*" Excitement rang in the man's voice. "*They are to the southwest. They were trying to make their way north, but the Graygual watch for them. Even coloring their hair, their mind power is easy for the Inkna to detect. They stay where they are, waiting for word of the Chosen. Of...the... Are you...?*"

A thrill rang through Shanti, blocking out everything else. Rohnan grabbed her arm with a claw-like fingers, his desperation to see more of their people showing in his grip.

"*Why are you here if they are there?*" Shanti asked

with a wispy voice.

"*I am sticking to a central location. I wait for the Wanderer. The violet-eyed girl. She's…one of them. One of… Are you…?*"

He wouldn't finish the sentence. He wouldn't come out and ask. The reason behind that had Shanti hesitating.

"*What is on your mind that prevents my power from reaching you?*" Shanti tried again.

His face closed down and his lips tightened.

"He is distrustful. We have not identified ourselves. This city is divided." Rohnan rose and backtracked a couple steps, picking up the knife where he had dropped it to dive for the man.

"This city is crushed under Graygual, Rohnan. Of course it's divided. But until I know what we're dealing with, I don't want to show our hand." To the man she said, "*I am looking for two boys—young men. One is large, with big shoulders and well-defined muscle. The other is shorter, though not by much, and thin. Lanky, almost. Have you seen these boys—young men?*"

An intense flare of terror rose from her light mental touch on Maggie.

"*Flak!*" Shanti swore, rising.

"*I know where they are!*" the man said in excitement.

Fear for the girls and elation both coursed through Shanti. "Rohnan, go with him. I will go to Maggie."

"We shouldn't split up, *Chulan*."

The man rose and motioned them on. He started jogging across the rooftops.

"*Flak*," Shanti swore again, looking down off the roof. Kallon waited just below. Down the street, around the corner from the Shadow's kill, a pair of feet disappeared into a doorway.

"Kallon," Shanti whispered down. "Kallon!"

He turned and backed up, looking at her. "The girls are in trouble and a man up here knows where the boys are. We must go. He takes the roof."

Kallon glanced down the street to where their people were jogging back. She felt his mental equivalent of a sigh. Rooftops meant they'd be out of the contest. A moment later Sayas appeared over the edge, then Mela. The rest followed, one by one, until they all gathered.

"*You are the Shumas, aren't you?*" the man said, having stopped when he realized the others weren't following.

"*Yes. Lead on. Some of us will follow. Some will go look for two girls that came with us.*" Shanti motioned him to go.

"*Oh, the ones with Tauneya? They'll probably be in the same place.*"

A wash of cold went through Shanti as she recognized that name, followed by another blare of terror from Maggie and Ruisa. "*Hurry!*"

CHAPTER 22

Shanti climbed down the ladder and stopped beside a worn door with peeling paint. Litter rattled as the breeze caught it, making little flapping movements down the alleyway. The nondescript building was situated in what Shanti assumed was a bad part of town. She'd had to watch her step along the roofs to keep from falling through in some places.

"This way." The man opened the door and stepped through. Light spilled into the alleyway, pushing the Shumas back against the wall.

Shanti pulled her sword as a flare of expectation came from Ruisa. She peered inside. A large room opened up before her. Worn and tattered couches and chairs lined the sides. Rugs, splotched with stains, covered the floor in layers, dotted with sleeping furs and bodies. Maggie and Ruisa sat next to each other near the door, still wearing their revealing clothes. Toward the back, each occupying a chair, sat Leilius and Xavier.

"What the bloody hell?" Shanti marched in the door, ignoring everyone else as she made her way to the two boys. Leilius flashed a grin that quickly melted away.

"S'am?" he asked, fear working into his expression as she got closer. "Are you—"

Shanti attacked him with a fierce hug, squeezing his bony frame as tightly as she could. She accosted Xavier next, unable to fit her arms around his upper body. She took a step back and then punched him in the chest.

"Ow, S'am." Xavier rubbed his pec. "Why?"

"I thought you'd died! What happened?" Shanti demanded.

"We can't have them in here," someone said near the door. "They'll find us."

"*So we meet again, eh?*" A larger woman sauntered into the room with half her large bust hanging out of her top. She planted her fists firmly on her hips. "*I tell you I be ready, no? Well now, here we are. You tell me the plan, and I tell you a better plan. Go.*"

"*Tauneya...how...?*" Shanti shook her head, mystified that the prostitute from the Hunter's camp so long ago would be in that city. "*Did you save them?*"

Tauneya glanced at Xavier and Leilius. "*One of us found them. They running around like idiots. Inkna no need eyes to see.*"

"*Is this the Wanderer?*" the man who had led them to the building asked. "*I thought so, but she wouldn't say. Yes, look! The violet eyes! I feel so lucky.*"

"How are they doing it?" Shanti asked, ignoring the man.

"Here." The man ran into another room.

"They fed us something, S'am," Leilius said. "Inkna patrol. They must've felt us like you do sometimes, and then they tried to kill us, I'm sure of it. We didn't get to see the gate. I tried to go out again, but they wouldn't let me."

"Tauneya knows about the guards around here," Xavier said as the man ran back into the room holding a long black stick in his hand. "They're all mapped out. And Ruisa is trying to poison them. Still, S'am…there are a lot of Graygual. At least five times as many as we have. If the Shadow don't show up…"

Shanti took what looked like a black root from the man. *"This disguises the mind?"*

"Yes," Tauneya said as she took a seat. She said something in another language. A man at the door ran out.

"They send lookout," Tanna translated.

"That is cooked weed." Tauneya pointed at the thing in Shanti's hand. *"Nasty weed. Call it ghost weed. Now know why, eh? It grow wild around this city—probably others, too. You have to cook a special way, then Inkna can't find you. Can't kill, eh?"*

"She got me, though." The man rubbed his temple. *"That hurt."*

"She powerful. More so than stinky Inkna." Tauneya nodded once.

"Can those with mind power use it?" Rohnan asked.

Everyone looked between each other. Finally it was Tauneya that answered. *"We never try. How could we?"*

"I doubt it," Kallon said from beside the door. *"If it disguises the mind, it must hinder the* Gift.*"*

"We can use it on the enemy," Sayas said.

"And they can use it on us." Shanti didn't need access to her *Gift* to be bred. Xandre getting his hands on that weed would be devastating in the wrong circumstances. *"Who else knows about that weed?"*

"The weed? Everybody." Tauneya shrugged. *"It be a weed, eh? But to cook the weed, now that is secret. We guard that with life. Have to. If Inkna knew, we would no longer have sliver of freedom."*

"It makes you feel really sick, though, S'am." Leilius rubbed his belly.

"Better than dead." Shanti's mind raced. *"Do the Inkna gather in one area? Can we get that weed into tea or food?"*

All eyes went to Tauneya. She ran a finger across her chin. *"Best I do is morning tea. It be too late for sex calls tonight. You won't get all, just some."*

"I'll take some. Maggie, Ruisa, learn how to make that tea." Shanti looked at the gathered Shumas. *"Who is going to volunteer to take the tea and see if they can*

still use their Gift?"

The three weakest raised their hands, then looked at each other, figuring out who would be best for it. It was Rohnan that took the stick from the man. "*My* Gift *is not as useful in battle.*"

Shanti stayed his hand. "*Your* Gift *keeps you alive in battle.*"

It was Rohnan's turn to slap her hand away, putting in more sting than he needed. "I am good enough now, *Chulan,* that I only need my *Gift* with you. Or the Captain, if I ever fight him."

"You haven't fought the Captain?" Kallon asked without expression.

"I do not care for being punched." Rohnan gave Shanti a level stare that spoke volumes. She didn't comment while he put the weed into his mouth. His face pinched together. "Bitter. And it burns."

"*How much does he need to eat?*" Shanti asked.

"*Without tolerance to it, two big bites should do.*" The man watched Rohnan with interest.

Rohnan huffed out a painful breath and put a hand on his chest.

"*It feels better than the Inkna mind power,*" Leilius said with a solemn expression. A few people around the room nodded.

"*Okay.*" Rohnan waited for a minute.

Almost immediately, Shanti's ability to feel his mind

faded. She mentally reached out, but touching his mind was like sand running through her fingers.

"*What do you feel?*" Shanti asked with a strange surge of fear. She reached out to touch him physically.

He shook his head. "*Nothing. Just…myself. My own feelings, no one else's.*" Bliss transformed his face. "*This is…nice. Although I feel like I'm going to throw up.*"

"*That doesn't go away,*" Leilius said with his hand on his belly again.

"*How long does it last?*" Shanti asked.

"*About four hours is average,*" Tauneya said. "*That is, if you no take anti-drug.*"

Shanti turned toward Tauneya slowly. "*This anti-drug…it works?*"

"*Mostly. Not completely. You still protected from Inkna, but they can feel. Judging by Inkna expression when they see us, something is off. But they have no pushed.*"

Shanti grabbed the weed from Rohnan and took a big bite.

"*What are you doing?*" Kallon said, rushing forward.

Her mouth started to burn. "*Ugh. This is gross.*" She took another bite. "*I'm going to beat Sonson.*"

⁂

"What does it mean, sir?"

Weary and saddlesore, Cayan flung his leg over the

saddle of the horse. Men staggered around him. They had pushed hard these last few days, but now their bodies were starting to give out.

Sanders stood straight and tall beside an expensive coach, refusing to accept his brain and body's plea to shut down. The man was a rock.

Cayan noticed the horses off to the side, tied to a tree and shifting in the night. He opened the door of the coach and found a note lying on the velvet bench seat. "Bring me some light."

Light bobbed as a lantern was thrust closer.

The note was written in Shanti's hand, instructions for how to proceed with the coach.

"Damn it, woman." Cayan handed the note to Daniels. He pushed away the fuzzy tiredness of his mind and focused on their *Joining*. All was quiet. As in, he couldn't read her at all. He could feel her, but even that was muffled, as if she was speaking through a sock. He didn't know much more other than she was alive and not in pain or danger.

"This…changes things, sir." Daniels held up the note.

"What is it?" Sanders asked, sparing a glance for the men tying up the horses. "Rachie, that horse—you're going to get kicked one day, son. You'd best watch yourself."

"Yes, sir!"

"Idiot," Sanders muttered.

"Shanti has found a way to hand-deliver me to the officer in charge of this city. Sanders, you'll be leading the men in the charge through the gate. Daniels—work it out."

"Yes, sir," Daniels said, only a sliver of tiredness entering his voice.

"Just you, sir?" Sanders asked, following Cayan through the men setting up a makeshift camp.

"No. Three non-*Gifted* men, the very best warriors we have. I'd take you but I need someone to lead the charge."

"No problem, sir. Who are you choosing?"

Cayan stopped and looked out at the night, flicking through countless options. The Graygual officers would be trained to the level of the Hunter, Cayan bet. They'd be quick and precise, with no emotion, and able to endure pain. He needed someone that wanted it with a passion. Someone good and fast, but that also wanted vengeance.

He blew out a breath. To Sanders he said, "I'll think on it. In the meantime, get everyone fed and settled down. They should get a couple of hours' sleep while they can."

"Yes, sir. What about the Shadow?"

"They should be here by dawn. If they're not, we go without them."

The first rays of the sun crawled up the roof closest to the front gate and over Shanti's boot. The creak of leather indicated soft shifts in position, of bowstrings being rubbed against hands or gloves. A fine coach trundled down the path toward the city led by a pair of exquisitely bred horses. The speed of the coach was much faster than when it had left the city the day before. The guards would think something was wrong.

The guards, roused out of their half-asleep stupor by the commotion, straightened up and stared for a moment. Recognizing the coach, one rushed out of the area, probably going to tell a higher-up. The two left behind rushed forward, ready to grab the horses and check in on the lady inside. If someone needed medical assistance, they'd want to direct her.

Everything was exactly as Tauneya had said. From the Inkna they'd overtaken, to the changing of the guards that was about to take place. The officer in this city wasn't like the Hunter. He didn't constantly change schedules and rotations. He had found what worked, and stuck with it. Every officer had their downfall. This officer was thinking he was smarter than the citizens of the town.

"Hold," Shanti said quietly. She checked in with Kallon at the back gate, the root having worn off by now. There would be no Inkna in the area to intercept.

Shanti and Sonson's teams had made sure of that last night before they settled down for a few hours' rest. Soon they would be missed. Soon. Not yet.

Kallon was calm and expectant. It meant Cayan's people were close, if they were not already infiltrating the city.

"They will come," Sonson said quietly in Shanti's ear. "They will make it."

Neither of them had felt the Shadow. This would be a very sticky situation if they didn't turn up.

"Here he comes." Shanti watched as the guard stood in front, waiting for the coach to slow. The driver, not the same one that had gone out, gestured the man out of the way. The Graygual had one moment of confusion before running in front of the horses.

Nervousness radiated through Shanti as Cayan must've wondered how this would go. He was going in completely blind, trusting her with everything he had. "Hopefully he's good on his feet, because I have no idea what'll happen in there."

"Even if Tauneya did know, you wouldn't be able to get the information to him," Rohnan said.

The horse slowed as it crossed the threshold. The running Graygual grabbed the reins and started walking the horses off to the right. He didn't try to open the door again.

"I hope he figured out how to wear black," Shanti

surmised.

"Let's hope he gets an audience before they realize the woman isn't in there," Sonson said.

"True." Shanti blew out a breath, working on finding calm so she didn't add to Cayan's turbulent situation. No doubt he sat inside, completely straight and tall, proving to his men that he was made of steel. It would help them. The reality wasn't helping her.

"Okay, take aim." Shanti sighted her borrowed bow. The change in personnel would happen any minute. "Wait until they are all on here."

Sonson gasped. "The Shadow Lord just made contact."

"Tell them to wait," Shanti said urgently.

"We can't communicate in the way you've devised…"

Shanti felt his swirl of various emotions, trying to warn them away. Instead, up over the rise in land, dust billowed before the heads of riders, and then horses, showed themselves. A line of multiple colors announced the hierarchy of battle-ready Shadow.

"*Flak!*" Shanti rose in her crouch, first checking to make sure Cayan was around the bend, and then sighting. "Here we go…" She let go of the bowstring. The arrow zipped through the air and stuck into the back of the Graygual trying to release the locking mechanism in order to close the gate.

She sent a warning to Kallon, their signal that it had begun. His answering message of *alarm* meant it was too early. "I *know* it's too early, Kallon," she muttered through gritted teeth. "What do you want me to do? Tell the Graygual to hold on a moment?"

"He can't hear you from here, you know," Sonson said. His fingers released. An arrow hit the Graygual running right in the chest. He grabbed it with clawed hands as he sank to his knees.

Fright and urgency pumped out of people in waves. "Here they come..." A swarm of Graygual ran in the direction that Cayan had disappeared, arming themselves even as they ran. One rubbed sleep out of his eyes. Another wiped off something spilled from his front.

"We disturbed their breakfast," Sonson said, firing. He loaded again, and fired. Again. And again.

"Everyone, fire!" Shanti yelled.

Fanned out around her, bows sang. Arrows flew through the air, hitting Graygual mostly in the back as they ran to their posts. With grunts, they died or turned, staring up at the rooftops with surprise on their faces. The smart ducked for cover; the rest reached for their swords and died in the process.

"This place is about to be swarming with Inkna," Shanti said, connecting more securely with everyone around her, and readying. She felt Cayan reach for her, obviously knowing something was happening and wanting to give her more juice.

"Not yet, Cayan," she murmured, planting her hands securely on the rooftop and bracing.

"He can't hear you either—"

A slap of mental power cut Sonson off. Like a blast of needle pricks, the pain hit them with force, battering their shields. What felt like acid slipped off her mind and dripped down her body, powerful enough to fray her thoughts. Another wave smashed into them, even rougher than the first. She felt Cayan's growl of power rising, thrashing against his control.

Soon, Cayan, she thought through the crashing of pain. *Very soon.*

"Almost—" Sonson said through a clenched jaw. "Almost…"

A surge of power fed through Sonson and rushed around their connection. It locked them more securely with those across the city and turned up the punch of what was growing in Cayan.

The Shadow Lord was in range.

"Hit 'em hard!" Shanti yelled, rising from her crouch and running for the ladder. "Kill them all!"

The line of horses thundered down the lane and fanned out, aiming right for the gate. Graygual tried to run forward, desperate to lock them out. The townspeople had taken the weed, though. They were unharmed by the Inkna. Arrows sailed through the air, striking arms, chests, faces, backs. Shanti felt Sanders crossing into the city. Surrounding him came the Westwood Lands army.

Shanti spread out her *Gift,* trying to get an idea of what the enemy was doing. As she feared, Graygual were rushing into the streets, armed and ready for battle. The last of Alena's poison had been served, but she had fallen short. They hadn't hit enough. Or maybe the Graygual were just too many.

Shanti descended the last of the steps as a Graygual ran at her. She blocked his thrust, whirled, and struck the man running up behind. Stepping out to the side, she kicked the first Graygual's face and got out of the way for Rohnan to jump down, slashing with his staff as he did so. The blade cut the Graygual's face in half.

Shanti *searched,* finding five minds that could easily be the one turning. She *struck* them all, making them pause for the archers to hit.

A sword caught the morning sun as it moved through the air. If it weren't for that, she would've missed it. She dodged out of the way. The blade barely missed her shoulder. She swung her sword across, cutting through his stomach before Sonson stuck him in the back.

"Stay with the original plan?" Sonson yelled over the din.

Shanti felt the horde of Graygual running through the city right before a gigantic roar shook the ground. She couldn't help a mad grin. "I hope Tauneya was true to her word and made sure people stayed in their homes."

Shanti ran to the edge of the building, getting a look at the carnage. Arrows continued to fly, some finding their marks, some sailing away. Across the drawbridge, huge and lumbering but with size and power no land animal could match, were the beasts of the Shadow Lands.

"We take the officers' quarters first!" Shanti ran around the bend as another roar shook the ground. Men screamed, and there followed a fierce, wet growl.

A rip of power scoured a cluster of Graygual running at Shanti on their way toward the gate. The enemy sank to their knees. There might be more Inkna in this battle, but with the Shadow Lord showing up to the party, there were three people at max power. The stakes had evened out.

"Let's go, let's go!" Hooves thundered across the drawbridge behind them. Shanti sprinted through a courtyard and ran around a decorative hedge. The coach waited close to the front entrance. Three dead Graygual by its side.

"Not quite perfect," Shanti said, feeling Cayan's exertion. He hadn't made it to the location without a fight, but he wasn't waiting for her. He was taking his opportunity.

A push of violence hit them through the connection as another thrust of power raked the area behind them. Their people were engaged in battle. They were running out of time for a coordinated attack.

Shanti leapt over a dead body and ripped open the door. An arrow flew right past her face and stuck in the wood beside her. She *jabbed* with her power, and then followed the Shadow Lord's lead and *scoured* the area before her with fire. A man staggered in the corridor.

"Go, go, go!" Sonson urged her.

Staying low and to the side, she ran as fast as she could, swinging her knife downward and into the back of the Graygual. Sonson sent out a blast of power, ripping a scream from two people. Denessa threw one more, taking out someone in the hallway on their right. Before them, through a series of archways decorated by the finest craftsmen, ran three Graygual with swords.

A low hum settled deep in Shanti's gut. From it rose the spice from the *Joining*. Power simmered as Cayan went completely tranquil. A moment later, tiny sparks of fire burst through her body.

He was preparing to fight. He'd found the officer.

"We gotta move!" Shanti yelled, letting Rohnan and Sonson clear out the Graygual running at them. "The officer is bound to have reinforcements. Cayan will be overrun."

CHAPTER 23

Cayan walked slowly toward a man slightly shorter than himself. Dressed in black and with seven red stripes, this Graygual would be one of the best.

"Who are you?" the man asked in a rolling accent.

"You must know, if you are speaking my language." Cayan watched his eyes. The way he moved. He was jerkier than the warrior from outside the Mugdock village, not as graceful, but he held his sword the same. His footwork followed a similar path.

A concussion of sound rocked the foundation of the building. Through the opened window men screamed right before a furious roar shook Cayan's bones. The officer did not so much as flinch. He did not even look toward the strange and new sounds. His focus was complete.

It would also be his detriment.

"The Being Supreme has been looking out for you since you took the Inkna town. He is highly intelligent and so far ahead of you."

"Then why don't you have better defenses?" Cayan thrust. The Graygual blocked and danced to the side and then at a diagonal back to him, creating an attack. Cayan blocked and followed the same footwork, advancing. Fast and clean, the Graygual wiped his sword through the air, took the block but then swung back, trying to catch Cayan on the backswing. He was ready. He jumped back and immediately peeled away to the side, blocking the next thrust and creating distance.

The Graygual was stronger in his footwork. That was not the way forward.

"These are better defenses. Tell me, how did you get in?"

Cayan rushed forward, hard and brutal. He thrust, felt his sword battered away, and then threw his fist. The Graygual's head whipped back. Cayan swept with his blade, catching air. The Graygual had dropped and rolled to the side. He was up a moment later with a red patch on his cheek and sober eyes. He hadn't seen that coming.

Welcome to a real fight.

Cayan didn't let up. He rushed again, using rough sword work, messy but effective. He clipped the Graygual's sword, then slashed through his shirt, before pivoting and kicking hard. His boot hit the Graygual's thigh, and the follow-through of his body knocked the Graygual's legs out from under him. He fell on his side, his sword out, ready to block. Cayan kicked his hand instead, then brought his sword down. The Graygual rolled just in time, getting the blade across his back.

He kicked his legs up then out, rocking his body up and landing on his feet. He took five fast steps before he recommenced the fight.

"Where were you trained?" The Graygual's voice was devoid of emotion, but Cayan could feel his incredulity.

"I come from a long line of warriors."

A shock of pain blanketed the room. Cayan knew this would happen, which was why he'd saved his strength.

He felt his men drop to the ground outside the door.

The Graygual's eyes twinkled. "Alas, even warriors must bow to the *Surchine.*"

Cayan *let go.* He threw off the control he'd been fighting with since Shanti had begun fighting. Almost without warning, a surge of power, so pure, so raw it brought tears of pain to his eyes, roared through his body. It bubbled out, filling the room with a force unlike any other. Through Shanti he felt all the others, including the huge force of the Shadow Lord. More power dumped into him, connecting him and making it grow. It swirled and expanded, rushing in his ears and pounding through his body. The unwieldy force whipped around him, half flirty with Shanti's power sharing his body, and half a brutal, destructive thing that would tear down everything in his sight.

He sent a blast of warning to Shanti. He could contain this, but he couldn't direct it. Once it was out, he was at its mercy. She would have to control the flow.

Too late now.

Another slap of pain hit him, making him take a step back. Anger rose, aggravating the power stuffed in his body. The door burst open, revealing two Graygual standing in front of three Inkna.

"You have no idea what you are up against," Cayan said, straining.

"Actually, I think you—"

Cayan *ROARED* with the power. It thundered through the room. Walls quaked. The Graygual officer screamed and clawed at his chest. Those in front of the Inkna tried to step forward. Instead, they fell, landing on their faces and bouncing. Blood splattered from a broken nose. Red dripped out of their ears.

The Inkna stared at him, their faces white in utter shock. Their shields and combined might withstood his raw power, but would they withstand Shanti's finesse?

He summoned more power, letting it boil out of his body and hover around him in the air. And then he felt it. Fizzing through the building. His hairs stood on end. The current tickled his neck and sent bubbles through his middle. Sparks danced within his power, set in motion by his other half.

He felt her, down the hall, running at him with all her might. Her people and the Shadow ran in behind, downing everyone ahead and killing everyone coming from behind. She bothered with none of that. She was here for him.

She thought he needed saving.

The air crackled as their collective power fed off each other. Cayan offered it up, let her assume control. As soon as he did, a surge flowed from one to the other, treating their bodies as one.

The hum between them started to vibrate. The ground trembled. The air above them sizzled. Power as cutting and agile as a whip shot out. It hit off the Inkna, making them stagger backward. One grabbed his head. The others clutched at the walls to stay upright. Another shock of power, finer this time, aiming the massive *thrust* for one tiny piece of their minds. Like a needle striking blown glass at high speeds, a crack formed in their shields and began to grow. All it would take was one more thrust.

Shanti barreled into them with bared teeth and her sword. She slashed through the first, spraying blood against the wall. A knife flew end over end, sticking into the eye of another, an excellent shot from someone behind her. Shanti kicked the last between the legs, making him bend before she hacked down at his exposed neck. He crumpled. His head rolled across the floor.

"What, you're waiting for me to do everything?" Shanti asked with a heaving chest. "You couldn't walk forward and stick your sword in them?"

He smiled. He couldn't help it. Like a vision from his dreams, she was the most beautiful thing he'd ever seen in his life, made all the better for the splash of blood on her cheek and the fire in her violet eyes.

"I wanted you to feel good about yourself. You know, think you were doing something for the war effort." He crossed the distance in a couple strides and grabbed her behind the neck. He planted a deep, bruising kiss on her lips, so damn happy to see her in one piece.

"I love voyeurism and all, but we have to go. My mother is old. I don't want her to have to get off her horse." Sonson suddenly disappeared from sight, having run to the right.

Cayan stepped away from Shanti and ran to the large, open door in time to see Sonson dig his sword into the stomach of a Graygual.

"Okay, let's go. We have a lot of trained Graygual in this city. It's not ours yet." Shanti started jogging out of the door.

Cayan followed. "How many are we talking?"

"Let's just say Sanders is probably swearing about the odds right now…"

⁂

"Bloody hell, they're like ants!" Sanders slashed through a black tunic before punching someone in the face. The nose cracked. His sword slid through the Graygual's stomach a moment later. "Push through!"

A swarm of Graygual ran at him from down the street. They were trying to push Sanders and his men back out through the gate. Only half of Sanders' force had even made it in. This was a shitstorm that had started way too early.

"Keep going!" Sanders yelled. "Push through. Keep going!" He blocked a sword, rammed his body into the enemy, then got caught in limbs. With a growl, he jerked his head forward. His forehead smacked off the Graygual's face. The man staggered back, ripping out of Sanders' grasp. Sanders stabbed him with his sword, brought his foot up, and shoved him back off the blade. He turned with another strike ready, only to find Kallon's face.

"You're lucky you're so pretty, or I would've run you through." Sanders kicked a kneeling Graygual in the teeth, belatedly realizing that the whole horde around him were already sinking to the ground in agony. "You lot are wonderful to have around. Especially the ones who don't speak my language."

"Eat this." Kallon thrust a shriveled black thing that looked like bark at his face.

"Get away." Sanders pushed Kallon's wrist away before hacking down without ceremony, killing the enemy while they were down. He'd wait to fight fair when he trained the newbie women. He only had so much restraint.

"Eat this. It'll prevent mind power from harming you." Kallon held the bark up again.

"Why didn't you say so—Lucius, get your team higher. They can't shoot anyone from there!" Sanders grabbed the tough thing and ripped through it with his teeth. "On the rooftops!" He moved the piece out of his cheek and kept chewing, using his free hand to kill whoever was close enough.

Sourness made his eyes squeeze shut before his mouth and then throat caught fire. "What the hell have you given me?"

"Xavier says it does not taste good, but it works."

Sanders forced himself to take another bite. "Whatever helps me kill those pansy sons of bitches. I have a debt to settle with the Inkna."

Kallon took the remainder and moved on, aiming for all the best fighters first and letting other mental workers distribute to the rest. After he had given some to Lucius, who didn't question nearly as much as he should, and moved away, the Graygual began to rise up again like weeds.

"You couldn't have just killed them?" Sanders asked in annoyance.

Kallon replied, but by that time the grunts and cries of agony had turned into war cries. Sanders blocked a strike, and then slashed, feeling his stomach start to gurgle as he ripped his sword across exposed flesh.

"Uh oh." His stomach dropped and bubbled in that horrible way that warned he was about to shit his pants.

He grabbed someone's shoulder, stuck his sword through a gut, ripped the man to the side, and tried to move off to a corner. Another Graygual filled in. Then two more. He slashed and hacked, better and quicker, and way more experienced, but there were too many.

Something feathered across his head. Like the dancing of fingers on his brain, something barely touched him. His stomach gurgled again. "Oh no." One of the women, still climbing onto the roof not far away, froze and then convulsed into a ball. Her fingers went white on the ladder and her eyes squeezed shut.

Inkna. Had to be.

"Get that girl!" Two men on the roof sank to their knees, their bows falling out of their hands. Leilius rushed to the girl with the black bark while pointing at someone on the ground.

"Mine!" Sanders yelled, barreling through Graygual

as if they didn't have swords. He slashed and hacked, getting sprayed with blood while completely ignoring what was going on with his own body. He shoved a larger man out of the way and yanked his blade from the man's side, letting him die in peace. He sighted three Inkna sitting atop horses up the road. "Now you're going to learn what it's like to fight a fair fight, you good-for-nothing—"

Sanders sprinted at them, his teeth bared. The horses started to prance and their ears flattened on their head. One whinnied and pawed at the ground.

"That's right, here comes danger!" Two of the Inkna were staring at him, frustrated expressions on their faces. A soft prodding touched Sanders' mind, but he barely felt it. Ten feet away, close enough to still get them if their horses started to run, and suddenly hooves flashed in his face. The horse had been spooked, and bucked.

Sanders dodged to the side, not deterred, and then froze. Another creature had bared its teeth, and it was much, much bigger.

"Oh shit." Sanders shrank back. Another horse reared, screaming. The Inkna fell off, nearly prone as he hit the ground. The back of his head smacked off the street and bounced. Blood splattered where his skull had hit.

"No!" Sanders stabbed down through him as another horse threw its owner. The Shadow beast roared again, a sound that chattered Sanders' teeth. The giant animal plowed into the final horse and swiped at the fallen man, scoring through his chest.

"We'll call that teamwork." Sanders gave the animal a salute.

The beast roared. Blood dropped from its large canines.

Sanders backed slowly toward the nearest wall, wanting eyes on that beast all the time. They were supposed to be good in battle, mostly only going for the enemy. Sanders couldn't remember what he was supposed to do if that *mostly* turned out to be his bad luck.

Arrows flew through the crowd, sticking into the Graygual and lowering them to the ground. Another splash of fingertips raced across his forehead. A great few in the army groaned and sank as another rush of Graygual entered the square.

"Get those men the root!" Sanders yelled, running parallel to the beast. It let out a ferocious growl before swiping at the back of a Graygual. Four lines of red parted the black. He arched and screamed before the beast's head ripped into the back of his neck.

Sanders looked around wildly, trying to find those Inkna. His men were standing now, though. Shanti's kin must've been taking care of it, though he couldn't tell to look at them. Unlike the Inkna, who hid away, the Shumas worked through the crowd, their movements slick and precise, and their sword strokes lethal.

Sanders ran around the melee, slashing at enemy on the edges of the battle. He reached the drawbridge and saw the line of men anxious to get to the fight.

"Damn it!" A black shirt ran at him. He ducked, stuck upward with his blade, and propelled himself to the right, ripping his sword out as he did so.

"Clear this area of our men and I'll blow the Graygual out!"

Sanders followed the voice and saw Maggie with a round metal canister. Next to her, on the ground in a stone bowl, glowed a small fire. The flames barely reached out of their confinement. Out of the canister hung a white string.

"Move!" Maggie yelled, waving her arm to the side.

"Clear out," Sanders yelled, grabbing the back of one of his men's shirts and yanking him back. "Clear out!"

Men dressed in blue ran where they could. A scream rose the hairs on Sanders' arms away to the left, then the Graygual in the square shrank down in agony. The Inkna must've been taken care of.

"Hurry!" Sanders yelled, shoving and pushing to take advantage of the mental workers. "Go!"

Maggie lowered her contraption to the fire, and

then quickly threw. The hollow metal sound when it bounced was quickly lost to the screaming of the Graygual. It rolled amongst them, bumping off someone's boot as he crouched down, clutching his head in agony. For a moment, nothing happened.

A loud explosion shook the ground. A spray of metal stuck in bodies like a deadly pincushion. Bodies flew up and out. A limb spiraled through the air.

"Grisly." Sanders grimaced. He wasted no time. "Get everyone in, hurry!"

With a roar of fervor, Sanders' men ran over the drawbridge. Their feet thumped as the surviving enemy scraped themselves up off the bloody street. One by one they finished the Graygual off, finally joining the battle after only watching.

"More come!" Sayas ran past Sanders with his sword in his hand. He looked up at the roof and made sweeping signaling gestures with his arms.

"I'm with you." Sanders took off after the Shumas, noticing a few more running to catch up. "With me, men. With me!" he yelled, moving the battle forward.

Around the corner spilled a sea of black. Like a tide during a storm, they crashed into the Westwood Lands men and Shumas rushing to meet them.

"Fire!" Lucius yelled, his arm swinging downward.

Arrows shot into the fray, downing Graygual by the dozens. It wasn't enough. This city had far too many.

The feathered pressure slid over his head. Damn Inkna again. The city was infested.

Sanders turned back to check behind and noticed an opening off to the side. Within it, standing straight and stiff, stood one of the buggers.

"Now I've got you." Sanders stuck his sword through someone, nearly missed someone else, but luckily was able to slice off a limb instead, and elbowed a man fighting with a grim-faced Marc.

"Thanks, sir," Marc called as Sanders continued on.

His eye on the prize, he ran at that Inkna with everything he had. A black shape zipped in from the side. Another came from the left. "No!"

A cat lunged, its mouth fitting perfectly around the throat of the Inkna and chomping down. The other cat waited for the now-struggling man to fall before dodging in to finish the kill.

"You filthy little—I need revenge!" Sanders shouted.

A huge *boom* shook Sanders to the core. The air crackled around them, making some of their hair stand up as if lightning was about to strike.

Sanders looked up at the sky, clear and blue, promising a chilly but beautiful day. The ground and surroundings rumbled, speaking of thunder. A flash of lightning.

The cats ran around him and then slunk into the shadows of the buildings, still hunting for outliers.

The rumble sounded again before the air within the battle fizzed. Piercing screams frayed Sanders' nerves for a second, the sound of agony so great a mortal man shouldn't live through it. The screams ended in a horrible gurgle of death, amplified in a chorus of pain.

"Help them!" Sanders called, running back into the fray. He raked his sword across a stomach and kicked someone in the nuts, before ramming the heel of his hand into someone's nose. The man staggered backward as blood gushed down his face. Sanders ran him through.

The air crackled again before a deep roll slammed into the enemy. More agonized screams echoed against the walls.

"Take cover!" came a woman's voice.

Something dropped from the roof behind the enemy lines. Down the wall, something else fell right before someone took off in the other direction.

"Get down!" Sanders screamed, running to the side.

Two huge blasts in quick succession tore at the buildings and sent debris flying through the crowd. A head bounced on the roof off to the left. Someone threw up, unable to handle the carnage. Everyone and everything paused, including the mental power, as the dust settled.

Sanders turned toward Lucius, hopefully still in earshot on the rooftops behind him. "Close that drawbridge. Don't let anyone out. We need to keep this information in here."

Lucius cupped his mouth and yelled, "But what if we need to retreat?"

"We won't!" Not with the Captain in this kind of a mood, anyway. When the thunder started rolling on a clear day, he was not one to mess with.

As if to punctuate Sanders' thoughts, another rolling *boom* rocked the city, followed quickly by strikes of pain and torture that turned quickly to death. The Captain knocked them down, and Shanti killed them. Effective.

"Okay, spread out. Let's push deeper into the city and take them down. Do not kill any innocents!" Sanders yelled.

CHAPTER 24

S HANTI RAN ALONG the building, sensing someone ahead on the right. Their *Gift* flared and sparked, revealing a high-powered Inkna hiding from the battle. She bet there were a lot of those who would hide and try to sneak away.

"We've got to prevent them from leaving," Shanti yelled at Cayan as he rocked out another huge burst of power.

As she slipped into the space between buildings she heard a disembodied "Mine!" The word fell away as she found the Inkna pressed against the wall. "Your sort should do yourselves a favor and learn to at least defend yourselves." She grabbed his shirt front and jammed her blade into his throat.

Stepping back, she cleaned her knife as he fell to the ground.

Sanders jogged to a stop in the mouth of the alley with an incredulous expression on his face. "Did you not hear me say *mine*?"

"Oh. I didn't realize that was you. And that you

meant this one." No time to lose, she jogged around Sanders and met up with Cayan again, working toward the enemy. "If they take information about the explosives, and about the root, we lose two huge advantages."

"Xandre will already know about the explosions." Cayan's surge of power smashed into a line of Graygual. Shanti rained down shots of white-hot pain, piercing their brains before quickly moving on. Somewhere in the distance, another blast concussed the air.

"What about the innocents?" Cayan yelled above the din, referring to the explosions.

"They are only using those in primarily Inkna and Graygual areas. Except for here, which are not homes." Shanti threw a knife, hitting a running Inkna in the middle of his back.

"Damn it, Shanti!" Sanders growled, keeping pace with her. "You are making it impossible for me to finally get some vengeance on these vermin."

Shanti grimaced. "Sorry."

"Sanders, take some men to the front and tell the Shadow Lord to close the front drawbridge. We end this now. Kill them all." Cayan slowed.

Shanti felt it then. Ahead of them, filling an entire few blocks of the city, both Inkna and Graygual poured out. Shanti turned back toward Sanders, to yell at him to stop, but he was already on his way to trap them.

"He made us think this would be easy. He lured us

into the heart of the city, and then he unleashed the majority of his army." Cayan shook his head as something close to wonder colored his thoughts. "Genius."

"That's not a good thing, Cayan."

"Yes it is. We can learn from this. He is challenging us. When we rise to these challenges, we will grow. He has nothing to challenge him. He will stagnate."

"Not true." The fighting around them died down. Shumas stepped up beside her before spreading out to the sides. The Shadow in their force followed suit a moment later, forming a thick blockade of power. Those who had taken the root fell to the back, and those who had not stayed in the middle, shielded on all sides by people who could fight the Inkna. "I keep beating him. He is the one that is growing."

"You keep beating his officers. A leader is only as good as the people under him."

Through her *Gift,* Shanti could feel the mass of people filling the streets. It had to be enemy—citizens wouldn't be leaving their houses. Easily double their number, perhaps triple, and Shanti bet these men could fight. They would be excellent.

A thick wall of power saturated the air like fog. It billowed out and surrounded them, pressing in on all sides.

"Get your mother over here, Sonson," Shanti said in a low voice, feeling the two dozen pokes and prods to her shields from extremely high-caliber Inkna. "Quickly."

Cayan ran his thumb along his blade as his brow lowered over unfocused eyes. Emotions flitted through him so fast that Shanti couldn't pick up on them. His tongue came out and slowly licked along his bottom lip, something he did unconsciously when he was working out a particularly hard puzzle. He moved to the middle of the street, where his men parted around him. Shanti followed to stand by his side. The mental workers changed their position, covering the sides, and the army shifted accordingly.

"They are mightier than our army," Cayan said in a wispy voice. "They have more power, and they have more swords. They also know this city." Cayan looked to the right, then left, pausing on a brick wall blocking off the entrance to an alleyway not far in front of them. "They have trapped us in like mice."

"This is not a good speech for your men, Cayan," Shanti said as adrenaline spiked in her body. "We can't quit now. We can't run. We won't make it."

"Xandre only thinks with his army. He thinks with might. He collects large cities, money, men…he collects all the things that would maintain his power. But he does not keep the faith of the people. He rules by fear; he does not rule by love. All he has is his army."

Shanti shook her head slowly, not understanding

his point, as a shockingly large number of Graygual marched their way. And this was the host of Graygual that had been narrowed down by Alena's efforts. By the weed slipped into the Inkna breakfast. They'd already slimmed the herd, yet still it was all encompassing...

"The Wanderer will unite the people with her suffering, and lead them with her love." Cayan's clear blue eyes focused on her. "Only when you allow yourself freedom of thought can you obtain the freedom of mind."

"What are you talking about, Cayan?" Shanti asked, panic starting to increase the speed of her heart. "You sound like Burson. We don't have time for this."

"Burson said those things. The Chosen will lead the people. But the Wanderer must unite them. We need you right now."

"You're not making any sense," Shanti said through clenched teeth.

His power pulled back in and wrapped around her. Like hands caressing her body, she felt his touch on the most intimate of places. Unexpectedly, the simmer within her rose and blossomed, filling her up and overflowing. It felt like a thousand kisses pressed on her bare skin before his lips slid across hers. He grabbed her power, something that felt like a physical thing, and brought it into him to that deep place where only she was allowed to go. He forced himself deep into her, their bodies only a shell of their united beings. "Call to the people, *mesasha*. Unite them."

Any doubt that flitted through her was immediately wrapped up in Cayan's confidence and carried away. She *felt* the rightness of this, because he did. She *felt* the path before her, because he was showing it to her. He had the deep well of power that she had to finesse and direct, and he had the vision that she had to realize. They were two halves melded into one. Her decisions and ideas had taken them to this point, and now he was directing them beyond it. That was truly what the *Joining* was.

She closed her eyes, not having to block out the encroaching enemy or the thought of losing everything yet again—Cayan was already doing that. He was shielding her from reality while she tapped into that place deep inside. She thought of her family, who had given their lives for their people. Her grandfather, who had stayed behind in that first battle so that he might guide the next generation. The ghosts of her people drifted around her, clenching her heart and bringing tears to her eyes. She thought of her people, reunited at last. Of Rohnan, prepared to give his life for her, and traveling the land to find her again and give it all over again if need be. Then the boys and girls who trusted her with everything they had. Who allowed themselves to be beaten and battered, to be tricked and fooled, to be shoved into battle and then marched to unknowing places, all because of their love for her. And their belief in her cause.

Tears came to her eyes as emotion rode everything. She felt the power rising up around her, carrying both her pain and hope, and then blasting out in all directions. It blanketed the city, sifted down into locked homes and wrapping around scared or angry citizens. She felt the people latch on, picking one emotion or more, and gripping with all they had.

"Now it is my turn," Cayan said softly. The blast of power sparkled. The hope turned into a tangible thing, injected with Cayan's confidence. Urgency fueled the power, not pleading for aid, but appealing for people to fulfill their own destiny, to grab their freedom with both hands.

He was giving them a silent call to action.

One by one, she felt people moving. They left their homes and walked outside. Some climbed the roofs. Some swirled in heat and vengeance. Some drifted with aid and healing in mind. She called the people; he would lead them. They were the Chosen.

"What the fuck is going on?" Sanders stalked up with a surly expression. "We've got a mass of Graygual headed this way, sir. You need to put that woman down."

Cayan stepped away from Shanti with the fizzle between them strong. In a voice that carried to the whole of the army, he said, "Today we unite the people against all odds. Today we claim our freedom. Together!"

A cheer went up, bolstered by the power that still blanketed the city. Locals on roofs pumped their fists as the army shouted. Across the city, Shanti felt the Shadow Lord and Portolmous organizing their people.

"Today, we fight!" Cayan started walking. Another cheer went up as the army started walking with him. People moved across the rooftops. Ladders were thrown over the sides and boards dropped between buildings, letting them travel where they would, unimpeded by brick walls.

A roar and the sound of running boots echoed all around them. Shifting leather and clinking metal announced someone coming. A blast of mental *Gift* slapped her shields.

An answering roar of pure, raw power erupted from Cayan in thick, heavy waves. As the Graygual came into sight, filling the streets and running at them with swords in their hands, the torrent of pain rammed them, dropping them to their knees. Another deep, earth-shaking blast battered them, shaking them to the ground with the awesome might. Shanti *whipped* and *slashed* with her *Gift,* using the power to splinter the Inkna shields.

Like an avalanche, the third force joined the mental

fray. Power rolled and heaved before crashing onto the Inkna. Their brains, exposed by Shanti, suffered from a dexterity of power that could only come with a lifetime of use. The Shadow people held apart those shields, preventing them from being reconstructed, while the Shadow Lord brutally *beat* and *scraped* at their fragile minds.

Arrows rained down from above as Shanti ran forward. Sword in action, she hacked down at a Graygual, cutting off his hand at the wrist. Whirling, she slashed through a ribcage and then kicked out, catching someone in the chin. She slashed down, chopping halfway through his neck before she ripped her sword out and shouldered into a Graygual.

Cayan slashed the Graygual's back, making him scream and convulse, allowing Shanti to knock him away. More arrows rained down behind enemy lines. Rocks flew from rooftops, along with anything else they could find.

"Push them toward the Shadow Lord," Cayan yelled, movements so fast they were hard to see. He slashed and cut, a perfect specimen. His muscle bunched and elongated, power and speed like none of these Graygual would ever have seen.

Shanti threw another shot of power at the Inkna, winding around the Shadow Lord's efforts and ripping away someone's sanity. She battered away a return thrust even as she blocked with her sword, flicked, sent the enemy blade flying, and stabbed through. She moved on to the next, then the next.

A blast shook the ground up the way. A part of a building broke free. A huge chunk of stone fell on a cluster of Graygual. Another explosion sent a spray of bodies into the street. A brick wall crumbled, creating a thoroughfare.

A few moments later, a roar issued forth from that broken wall. Two beasts ran through, one after the other. They smashed into the crowd like rabid animals. A few locals scrambled back onto the roof, now thinking better of joining the fight at ground level.

A clatter came up behind them. Hooves falling in a strange, haphazard sort of way ran on the hard street. Shanti cut down a Graygual in front of her before shaking her head. How that bloody horse always managed to turn up in the middle of the action, she had no idea.

"I'll take out the Inkna," Shanti shouted as she ran to the side, hoping it was actual hooves and not their echo she was hearing. Her horse, the Bloody Bastard, nearly pranced out of the line of Westwood men, shaking his head and rearing up, throwing off everyone's attempts to capture him and ride him to the battle.

She whistled, a high, shrill sound. It was met with a

neigh as the horse stomped toward her.

"Be careful!" Cayan yelled after her.

Sheathing her sword, she took a running leap before climbing onto his back. He hadn't been saddled, so she grabbed a fistful of his mane and held on for dear life.

Cheers went up as the Bastard ran headlong into a crowd of Graygual.

"Go around, you stupid animal!" Shanti yelled, ripping out her sword again and slashing down. It bucked and kicked out, catching someone's head with its hooves. Despite their desire to take Shanti down, the Graygual backed away from the crazed animal.

One of the cats ran next to it for a moment before turning into a dark alley and lunging. A beast roared behind them before a scream cut off abruptly.

"There goes the neighborhood," Shanti muttered as she hacked down at a Graygual that had veered too close.

They reached empty space amid the chaos, the line that always existed between the Graygual and the Inkna. Another clatter of hooves had Shanti turning. Rohnan came right behind her, riding a horse that had also been stolen from the Graygual.

"Don't like being alone anymore, huh?" Shanti asked her horse, who was sounding his strange equine growl.

"The Inkna are occupied by the Shadow Lord, but

there are still a lot of them," Rohnan said as he came alongside her, running through the almost empty street.

Shanti held on while the Bastard jumped over a washbasin that had crushed a Graygual skull. "Go *around,* you bloody animal."

They took a bend too fast, having Shanti almost rolling off her horse, when they found the Inkna. Stationed in a line, three deep, they stood straight with their eyes closed, fighting the battle from a distance. In the middle, leading the mental effort, was a Master Executioner.

"Xandre pulled out the big dogs," Shanti said, grinning as half of them snapped their eyes open. The smile melted off her face. "Sanders is going to be pissed I didn't bring him."

Her horse crashed into their line, trampling two men and scattering the others. Like angry hornets, power struck her head in quick succession, pounding her. She ripped off some weed with her teeth and chewed it hastily. Her horse reared and kicked out. His hoof made two Inkna duck and two more roll out of the way. She fell off the back, feeling the burn as the weed and saliva slid down her throat. Her body hit the ground. Dull pain shot up her arm to her shoulder.

"*Chulan.*" Rohnan crawled toward her on the ground, getting battered mentally. He took the remaining weed out of her hand and tossed it into his mouth.

The intense pain dulled. Then turned into nothing more than pressure.

Shanti stood up and wiped a speck of blood from the corner of her mouth. A few of the Inkna's eyes rounded. In the Graygual language, she said, "*Uh oh, now what?*"

Rohnan rose up next to her. His staff started to whirl.

"No you fucking don't!" Sanders sprinted into the area with his sword in hand, blood splattered across his front. "I claim Betty's twin!" He took a running leap and tackled the Master Executioner.

Shanti moved into the group with sword slashing, taking them out as quickly and efficiently as she was able. Pressure pulsed against her head, threatening pain, but none of it reached her, and none of them could fight.

Rohnan hooked his blade around a neck and yanked as the Bastard kicked someone in the chest. Sanders abandoned his sword and took to them with his fists. There were tears in his eyes and vengeance on his mind. Shanti and Rohnan knew exactly how he felt.

From beginning to end, it lasted no more than ten minutes. The three of them and two horses stood panting, looking down on the biggest collection of Inkna Shanti had ever seen in one place. "Xandre really wanted me dead," she said into the eerie silence.

A cough took her out of her reverie. She looked up and started, seeing the rooftops littered with people staring down. Some had bows, some a collection of household items, and all were silent. Not all were looking at her, though. Some were looking at Rohnan, who was petting and calming his horse, and a great many were watching Sanders, standing amid the bodies, his white shirt soaked in blood, with pain and suffering etched on his face. When he looked up from the Inkna, his face transformed into one of rough tranquility. He was not at peace with what had happened to him, but he could come to terms with being the victim.

Shanti bet that a great many people staring down on them could sympathize with the emotion so clear on Sanders' face.

"We're not done yet," Shanti said, sighing. "There are still a few Inkna hiding around the city, and a great many Graygual."

"With the amount of mental power we have, *Chulan,* they don't stand a chance," Rohnan said.

"Even so. Let's go clean out the rest of the trash." She took a running leap onto the Bastard, then dug her heels into his sides. The animal took off, his hooves clattering against the cobblestone. A Graygual stepped out, and then another. She slashed down with her sword as she ran by, then held on for dear life as the Bastard jerked to a stop so he could kick out, clipping one of them with his hoof. The Graygual crumpled to the ground, his face ruined.

"Blasted animal, you're going to end up breaking my neck!" The roar of fighting and battle raged as she turned the corner, metal clashing against metal, but whole sections of enemy were screaming as they sank to their knees. The Shumas and Shadow were taking advantage of their mental might.

She waded into the middle, slicing a neck before hacking through a shoulder. She struck a black-clad chest, unable to help mentally because of the weed. The Bastard reared, punching faces with his hooves before kicking out and knocking down more enemy.

A peal of thunder boomed outward from Cayan, taking those around her to their knees. The Bastard reared and screamed before galloping out of the way. He didn't go far, though, a warhorse down to his bones. Instead, he bobbed his head and waited for the next opening.

"You're insane, horse, you know that?" Shanti swung her leg around and jumped. She hit the hard ground, slashed through a writhing Graygual before meeting up with Cayan. Another burst of power rocked out, taking out a large faction of enemy. His men then waded through, protected by the weed, and finished them off.

"Victory is ours," Cayan said, out of breath but not

showing any sign of fatigue in his bearing. "The Shadow Lord is still using large amounts of power, but we've done it. They don't have the resources to stop us."

"We've won." Shanti sighed. "We're still alive."

The fall of rocks and debris from the rooftops lightened. The screaming subsided as the Graygual died. "Yeah!" one of Cayan's men shouted, raising his sword. Another, his bloodstained face weary, but eyes bright, lifted his sword into the air in response. A cheer went up around them, the people on the rooftops holding up their fists in victory along with the soldiers.

"We did it," Shanti said, feeling the smile bud and the relief wash over her. "Somehow, we did it." She felt danger gliding toward her, and turned to smile down at her big cat, invisible to the *Gift* even if she'd had it. She scratched his head and then his ears before bending down to hug his neck. "We did it." She sighed in relief as tears came to her eyes.

"The people helped." Cayan looked up at the rooftops. "This victory will be talked about. It's the beginning. This land will take back its freedom, starting with this battle."

CHAPTER 25

"I HEAR SONSON won," Cayan said as they made their way to a large patch of grass in the city park.

Shanti threaded her hands through Cayan's as they passed the drawbridge, still raised with the gates locked. Two days had gone by since their victory, and while no one had tried to get in, there were still Graygual hiding inside the city that were trying to get out.

"The competition is not over yet. I catch up to his numbers a bit more every day."

Shanti let her walk sway, bumping into Cayan's big arm. He took his hand out of hers and draped it over her shoulder. "The people are in awe of Sanders. They'd heard stories of him already—the Inkna hate him, after all. They got to see him in action."

"He's still…messed up from being tortured. I think this will help a little. The weed does, anyway."

Cayan stopped them and turned Shanti toward him. She closed her eyes as his fingertips slid across the bottom of her jaw, tilting her face up to him. His lips were warm and full, opening hers. His tongue flitted in playfully. All too soon flirty turned passionate, his hands coming around her with need. He backed off as heat kindled in his blue eyes and burnt through his body. "Marry me, *mesasha*. Say you will."

Shanti couldn't take her eyes away from his. She felt light and giddy, but she didn't feel like giving in just yet.

She shrugged a shoulder. "How can I consent to giving you my hand? You haven't fought Kallon for permission yet."

The fire sparked, a different kind of heat. His dimples etched his handsome face as he smiled. "You want me to prove my dominance, is that it? He mentioned that the women fighters of your land make men prove their worth."

She tried to keep the surprise out of her expression. His smile brightened, and she felt it through her body. How annoying.

"C'mon, I'll go make a man of him right now." Cayan looped his arm around her shoulder again.

"He's harder than you think. You are technically better, but he has a stupid amount of patience."

"I have patience, too, *mesasha*. I have to with you."

"I'm nothing compared to him."

They found Kallon amid a large group of people. Shumas, Shadow, and a bunch from the Westwood Lands created a circle. Around them stood people from the city, watching a little sport or possibly curious about the prowess of these new people.

As Cayan walked through the circle, Kallon said, "I will be using my power, Captain."

"Weapons, or hand to hand?" Cayan asked as he gently directed Shanti to the sidelines.

"I'll take it easy on you—hand to hand." Kallon didn't smile, but his eyes sparkled. Maybe he was loosening up a little.

Leilius, Gracas, and Xavier crept out of the bushes and blended into the crowd. Cayan tied back his hair, and Kallon did the same.

The two men squared off. One was lithe and graceful, as were most of Shanti's people; the other was tough and brawny, as were many of Cayan's. Hands stayed at their sides. Shanti felt her mirrored power start to burn, then rise, playing with its mate, asking Shanti to do the same.

She refrained from connecting with Cayan, making sure not to steer his power. This had to be one on one. It was only fair, and was really the only way Kallon had a chance.

"Cayan will still win," Rohnan said next to her.

"Probably, but without someone to help direct his *Gift,* Cayan is nearly useless with it."

"Not useless. He takes everyone down, not just his opponent."

"He'll do it," Xavier said, pushing another Shumas

out of the way so he could sit next to Shanti.

"Xavier, you might get blasted with power up here," Shanti chided.

Xavier held up the weed. "I'm good. I want to see this fight. I want to pick up on some tricks."

Shanti's power lurched in her chest. Cayan's body flexed suddenly, head to toe, his muscles straining his shirt. Then Kallon was moving, hands and feet lightning fast. He kicked, hitting Cayan in the upper thigh, and then struck. Cayan dodged the blow and blocked the next.

"Why doesn't he hit back?" Xavier asked with urgency. "He can hit harder than that. He's faster!"

"He is adaptive, no?" the Shadow Lord asked from Xavier's other side. "He's learning?"

"Yes," Shanti said to the Shadow Lord, her eyes not leaving the fight. She held her breath as Kallon advanced. She knew the move; he was stabbing with all his power in one tiny spot on his opponent's shield, hoping to shatter the barrier then rake the mind, while using a circular bodily attack. It was much more effective with a sword, but the opposite style in head and body confused the mind into making mistakes. Shanti used the same move, and she had learned it from Kallon.

"He never charges *me*; he always waits until I attack him." Shanti leaned forward, bracing her elbows on her crossed legs. "Annoying."

Cayan warded off another series of attacks, blocking and moving expertly. Anyone could see that he wasn't engaging on purpose. Tingles worked through Shanti's body. She wondered what he planned to do. He'd never done this with her. He'd always fought back. "It's like I don't know these men."

"They each drop their bravado with you, *Chulan*. They just fight. Here…" Rohnan let his words travel away.

"They are sizing up their dicks," Mela said, leaning forward. Sayas laughed next to her.

"Do you see how he is slowing his movement, Xavier?" Shanti asked as Cayan warded off another series of attacks. "He is deliberately allowing his opponent to see his moves, just to see how he reacts. I don't advise this unless you are absolutely certain you have the upper hand. You do that with someone like Cayan, and he'll use it against you and kill you before you realize he's playing you."

"Will Kallon know what he's doing?" Xavier asked.

"He knows. He is doing the same thing while trying to weaken Cayan's mental power. He's playing for time. He doesn't realize Cayan's strength."

"Here we go," a male voice said behind them.

"The Captain just got serious," Rohnan murmured. "I do not envy Kallon what is going to come next."

No one did. In a heartbeat Cayan was done with his

learning. He was on the offensive, his movements speeding up to his normal pace, his punches and kicks harder, and his body taking on that liquid grace he was known for. It was now Kallon who was trying to turn defensive measures into attacks.

"He is fast," someone breathed.

"Yes, for such a big man," someone else added.

The crowd sucked in a breath as one of Cayan's punches landed in Kallon's side. The breath whooshed out of his lungs and his eyes took on a crazed look. He was probably bashing Cayan mentally to buy himself a second. Cayan shook his head, his brow furrowing, trying to push his physical advantage but needing to spend more effort mentally.

"Kallon is at full power. He is no longer taking Captain's measurements," Tanna said behind Shanti.

Kallon held back a little, doing with Cayan what he'd always done with Shanti. "There. Now. Let's see what Cayan does," she said.

Cayan advanced. He was power and strength, ready for the other man to submit. A pulse of pure thunder ripped from him, blasting the other man with such force that Kallon stepped back. The crowd shriveled together, feeling the blast themselves, trying to block as a group.

Cayan's body launched at the other man, another pulse shooting out, the crowd groaning right along with

Kallon. Everyone reached for each other, wanting to connect and merge power, needing to fortify their shields. Weed was produced quickly, everyone who had it taking a bite to ease the pain—the burning and stomach churning was better than a blast of Cayan's might.

Cayan started landing punches, hard strikes to meaty areas, bruising tissue and bone, all easily healed with time and Marc's remedies. Shanti's power surged and boiled, wanting release, reaching for Cayan, wanting to merge with him and fight together.

Kallon backed across the clearing, unable to fight back, or to retreat from both the physical and mental assault, outmatched in both. He took a knee and put up his hands, trusting Cayan to stop his advance. Cayan did, standing over the other man panting, worn out and worked hard.

"Our Captain is scary, right?" Rachie said from somewhere with pride in his voice. "I'm right to be scared shitless of him!"

Kallon stood slowly and rolled his shoulders. He put a hand to his side. "At least you don't bite."

"Don't drag me into this!" Shanti said as she stood. Smiling, she clapped Kallon on the back, harder than she needed to.

"Thank you," Kallon said, wincing.

"Shanti Cu Hoi," Cayan said in a strange voice. He

dropped to a knee before her. "Will you marry me?"

With a flush, Shanti tried not to notice all the people staring at her. She swallowed as Kallon stepped away, giving them room. She opened her mouth, maybe to say no, but "Yes" tumbled out of her mouth.

Clapping and cheers filled the clearing. Cayan's lips connected with hers again, sweet and delicious. "Finally," he said, his smile so bright it could block out the sun. "C'mon, let's head back. There's something I want to show you."

"I bet it's big, and I bet she's already seen it," Mela hollered. Everyone laughed as Shanti hurried Cayan away from the group. They'd only get raunchier, which wasn't as big of a concern as them getting grabby.

Alena stopped them, still looking tired from so long without sleep when she was alone in the city. "S'am. From what we've seen, it seems my poison hit about as many as we thought it might, but…"

"It helped," Shanti said firmly. "You couldn't be expected to rid a whole city of Graygual with one pot of stew."

Alena shrugged and looked at the ground. "High expectations. I just wish I could've helped in battle—" She'd been kept back until the city people had taken to the rooftops.

"We can only do so many jobs, Alena." Cayan leaned forward, catching her eyes and making her shrink back. "You did good. You fulfilled your place within this army. Shanti's Honor Guard has never done things the normal way. You are the only one who notices. Trust me."

"That's certainly true," Shanti said, covering the woman with a blanket of support. "Now go learn to use that sword."

"Yes, S'am," Alena said, hurrying away.

"She's dedicated," Cayan said, noticing Marc sitting by himself. "As is he, when he wants to be."

"He's taken it upon himself to learn more about the *Gift*. I think he's under the impression that I won't make him fight if he finds another useful skill."

"My men are experienced, and he's the doctor. They weren't going to sacrifice their chance to get healed if they got injured. I don't blame them. You put him at too much risk."

"Usually there isn't a choice."

"Captain!" someone hollered, urgency in his voice.

Shanti's stomach flipped over and worry started to eat away as she recognized the pain pouring out of the man. She spread out her *Gift*, feeling more sorrow and some confusion.

"Sir, it's the prisoner."

Cayan started jogging immediately, and Shanti followed right behind him. They covered the distance to the officers' quarters in no time. When they got there, they both slowed, taking in the broken door hanging on one hinge. Shanti stepped through after Cayan and immediately felt her stomach drop to the floor.

There, on the ground with blood coming from a hole where his eye should have been, sprawled Daniels. Tomous was strewn on the floor across the room, one of his arms at an unnatural angle.

Heart in her throat, Shanti rushed to him, feeling for a pulse on his neck. Her *Gift* was pulled away, covering the city and then identifying each mind as Cayan *searched* for the prisoner. A pulse pushed at her fingers, strong and sure.

"Get Marc," she yelled. One of the Westwood men peeled from the door and took off at a run. "There's no point, Cayan," she said, touching Tomous' arm. It was hot to the touch. Only an idiot wouldn't know it was broken. "He can hide from your *Gift*, remember."

"Fuck!" Cayan picked up a chair and threw it against the wall. He walked toward the window and looked out, pain coursing through him as Daniels lay on the ground behind him. "How did this happen?"

The man who had summoned him, solemn and heartbroken, spoke up in a rough voice. "Tomous was guarding him. Daniels came to question him, I believe. We heard a commotion and came to see what was the matter. We found them like this. No one went by us."

Shanti looked around the room, feeling the grief

from Daniels burying into her chest. She rubbed her eyes as Kallon and Rohnan came running, feeling her through the link. Rohnan stepped into the room and then found the object of her pain. He paused, and then slowly walked to the wall and leaned his back against it, looking at the ground.

"Summon someone from this town that knows this building," Cayan said with murder in his voice. "I want to know how someone could get out."

"Yes, sir." The man hurried from the room.

It only took a few moments for a skinny man with scars up and down his arms to skulk into the room. His hollow eyes and missing teeth accentuated his slumped shoulders. It didn't take her *Gift* to know that he was emotionally dead from some trauma or other. It didn't take her experiences to know that the Graygual had something to do with it.

"*This room?*" the man said in a scratchy voice ruined from hours of screaming. The man dragged one of his feet as he made his way across to the far wall beyond the fireplace. He touched a decorative ornament and then pushed on a brick at the fireplace. A door latch disengaged within the fireplace, opening a crawlspace. "*Goes through to a tunnel outside.*"

"*Why wasn't I told of this?*" Cayan demanded in the traders' language.

The man shrugged and stared at the distant wall. "*I

was tortured for that information once. Seemed a shame to just offer it up. Lazy, that."

A blast of power scoured the room, making Rohnan stiffen.

"Yeah, that'd be about it," the man said. *"Yours would probably hurt more. You got more power."*

Cayan stalked right in front of the man, trying to bend to catch his eye. *"Do you want death? Because I can grant it right now."*

"Cayan," Shanti warned, working her *Gift* into Tomous to try and ease the pain keeping him from making it back to wakefulness.

Cayan straightened up and exhaled. *"How many more of these tunnels exist?"*

"Two. One in the guardhouse in the front, and one in the mistresses' chamber at the other end of this building."

Cayan's whole body flexed and another blast of power leaked out of him. He looked at Kallon. "Seal those up, and then scrub this city free of Graygual."

Kallon, despite never having answered to Cayan before, nodded and jogged out of the room. Cayan knelt by Daniels slowly, his face a terrifying mask of rage. Inside of him, though, something was breaking. Grief was rising up and threatening to overwhelm him.

Before Shanti could get up and go to him, Rohnan was there, laying his hand lightly on Cayan's shoulder. They'd lost a few dozen men and women in the battle, all hard to bear. They'd grieved together, buried them, and sang to remember them. The pain was acute, but in this, they'd thought themselves safe. They were shut in a city with excellent defenses.

They should've been safe.

But with Xandre, they would never be safe.

"He has his prize back," Shanti said as she noticed clean slices on the ropes on the floor. "And he had help."

"You think this is the inner circle?" Cayan asked as he hung his head, not shrugging off Rohnan's hand.

Shanti knelt beside him. "No one outside this city would've known where we kept him. He was in here because people would think we took this room. They wouldn't suspect he did. No. I think this was an inside job. He had help."

Cayan leaned toward her a fraction. "None of my men, or your people, would know about that tunnel." He straightened up as Marc ran in with wide eyes.

He saw who was on the ground and sagged. "No."

"Our rest is over," Cayan said. "We need to let down the drawbridges, get this city back on its feet, and find Xandre. This ends. I will not lose any more to these side battles. I want him dead." He stalked out the door without a word, on the verge of breaking and not wanting his men to see. He had to stay strong for them. It was his burden to bear.

Shanti sat next to Daniels quietly. Rohnan lowered himself down behind her and threw an arm around her shoulders. Cayan was right. This needed to end. The more they stalled, the more people they would lose. Xandre would just get better and better. He had probably fortified a few of his cities, and he'd only lay more traps. Eventually, they would have no one left.

"It's time to hunt," Shanti said quietly as a tear tumbled down her cheek. "He's somewhere, and we will find him. Keep your eye out, Rohnan. If the person who did this is in our army, his emotions will give him away. He'll lead us right to Xandre."

"Do we tell the Captain?"

"No. We tell no one. We let him go unchecked, right through Xandre's back door."

They sat for a moment, huddled together, mourning their loss. After a while Rohnan said, "I am ready for this to be over, *Chulan*. I am ready for my life to begin or end. I am tired of this half-life."

"Me too, Rohnan. Me too. It won't be long now."

THE END

Check out KF Breene's website for her other titles:

kfbreene.com

Printed in Great Britain
by Amazon